Pr...

"Bex is ...., the author puts her insider knowledge of the skating world to good use, filling in the background and participants with very realistic details. A new Bex Levy mystery is a real treat; so settle in for an evening of skating, murder, and entertainment."
—*The Romance Reader's Connection*

On Thin Ice

"Fans of figure skating will laugh out loud at the descriptions of the skaters, attitudes, costumes, and stunts. Non-fans will revel in the finely crafted mystery. Bex Levy is a great protagonist who is prone to talking to herself, putting her foot in her mouth, and slashing at people with blades of sarcasm. Alone, the humor in *On Thin Ice* makes it a good book; combined with the interesting characters and suspense, it is a great book." —*The Best Reviews*

"I enjoyed the characters and their interactions as well as the skating intertwined with the mystery . . . well-crafted."
—*Books 'n' Bytes*

continued ...

Murder on Ice

"If you are even a casual fan of figure skating, you will love this book. The author . . . really knows the behind-the-scenes dish. . . . The character of Bex is one of the best amateur sleuths to come along in some time. . . . The mystery is interesting, and the investigation is so entertaining that you'll be glad you're along for the ride. I'm already impatiently awaiting the next book in this series."
—*The Romance Reader's Connection*

"Alina Adams gives a glimpse into the rivalries, the animosities, and the bickering that goes on in the world of amateur figure skating. The protagonist scores a 10 as one of the better leads to come along in years. She is perky, has a delightful sense of humor, and leaves no stone unturned in her quest to find a murderer. . . . *Murder on Ice* is a winning amateur-sleuth tale starring a delightful self-deprecating heroine."
—*The Best Reviews*

"Adams uses her extensive knowledge of the real-life world of competitive figure skating to create a very realistic background for this murder—and possible blackmail—mystery complete with hints of dark humor. A likeable, down-to-earth heroine makes this a must-read for cozy mystery fans with a fascination for figure skating."
—*Romantic Times*

"Adams's style is light and breezy, and the book moves right along. She wickedly portrays the behind-the-scenes backbiting and jealousies of television personalities, both on- and offscreen. Readers who enjoy a lighter mystery and those who are intrigued with the rumored infighting in the world of competition figure skating should enjoy this one!"
—*Books 'n' Bytes*

"*Murder on Ice* mirrors events from the [2002] Winter Olympics. Corrupt judging, cutthroat battles between the skaters, and the behind-the-scenes viewpoint all help to add depth to this unique mystery.... This marks the first book in the new Figure Skating Mystery series. It is shaping up to be an addicting collection of books."
—*Roundtable Reviews*

Berkley Prime Crime titles by Alina Adams

MURDER ON ICE
ON THIN ICE
AXEL OF EVIL
DEATH DROP

Death Drop

ALINA ADAMS

BERKLEY PRIME CRIME, NEW YORK

THE BERKLEY PUBLISHING GROUP
Published by the Penguin Group
Penguin Group (USA) Inc.
375 Hudson Street, New York, New York 10014, USA

Penguin Group (Canada), 90 Eglinton Avenue East, Suite 700, Toronto, Ontario M4P 2Y3, Canada (a division of Pearson Penguin Canada Inc.)
Penguin Books Ltd., 80 Strand, London WC2R 0RL, England
Penguin Group Ireland, 25 St. Stephen's Green, Dublin 2, Ireland (a division of Penguin Books Ltd.)
Penguin Group (Australia), 250 Camberwell Road, Camberwell, Victoria 3124, Australia (a division of Pearson Australia Group Pty. Ltd.)
Penguin Books India Pvt. Ltd., 11 Community Centre, Panchsheel Park, New Delhi—110 017, India
Penguin Group (NZ), Cnr. Airborne and Rosedale Roads, Albany, Auckland 1310, New Zealand (a division of Pearson New Zealand Ltd.)
Penguin Books (South Africa) (Pty.) Ltd., 24 Sturdee Avenue, Rosebank, Johannesburg 2196, South Africa

Penguin Books Ltd., Registered Offices: 80 Strand, London WC2R 0RL, England

This is a work of fiction. Names, characters, places, and incidents either are the product of the author's imagination or are used fictitiously, and any resemblance to actual persons, living or dead, business establishments, events, or locales is entirely coincidental. The publisher does not have any control over and does not assume any responsibility for author or third-party websites or their content.

DEATH DROP

A Berkley Prime Crime Book / published by arrangement with the author

PRINTING HISTORY
Berkley Prime Crime mass-market edition / October 2006

Copyright © 2006 by Alina Sivorinovsky.
Cover art by Teresa Fasolino.
Cover design by Lesley Worrell.
Interior text design by Kristin del Rosario.

All rights reserved.
No part of this book may be reproduced, scanned, or distributed in any printed or electronic form without permission. Please do not participate in or encourage piracy of copyrighted materials in violation of the author's rights. Purchase only authorized editions.
For information, address: The Berkley Publishing Group,
a division of Penguin Group (USA) Inc.,
375 Hudson Street, New York, New York 10014.

ISBN: 0-425-21266-1

BERKLEY® PRIME CRIME
Berkley Prime Crime Books are published by The Berkley Publishing Group,
a division of Penguin Group (USA) Inc.,
375 Hudson Street, New York, New York 10014.
The name BERKLEY PRIME CRIME and the BERKLEY PRIME CRIME design are trademarks belonging to Penguin Group (USA) Inc.

PRINTED IN THE UNITED STATES OF AMERICA

10 9 8 7 6 5 4 3 2 1

If you purchased this book without a cover, you should be aware that this book is stolen property. It was reported as "unsold and destroyed" to the publisher, and neither the author nor the publisher has received any payment for this "stripped book."

Prologue

At first, no one realized he was even there.

Though the Pasadena Dome in Southern California could accommodate up to fifteen thousand spectators, on the morning of the Senior Dance Compulsory run-through at the U.S. Figure Skating Championship, the only people in the arena were the five dance teams making up Practice Group "B," their coaches, a handful of parents, and about fifty hard-core skating fans—middle-aged women bundled up in sweatshirts and fur-lined parkas who believed that their All-Event Nationals Tickets really, really meant All-Event.

They had the Championship's program on their laps, a thermos full of coffee in their left hand, and a pen in their right, ready to jot down who'd deigned to attend the early morning practice, which team was skating to what music, and how their edges looked compared to their opponents' twizzles versus the other's Choctaws and Mohawks. Some of the fans even had laptop computers for on-the-spot Internet reports. They were the easiest ones to spot, since they absolutely had to be sitting next to a phone jack, and tended to get very cranky if blocked.

They also liked to sit in the front rows, since that made it easier to eavesdrop on what the coaches, standing at the barrier, were whispering to their students on the ice. The bulk of the advice seemed to be, "Push. Push. Push!," making most dance practices feel more like natural childbirth classes, especially when that advice was often followed by, "Just ignore the pain for now. It will be worth it in the end."

The dancers all listened keenly, nodded intensely, blew their noses, took a sip of bottled water, then joined hands and whipped around to—more often than not—make the same mistake, prompting the coaches to groan and that groan to echo off the cavernous arena. At that Sigh of Ultimate Despair, the skaters' parents, who previously had been sitting hunched over in their seats, trying to calculate how many hours of sleep they had lost per lifetime after a decade of racing to 5:00 A.M. practices, would snap to attention as if slapped and commence staring pointedly at their offspring, as if their focus—and their focus alone—was what might keep the kids upright for the duration of their event.

"That concludes practice time for the Paso Doble. Our next dance will be the Killian," intoned a sleepy announcer's voice as the arena was engulfed in shrill and painfully peppy music. The Killian was a march, and one of the fastest ice dances in existence. While two sequences of the Ravensburger Waltz took fifty-eight seconds to skate, and two patterns of the Tango Romantica filled a leisurely, practically restful, one minute and forty-three seconds, the Killian required six sequences to be whipped through in exactly fifty seconds.

On cue, all of the couples who'd previously been facing each other for the Paso Doble, turned so that both were facing in the same direction, the man's right hand clasping the lady's right palm and pressing it to her hip, his left hand extending her left arm across the front of his body. Their expressions of fiery, Spanish intensity morphed into mindless, noncountry-specific glee, and off they went in a counterclockwise circle, cheerfully pretending that their hearts weren't ready to explode out of their chests from exertion, or that the squishy feeling in their socks was merely wholesome sweat rather than blood from freshly opened blisters.

This time the scream emanating from their coaches was, "Cross behind! Damn it, how many times do we have to go over this? Cr! Oss! Be! Hind! Boot! Touching! Boot! It doesn't do anybody any good if you cross behind without the boots touching!"

The dancers all listened keenly, nodded intensely, blew their noses, took a sip of bottled water, and tried their best.

As the practice drew to a close, the mood in the arena grew more desperate. Coaches who'd spent the past year trying to get their points across realized that they had literally four more minutes to make an impression. Skaters who'd spent the past year just ignoring the pain, understood that they had four more minutes to get their steps right, or all that suffering would amount to nothing. Their parents were already giving up on this season and making plans for the next—maybe a new coach was in order; maybe a new partner. The spectators started typing their concluding thoughts onto the Internet. It wasn't until after "Group B" finished their run-through, and "Group A" stomped in to take their place, bringing with them a new contingent of frustrated coaches, sleepy parents, and rabid fans, that anyone even noticed the abandoned baby.

He was so tiny, he couldn't even hold his head up in his car seat, needing to be propped up by one of the straps. He wore a newborn-size blue snowsuit with a hood, gloves, and booties, and seemed not so much scared as befuddled by the crowd that gathered around him after the first yelp. He blinked, sleepy and unfocused, then arched his back, yawned, stretched, and smacked his lips.

"He's hungry," one of the skating moms said. But seemed stymied over what to do about that fact.

"He looks like he's all by himself," came another statement of the obvious.

"We should call someone."

"I wonder where his mother is."

"We should get someone."

"Yes. Someone should get someone."

Eventually it was the referee who decided that his authority to make all calls for a given event included determining the fate of a baby abandoned on his watch. He picked up the surprisingly light car seat and moved toward the Championship's accounting office. He called the police, telling them they had an unaccompanied infant on their hands, with no idea of who or where the mother might be.

However, twenty minutes later, when the LAPD arrived, the referee nervously had to tell them that now he actually did have some idea of who, and even where, the mother might be.

He thought she might be Allison Adler, a nineteen-year-old former national ice-dancing champion who was now hanging, dead, from the ceiling of the costume room, a red leather belt with sparkles on the buckle tightened around her neck.

One

Rebecca "Bex" Levy, crack 24/7 Television Network figure skating researcher, was in the arena when the abandoned baby was discovered. She was, however, at the other practice ice surface, the one hosting Ladies Practice Group "A," rather than at the one for Compulsory Dance Practice Group "B." There was a very good reason for that. It was because nobody cared about Ice Dance.

Well, that wasn't 100 percent true, technically. The skaters cared. Their parents cared. So did their coaches, and even a few hard-core fans. What Bex meant to say was that *television* didn't care about ice dance. Which meant it barely existed as part of the National Championship.

Certainly, 24/7 broadcast the Free Dances, which were worth 50 percent of the score. Well, the top three free dances (the top two if the Bronze medal girl wasn't pretty enough for close-ups). But they didn't even show the Original Dance, which was worth 30 percent, so they certainly weren't going to show the two Compulsory Dances, which were worth 10 percent apiece and featured every single couple skating the exact same steps, with only three pieces of music to choose from, besides.

Though Bex's boss, Gil Cahill, usually insisted she attend all the practices—regardless of the fact that there were always two going on at the same time—even Gil made an exception for the compulsory dances. Gil wasn't interested in the criteria and rules used to judge them, so he decreed that no one in the audience would be either. He told Bex that she could go ahead and skip that "Special Olympics exhibition" to focus on the Ladies, who were, after all, the marquee event.

This Nationals featured a particularly exciting (read: ratings worthy) matchup, with the defending Silver and Bronze Medalists from the year before gunning for the newly vacated U.S. Ladies' title. And since Jordan Ares and Lian Reilly were both in the practice group scheduled for the same time as the compulsories, that's where Bex was, sitting in the stands, dutifully taking notes on the teenagers' jump content.

At least that's what she should have been doing. Wrapped in her red, white, and blue 24/7 parka, a knit black cap pulled down over her ears, and clutching a pen in one gloved hand as she balanced her notebook on her lap, it certainly did look to the world as if that was exactly what Bex was doing.

In actuality, after scribbling down, "Lian landed one out of every six triple-triple combinations she tried," and "If Jordan keeps doing her triple Lutz that close to the boards she'll end up in the judges' laps ... maybe that's the point?" the bulk of Bex's attention was occupied by observing the most recent personal development in the Life of Reilly.

Lian, it seemed, had a new boyfriend.

Now, usually that wouldn't be such a big deal. In the

real world, eighteen-year-old girls were known for getting new boyfriends. Some were known for getting a new boyfriend every week. But in this case, Bex was willing to bet the strapping young hunk in question was also Lian Reilly's first-ever boyfriend. Because this, after all, was skating. And it was Lian.

Lian was special. Or so her mother, Amanda, kept telling anybody who would listen. Lian was destined for greatness. And Lian had decided, at a painfully early age, that greatness meant becoming a skating legend. From age three, Lian had spent every afternoon, then every afternoon and morning, then every afternoon, morning, and whatever time could be squeezed in between, at the rink. She made her mother drive her to ballet lessons and costume fittings and stylists. She made her mother chaperone her to local and international competitions. And she allowed her mother to pick up the tab for the privilege. At first, Amanda endured the insane lifestyle because she loved her darling girl beyond reason (having adopted Lian from a Chinese orphanage as an infant, Amanda believed they were destined to be family). But even she eventually reached her limit and rebelled. Amanda made a deal with her daughter: Lian would have to win the upcoming Nationals, or they were quitting and going home. Lian agreed, because she saw that, this time, Mom meant what she said, and Lian had no choice. Which meant that, this season, Lian had put even more effort than anyone previously guessed possible into her training. Which made it extra surprising that along with the extra work, she'd also somehow managed to sneak a boyfriend onto the schedule.

And not just any boyfriend. Little Lian had gotten herself the pick of the litter: Cooper Devaney, U.S. National Men's Champion, or, as his fans liked to scream from the stands when he came out onto the ice, "Super Cooper!"

He was twenty-two years old, six feet tall, with wavy,

sandy brown hair, hazel eyes, a dimple in his chin, biceps to make Popeye weep, and a butt so tight he didn't even incur a mandatory costume deduction for wearing tights. (The latter was two years ago for an ill-advised *Romeo and Juliet* routine. Since then, Coop had switched coaches and choreographers and now preferred simple, tight black pants, and red, tight T-shirts that showed off all his best assets simultaneously.) In the real world, Cooper Devaney would have been a heck of a catch. In skating, he was a god.

Which made it even odder that Lian had somehow landed him. Unlike her, Coop had a rep for being quite the player. According to notes a former researcher recorded in his file from a Nationals ten years earlier, *"The standout in the Novice Men's event was Southern California's Cooper "Coop" Devaney. Solid jumps (three triples), nice spins, good footwork, but the charisma!!!! Twelve years old, and he had girls screaming for him in the audience at exhibition! Watch this kid. He's going to be a star!!!"* According to gossip, he'd dated half the Junior World Team until he made his first Senior one, then promptly traded up—and never looked back. His previous girlfriend was Allison Adler, the ice-dance champion. But that ended, as far as Bex knew, almost a year ago, when she quit skating. Asked to make a bet on which girl he'd go for next, Bex would have put her money on Jordan Ares. While Coop had been working his way through the female side of the Senior World Team, Jordan had been doing the same with the male (to be fair, her options were much more limited, and she had been forced to go for a few coaches and officials just to keep things competitive). It was about time they hooked up, if only so both could check the other off their to-do (literally) lists.

Except that, surprise! it was Lian whom Coop went for, not Jordan. And the newly knighted girlfriend could not have looked more thrilled. Even half an arena away, Bex recognized the infatuation. Lian didn't land a single jump without glancing over her shoulder at Coop. She waved to him from the barrier while she was supposed to be catching her breath and listening to her coach. Twice, she skated over to another girl on the practice, casually struck up a conversation, then giggled, covered her mouth with one hand, and pretended to surreptitiously point Coop out in the stands. He smiled and gave her a thumbs-up both times, utterly unembarrassed by the attention, which, of course, made Lian giggle more.

Neither Lian's coach nor her mother appeared as amused by the performance art as Bex was; but, for probably the first time in her life, Lian did not really seem to care.

"They're not having sex yet."

The sweeping Anna Karenina coat, complete with gold, gilded buttons down the front and a fur collar to match the trimming on the sleeves, not to mention the "Seven Sisters Sorority" accent most certainly belonged to Mrs. Diana Howarth, skating's grand dame and half of 24/7's announcing team. But the sentiment expressed did not exactly gel with the persona she'd spent thirty years cultivating. Diana was often referred to as the Grace Kelly of skating. She was blond, refined, poised, and elegant. She wasn't someone you expected to observe, "That girl hasn't been popped, I'd put money on it."

Bex turned around in time to see Diana and her husband, Francis, grandly occupy the two seats directly behind Bex. Francis leaned over her shoulder for a peek at Bex's notes. He pulled a pen out from his inside black blazer pocket and proceeded to scribble Bex's observations into his own research binder so that, in several hours, Francis could sincerely believe he'd actually watched the entire practice and come to those conclusions on his own. Diana, meanwhile, whispered conspiratorially and, if Bex did say so herself, rather gleefully, into Bex's ear, "You can always tell a virgin by the way she skates."

"Hm," Bex replied, noncommittal, actually eager to hear the scoop, but afraid that Diana was just testing to see if Bex would take the bait—a sort of Princess and the Pea assessment of class-worthiness.

If it was a test, then Bex must have passed something, because Diana went on, "Look at Jordan Ares over there. Nothing virginal about that girl. Look how relaxed she is when she skates; it's like she's had a full-body massage. She is one fluid, languid bit of slowly dripping syrup, head to toe."

Bex nodded. And prayed very hard that Diana wouldn't decide to repeat her metaphor on the air during the Ladies' Short Program. Bex could already imagine Gil screaming at her through the headset in response, "What the fuck is she talking about? Are we selling Mrs. Butterworth here? Am I supposed to put Jordan Ares on my pancakes? Has Diana lost her mind? Bex! Do something!"

"Now, Lian Reilly, on the other hand," Diana said, "look at how she skates. Short, tight little steps. Jumps that barely get off the ground. Pinched face, darting eyes. She nods her head in time to the music, goodness—you can actually see her counting the beats instead of letting it wash over her and succumbing to the rhythm. She's ready to burst, but with no place to go. A bottle of champagne with the stopper jammed down its throat and glued for good measure."

"A bottle of champagne?" the imaginary Gil's voice in Bex's head shrieked, "Now it's 'Dick Clark's New Year's Rockin' Eve'? Have you all lost your minds down there?"

Diana said, "Lucian Pryce, he's a coach out in Colorado, ever met him, Bex?"

Bex nodded. "He's Toni Wright's former pair partner

and Rachel Rose and Robby Sharpton's old coach. I interviewed him for my piece on skaters who dropped out of sight right when it seemed they were at the top of their game."

That piece had been Bex's first attempt at field-producing, and it was supposed to be screened during this Nationals broadcast.

"Lucian," Diana said, "always encouraged his girl skaters to sleep around. Not have a steady boyfriend, mind you—that would distract them from training, and nobody wants that. But he encouraged them to cat around, no commitments, like a boy. Lucian believed it made them skate better. He liked to say: *Nothing duller than a tightened-twat virgin on the ice.* I must admit, I agree with him."

Bex immediately stopped praying that Diana would decide to call Jordan syrup or Lian champagne, and told God both were okay—as long as the expression *tightened-twat* never occupied the air between Diana's lips and a 24/7 microphone.

"But look at that lovely boy." Francis finished copying Bex's notes and surfaced into the conversation as if newly awake. He indicated Coop, sitting in the stands across from them. "Cooper Devaney practically erupts with an erotic charge from every pore. Surely you don't think an Adonis like that is allowing his vigor to go to waste?"

Bex thought it was bad enough when her parents gave her the obligatory birds and bees talk in the fourth grade. Hearing Francis and Diana Howarth, both sixty-plus years old, use the words "twat," "dripping," "erotic charge," and "vigor" was enough to make Bex want to cover her ears with both hands and loudly yodel.

Fortunately, she was saved from doing a *Sound of Music* medley or listening to any more of their disturbing discussion by the sandstorm of gossip that was washing over their section of the arena like a quickly creeping fog.

Gossip, Bex had learned after more than a year on the job, could be—and often was—a physical, tangible thing. It started with one person, then grew at a nuclear rate until it became a life force of its own, an audible hum picked up by dogs, seismographs, and people whose livelihoods depended on knowing everything that was going on in a ten-acre radius.

Bex first felt rather than heard the gossip, like a vibration. She felt the people around her, previously milling in a somnambulistic stupor as befitting the first practice of the day, suddenly perk up. Their heads tweaked into the air like a newborn bird's. They, too, could sense the gossip coming, and they wanted to be ready to pick up the first whisper. It came from the other arena. It came in loose words, in snatches of phrases:

"Baby boy . . ."

"Nobody knows . . ."

"Has to be hers . . ."

"No one suspected . . ."

"Why here?"

"Tragedy . . ."

"Allison Adler, I hear . . ."

"Tragedy . . ."

"Who do you think the father was?"

"Well, with a girl like that . . ."

Bex didn't need to hear any more. She, along with Francis and Diana—whose radar, after all, was even better tuned than hers—were already out of their seats, heading for the source.

Just like the game her mother taught her when Bex was a kid, where one person hides an item and then directs another person to find it by turning the music up on the stereo the closer they got to the hidden object, Bex simply followed the gossip growing louder and louder, until she was standing outside the referee's office, next to the costume room, which was now blocked off with yellow police tape. Behind the glass door of the referee's office, Bex could see several blurry figures deep in conversation. One of the figures wore the brimmed cap of a police officer. He held a notebook and pen and was nodding his head as another blurry figure gestured emphatically and waved his hands in the air. Which meant only one thing: Bex needed to get into the referee's office.

"Excuse me," she said, pushing aside the four-layer-deep crowd, using her research binder to pry them open like a crowbar against a creaky door. The rare people who dared so much as flash a peeved look in response to her rudeness, Bex instantly quieted by shoving Francis and Diana in front of her. A few rubberneckers might get up their nerve and question Bex's right to shove her way in like this, but everyone knew figure skating royalty when they saw it. If Francis and Diana Howarth wanted into the referee's room . . . better step aside, little people of no importance.

As Bex expected, the referee room's door wasn't even locked. The mob outside was staying put on the honor system. Bex, however, was able to turn the knob and walk right in, Francis and Diana in tow. Oh, those naive law enforcement types, who expected the gleam of their badge and the sheen of their authority to work on television employees.

"Can I help you folks?" The officer in charge appeared to be in his midforties, Asian, with thick fingers that made the pen he was holding look like a drinking straw in comparison.

"Miss Levy? What are you doing here, dear girl?" The officer's interview subject was the head referee, Harris Knox, a seventy-year-old, forty-six-year veteran of the sport whose biggest claim to fame was having worked Francis and Diana's first Olympic Pair Gold Medal win, and—in his telling—keeping the crooked Soviet and other Eastern bloc judges from cheating the clean-living Americans out of their rightful championship. Knox liked to boast that he'd been around skating so long, there was nothing he hadn't seen. It appeared, however, that the events of the morning were challenging his assessment. The poor fellow looked as if the gray in his hair and each wrinkle holding up his eyes were consequences of Allison Adler's stunt. To Bex, used as she was to hearing Knox proclaim every result and split decision with unquestionable conviction, it felt like the quavering voice and stunted sentences stumbling out of his mouth were a bad movie dub from the original Japanese.

Bex smiled politely at Knox but focused her energy on the policeman. He was the only one with the authority to throw her out, after all.

"Good morning," she chirped, "I'm Rebecca Levy, chief researcher for the 24/7 network. What seems to be the situation here?"

This was the part where Bex usually got thrown out, by the way.

But much to her surprise, the officer did no such thing. He simply indicated Knox with his pen and said, "Just getting the details. Stick around; better than having him repeat himself, right?"

Bex didn't know how to respond. This was not how these things usually went. As a rule, Bex would ask the authorities for info, and they would laugh heartily. Well, not out loud, but she could see their collective chests vibrating from the suppression effort. Then they would either tell her to get lost, to read the newspaper like everyone else, or, at best, to talk to the Public Relations Department. If she chose the latter, Bex would usually get even less information than if she'd stuck to just reading the newspaper.

No one had ever invited her to sit in on a statement before. Which obviously meant that something strange was going on here. And Bex intended to find out what it was as soon as she took advantage of the immediate situation and found out how much Harris Knox knew. She only hoped nothing would happen to upset whatever rapport she seemed to have accidentally engendered with the fuzz.

"Where's the baby?" Francis demanded. "We heard there was a baby."

Something like, you know . . . that.

"I had one of the mothers take him to the skater-hospitality area. Much warmer up there than down here," Knox replied before the cop had a chance to advise whether he could.

"What about the body?" Diana this time. Bex was beginning to understand why the Howarths made such a successful pair team. With one constantly trying to outdo the other, they must have practiced harder than any other skaters on the planet.

This time it was the policeman who answered. "We had Miss Adler taken down to the morgue. We're waiting for a positive identification. Her father has been called."

"You mean it might not be Allie?" Bex figured if Francis and Diana could blurt out whatever came to their minds, she might as well join in the fun.

"Oh, it's Allison, all right," Knox nodded feebly, eyes shifting, agonized, in the direction of the costume room. "I saw her. I saw her . . . hanging."

"Why would Allison Adler commit suicide?" Diana demanded, as if personally offended that someone could besmirch the National Championship in such a manner.

"Actually, I was hoping you three could tell me." Officer—his name tag read "Ho"—turned to Bex, Francis, and

Diana, notebook open, pen poised, interest in Knox fading. "I mean, I watch the skating shows sometimes—my wife, my daughter, they're big fans—and I hear you two talking about the skaters. Sounds like you know all about them. And you, Miss . . . Levy, was it? You're the researcher? So you'd probably know all about the skaters, too, right?"

On the one hand, Bex was thrilled that someone seemed to actually understand what her job entailed without her needing to explain it. On the other hand, she hated that now that the opportunity was finally here for her to flaunt her expert knowledge in front of an officer of the law and thus prove to all the cops she'd known before that Bex, too, could be useful in a murder investigation, she had so little to offer.

"Well, yes." Bex spoke as slowly as possible, trying to prolong her moment of presumed authority. "But, you see, I mostly research skaters who are going to be in the current championship. And Allison Adler wasn't scheduled to compete this year."

"Why not?" Officer Ho asked, his face unreadable and as of yet, not disillusioned.

"I don't know," Bex was forced to confess. "Allison and her partner—her dance partner, she was an ice dancer"— at least Bex knew that much—"Allison and her partner broke up last year. They never really gave a good reason formally."

"What about informally?"

"He was too old for the girl," Francis opined, unbidden. "How old was Allison Adler? Eighteen? Nineteen?"

"Nineteen," Knox piped up. Then sheepishly explained, "I remember because she was no longer age-eligible to compete at the Junior World Championship."

"But that was exactly the problem," Francis announced triumphantly. "Allison was age-eligible for Junior Worlds, but that geriatric she skated with aged out aeons ago!"

"Geriatric?" Ho inquired politely.

"Sebastian Vama," Diana translated for the Francis-impaired. "Allison's partner. He was a bit older."

"I think he was forty-two," Francis harrumphed.

"He's twenty-six," Bex corrected. It was her turn to sheepishly explain, "He was twenty-five last year when I interviewed him before Nationals. I remember because he went on and on about the poetic significance of reaching a quarter-century mark."

"And that," Diana pounced, "was actually a bigger problem than his age. A loon, that's what Sebastian Vama is. His feet maybe on the ice, but heaven only knows where his head is most of the time."

"He can be a bit . . . obscure," Bex conceded.

"Obscure?" Francis snorted. "I interviewed the so-called boy live on the air after the last National Championship, and his response to my perfectly reasonable, predictable, downright banal question of "Though this will be your fourth World Championship, it is your first as the American Gold Medalists. How does that make you feel?" with a deadpan, "I feel like a quote by Ralph W. Stockman." Naturally, I did not quite know how to respond to such a non sequitur. So I merely bided my time, waiting patiently for what I assumed would be an immediate clarification."

Actually, the way Bex recalled it, Francis defined biding his time as turning his head to peer into the camera, all but imploring the audience at home to step in and help him out. The pause dragged on interminably. Finally, with a sigh part condescension, part genuine psychological pain, Sebastian put Francis out of his misery and quoted, "Ralph W. Stockman: *Be careful that victories do not carry the seed of future defeats.*"

Francis continued looking strapped for a reply. So Vama shrugged and suggested, "Very well, to put it in terms you might understand: I feel like . . . a Diet Pepsi." And then he laughed uproariously—still live on the air, as if his quoting a commercial from a late 1980s Super Bowl was the height of continental wit.

"He is an excellent ice dancer, however," Diana defended.

"Was," Francis said. "He hasn't skated with anyone since Allison. He is much too old to start over again."

"Is he around?" Officer Ho asked. "This Sebastian guy? I'd like to speak to him."

"He should be," Bex offered. "He's here working as assistant coach under Idan Ben-Golan. That's Allison and Sebastian's old coach. He's helping Idan out with Coop Devaney. The men's practice starts in a few minutes. I bet they're over there."

On that score, however, Bex proved to be mistaken.

Idan Ben-Golan was not over at the men's practice. He was standing outside the office, banging the glass on the door once with his fist before realizing it was unlocked and storming right in.

"Where is the baby?" he demanded, his Israeli accent making the question sound like more of a threat than he'd meant. At least Bex hoped that was the case. Because he looked out of his mind.

Granted, on a good day, the thirty-three-year-old coach appeared out of place at an ice rink. In a sport where suits and Republican haircuts were the de facto dress code, Ben-Golan's shoulder-length flowing blond hair was bound to draw attention. In a sport so Caucasian that Asians were still considered exotic, his sun-scorched skin marked him as an outsider. And in a sport where fractures and shredded tendons were the expected injuries, one ear shot off by an enemy sniper during his Israeli Army days made it clear that this was no ordinary figure-skating coach.

But Idan Ben-Golan didn't usually look insane, just intense. He had this way of gripping the person he was speaking to with his gaze and refusing to let go until he was finished. It was creepy and more than a little disconcerting. And that was when he was just shooting the breeze. Apparently, when Idan really wanted something, the gaze could be turned up tenfold.

"Where is my baby?" Idan repeated, narrowing in on Knox. It sounded like the same question. But in Bex's world, there was a chasm of difference between "Where is *the* baby?" and "Where is *my* baby?" She didn't think this was a mere English-as-a-second-language translation problem.

"He's your baby?" Bex and Officer Ho leaped on it at almost exactly the same time. Bex was happy to see that an officer of the law was with her on this.

"Where is he?" Idan faced Knox. "They said you are the one who found him in the arena. What did you do with him?"

"Come on," Officer Ho offered amiably. "I'll show you."

Knox asked to stay behind—"I have to work the next event, you see, and I really would like to . . . if it's all right, of course. I really would appreciate the chance to gather myself together and such." Ho gave Knox permission, agreeing that he'd already told him everything he knew, then led Idan out of the room, upstairs to the next level. Naturally, Bex, Diane, and Francis followed without being asked, although Bex guessed she was the only one wondering why Ho was being so obliging to every request.

Ho opened the door to the hospitality lounge and there, next to a random skating mother plucked for diaper duty, was the baby of the hour, still strapped into his car seat, though with his outer clothing layer now off and a bottle of formula dangling between his lips. Without another word, Idan rushed over to snatch the infant out of his seat. He unbuckled the straps and held the boy up in the air, as if actually feeling the baby's weight was the only way to convince himself that the tot was fine.

Noting everyone watching him, Idan finally calmed down enough to stop asking the same question over and over and, somewhat embarrassed by how crazy he'd acted only a few moments before, explained, "His name is Omri. He's my son."

Behind her, Bex heard Francis chuckle. He leaned over and twittered in Diana's ear, although the message was rather unsubtly meant for all of them. "My, my, my, I do wonder how Miss Cash of the Pan feels about that. . . ."

Two

Idan, it was clear, did not find Francis's comment at all amusing. He lunged forward and, despite the baby tucked under one arm, football-style, still managed to, in the blink of an eye, constrict both palms into fists—though he did keep them at his sides. For now. "What did you say about my wife, Mr. Howarth?"

To his credit—or shame, Bex couldn't decide which—Francis wasn't frightened or discomfited in the least. "I simply asked how your lovely wife feels about your siring an infant with, apparently, your barely legal student. It's a reasonable question under the circumstances, wouldn't you agree?"

"And what exact business of yours would the emotional state of my wife be?"

"Is that why Allison Adler was found dead this morning?" Ho inquired, undaunted by constricted fists or unrestricted cattiness.

Realizing that he was the one being addressed, Idan

startled and, just as quickly as he'd curled them, forced his fingers to hang limply and unthreateningly by his sides. He slipped the baby out from under his arm and cradled the little guy against his chest, chin resting atop the boy's head. His eyes darted, fully aware that everyone in the room was staring at him with a combination of curiosity and fear, and cognizant that his behavior was perhaps not painting the most innocuous of portraits.

"Allison," Idan repeated. Bex imagined she could hear him ordering himself to sound calm, rational, and not at all at fault. "Yes. I heard about Allison, of course. That is how I knew that Omri was here. I—I do not know what to say. It's horrible. She was a good person, a good girl. I am very, very sorry. I don't know what caused—"

"Any idea why Allison was at the rink this morning, Mr. . . ." Officer Ho asked the obvious question.

"Ben-Golan. My name is Idan Ben-Golan." He jiggled the baby as if to calm him, although Omri showed no sign of crying or even of thinking about it. He simply sucked on his sleeve and stared forward.

"She wasn't competing, was she, Mr. Ben-Golan?" Ho followed up.

"No. No, she was not."

"Then why was she here?"

"She was dropping off Omri."

"Dropping him off, sir?"

"I—Allison. Allie was preparing to leave Los Angeles. She was going to leave this morning, and she was leaving Omri with me. For good. We agreed that it was for the best. It is what we agreed on."

"Where was she planning to go?"

"I don't know," he claimed. "She just needed . . . she wanted . . . Allison, you see, she had a very difficult year. She had a lot on her shoulders."

Francis quipped, "Isn't that rather uncomfortable? Gestationally speaking?"

Idan pretended he hadn't heard. Bex figured it was either that or actually hit Francis this time. And that wouldn't be good politically. Not only might it make him look guilty in Allison Adler's death, but also no skating coach could afford to make an enemy of Francis Howarth. A negative word from Francis during a live skating broadcast, and it was bye-bye endorsements. Instead, Idan told Officer Ho, "I would like to take my son home now." Turning to the woman who'd been feeding him earlier, he said, "Thank you very much for your help. I appreciate it greatly."

"I'm afraid I can't let you do that," Officer Ho said.

Idan already had the car seat in one hand and was headed for the door. He said, "I will be happy to answer any questions you may have for me about Allison, but at a later date. My son is tired and—"

"How do we know he is your son?"

"What did you say?" Idan's barely suppressed rancor performed a 6.0-worthy triple jump and barreled straight into Officer Ho.

Who didn't so much as flinch. He said, "What I have right now, Mr. Ben-Golan, is it? What I have on my hands right now is a dead girl—suspected suicide—and a baby, suspected to be hers. But frankly, I don't have anything to prove that. Just like I don't have anything to prove that this little guy belongs to you."

"Do you think I go around kidnapping strange children for my own amusement?"

"I think," Officer Ho replied, "that I am obligated to find out who the boy belongs to before I hand him off to the first bidder. Surely, as a father, you appreciate my being cautious in this manner."

Idan gently set Omri back down in his car seat, the force of how hard he'd wished to slam the safety contraption down visible in the tension vibrating through his forearms. "This is ridiculous. Why would I claim a random child?" When Officer Ho didn't answer, Idan threw both hands dramatically in the air and announced, "Fine. We will play your game. What do you need to see from me, sir?"

"Some sort of legal documentation should do the trick."

"I do not walk around with my boy's birth certificate, if that is what you mean."

"Perhaps you could go get it, and bring it here."

"And leave him alone with you people?"

"He seems well cared for. You said so yourself."

Idan let loose with a few words Bex couldn't quite recall from Hebrew school, but whose meaning was crystal-clear. "Very well. I am going home. Right now. I will be back shortly. Do not dare take him out of here before I come back."

"We'll keep an eye on him for you."

Bex would have said that Idan stomped out of the room, except that he was too graceful for such a linebacker of a word. Idan moved like an unfurling flag; the slightest twitch of his finger appeared to emanate from a single, perfectly balanced center. He stood as straight as might be expected of a former soldier, and moved as stealthily as someone trained to silently creep past the enemy. He was nearly sea-otterlike in that respect, simultaneously aquatic and feline. It was the latter trait that had held him in good stead when Idan Ben-Golan, at the unheard-of ancient age of sixteen, decided that he wished to represent his desert country at the Winter Olympics in figure skating. He had no figure skating experience. Israel had no regulation-size rinks. Idan did not let those things stop him. He bought videos of previous competitions from the United States, transferred them to PAL format, watched closely, took notes, then went onto a rink one third the size of an Olympic rink and proceeded to teach himself jumps and spins. He represented Israel at the subsequent Olympics because there was no one else to challenge for that dubious honor.

He came in dead last. His technical scores, if the judges could have managed it, would have been in the negative numbers. And yet, when it came to the artistic portion—the in-between parts designed to connect jumps to spins, trick to trick—even those who'd temporarily forgotten about figure skating's reputation for good manners and actually laughed out loud during Idan's programs had to admit that he had . . . something. Working without a coach schooled in the "right" way to execute a maneuver, he'd come up with moves and body positions that were truly innovative. Unaware that some skaters merely used their music as an audio prompt to remind them when to start their program and when to end it, Idan choreographed every single beat, not allowing a measure to go by unacknowledged. He may have finished the Olympics in last place, but he left the competition with several requests to consult (just consult, no one was willing to trust him outright quite yet) on the programs of those who'd placed well ahead of him.

It took nearly a decade (three years of which he spent doing military service) for Idan to work his way up to solo choreographer, and another five years for him to move into coaching. But over the past three seasons, he'd guided both Cooper Devaney and the dance team of Adler & Vama to U.S. titles. He won the PSA's "Rising Star" Coach of the Year Award. And along the way, he married the richest woman in skating.

Her name was Pandora Westby, a.k.a. Cash of the Pan. Her wealthy father had indulged his little sweetie's dream of becoming a champion figure skater by building an entire training facility purely for her enjoyment (they accepted other, paying customers, too, but the reality that their training center was always in the red was never a source of concern for the Westbys). When that dream failed to materialize after repeated tries on Pandora's part to simply qualify for Nationals, much less the Olympics, all that lovely money was recycled into Pandora's attempt to build her own champions. She sponsored various up-and-comers over a period of seventeen years. Always young men. Always handsome, always muscular, always at her beck and call. One incomparable year, she arrived at Nationals surrounded by her own private harem; Pandora, wrapped in a floor-length silver fur coat, and a six-pack of towering young men at her side, all dressed in tops so tight-fitting, they might as well have been shirtless.

Idan Ben-Golan, for the record, was never one of the boys. Which was why the wedding announcement, two years earlier, of the thirty-one-year-old coach marrying the forty-seven-year-old diva came as such a shock to those in the skating world who prided themselves on knowing not only everything that happened, but everything that was going to happen as well. The rumors began swirling instantaneously, with only a pair of details accepted as written in stone: She was after his body, he was after her money (and maybe her American citizenship, too—that part was open for further discussion).

Bex could only imagine what sort of firestorm the dirt about Allison and Idan's baby was already igniting in the arena. She was about to step out for an earful when a uniformed policeman blocked her way and, addressing Officer Ho, pointed his thumb at a husky man dressed in a baseball cap and gray-hooded rain slicker not quite broad enough to zip comfortably over his ample gut. The cop said, "Girl's dad is here."

"Ralph Adler." He shuffled inside and introduced himself awkwardly, not sure whom he should be addressing, which caused his eyes to ping-pong over every person in the room. He looked at the baby for a beat longer than he did at anybody else, so that it almost seemed like he was addressing the infant when offering his name. Which made sense, in an odd way, since they were, after all, related.

"Hello, Mr. Adler, I'm Officer Ho. I am very sorry about your loss."

"Ralph Adler," he repeated, still staring at the baby. He shook Ho's hand without looking at it, and only noticed that he'd done it when he felt Ho disengage. His own hand was still frozen in midair. He looked at it in surprise, then stiffly lowered it to his side. "I'm Allison's dad," he mumbled to no one in particular.

"Yes," Ho agreed. "Thank you for coming, sir."

"I didn't know," Ralph looked around, dragging his plea like a roll of cloth meant to envelop Ho, Bex, Francis, Diana, the baby, and his temporary caretaker.

"You didn't know your daughter intended to commit suicide?" Ho prompted.

"Yes." He nodded his head, then changed in midgesture to shaking his head. "No. I didn't know she was going to kill herself. I didn't know about the baby."

"It's a rather difficult condition to hide," Francis drawled. "Especially in spandex."

Ralph tugged on the hood of his rain slicker. It fell back to reveal a mostly bald head, with only a half moon of wispy, blond hair along the base of his skull to indicate where pinkish scalp ended and sunburned neck began. Ralph ran his fingers through the remainder, scratching until he drew blood. He said, "Allie moved out almost a year ago. Right before Worlds. The Worlds she didn't go to. We had a fight."

"About the baby?" Diana interjected.

Ralph had to turn around to look at her. The question obviously bewildered him. "No," he said slowly. "No. I didn't know about that. I said that, right? I didn't know."

"So what was the fight about, Mr. Adler?"

"Worlds. Allison—she said she wasn't going to Worlds." He looked helplessly at Francis, figuring the former champion would understand his confusion. "I didn't—I couldn't figure out what she was saying, at first. What did she mean, she wasn't going to Worlds? She and Sebi just won their first National title. This is what we've been working for since she was a little girl. National champion, World champion, that was always the dream. Well, Olympic champion, that's number one, I suppose. But you need to go to Worlds first." To Ho, Ralph helpfully explained, "It's almost impossible to come out of nowhere and win an Olympic title without first earning a World title. It happens once in a while, but not often. Especially in Dance. You really have to pay your dues and wait your turn in Ice Dance. As long as Allison and Sebi were the American runners-up, we couldn't expect the judges to take them too seriously. They were top ten the previous year, which is excellent, we knew that. But they needed that title to really contest for a medal. We were thinking top five, last year, then this year. Who knows? They could have . . ." Ralph trailed off, remembering that none of it was going to happen now.

"Did Allison say why she'd decided not to go to Worlds?" Diana asked, trying to sound like she was just helping Officer Ho out, but primarily for her own curiosity.

"She wouldn't." Ralph looked at the baby again, making the connection. "She wouldn't tell me why. I kept asking, but she wouldn't tell me."

"And so she left home?"

"I didn't tell her to go!" Ralph veered from befuddled to frantic. He focused on Bex. She guessed that being the youngest person (save Omri) in the room left her to play the part of Substitute Allie. "I never told her to go. I wouldn't do that! Allison and I are a team. We always said that: We're a team." To Ho, he said, "I'm not her biological dad. He left when Allie was a baby. I married her mother when Allie was three. That's how she started skating. I started her. I wanted to, you know, what do they call it? Bond? I wanted to bond with her. And I figured, all little girls love figure skating. So I started taking Allie to the rink. It became kind of our thing. Every Saturday morning, we'd let her mother sleep in and we'd get Allie's skates and her sweater, and this little yellow hat she really loved—it looked like it was made out of bananas—and we would go to the rink. Allie would skate and I'd sit at the barrier and watch. I always got her a cup of hot chocolate from the vending machine. I'd give her a sip every time she made it all the way around the rink without falling down. It was our thing."

"Did Allie like skating?" Bex asked. To an outsider such as Ho, it may have sounded like a strange question to ask about a girl who'd dedicated three quarters of her life to the sport. But after interviewing every competitor at Nationals, Bex possessed a long list of competitive skaters who'd told her everything from "I hated skating when I first started" to "Yeah, it used to be fun, but now it's like my job, you know?"

"She liked it," Ralph, who knew exactly what Bex was asking, insisted. "She did like it. She's the one who asked for lessons. And she's the one who wanted to keep on going after her mother died. Allison was twelve when her mother died. After that, it was just her and me. Team Adler. One year, her first one at Nationals, she made it in Novice Dance. We even had hats made up—'Team Adler.' Sebi wore one, too. Everyone got a kick out of it. We made people laugh when we wore them."

"No wonder you were surprised when she decided to quit," Ho sympathized.

"I felt like I'd been smacked across the face. You know

people say your ears ring when you get punched? My ears were ringing. I couldn't hear. We'd sacrificed so much for her skating. Allison gave up the most, sure. She's the one who had to get the bruises and put in the time and suffer the rejections. But I put in, too. I drove her to the rink and back twice a day, seven days a week, every day but Christmas until she got her license. I stood next to her when she looked at the results board and ended up lower than we both knew she deserved. I had to talk her up when she was down, keep her going and focused. And then there was the money. So many of the people in skating, they have so, so much money. I didn't realize it when we started. Admission and skate rental once a week isn't really going to break the bank, and we weren't poor. I do sales. Biotech sales; market is always good. We live pretty well by most people's standards. I just didn't know skating would cost so much. Not just the lessons and the skates, but the costumes and the travel. That's what killed me in the end. The travel. Plane fare and hotel and food when you get there. Not just for us, the coach, too. We had to sell the house. Got a smaller apartment. And I haven't bought a new car in more than ten years. I practically say a prayer every time I stick my key in the ignition. We never went to the movies. We shopped for our clothes at the secondhand stores and our food at those bulk places. But it was all supposed to be worth it in the end. Allison was going to the Olympics. That's what kept us going. I gave up so much because Allie was going to the Olympics. What the hell am I supposed to do now, huh? What was it all for? Tell me?" Ralph demanded. And then, looking at Omri, he swore, "I'm going to kill that son of a bitch, that's what I'm gong to do. Where the hell is he, anyway? Have you told him yet?"

"You mean Omri's father?" Ho asked.

Ralph nodded, the fellow apparently not even being worth a grunt.

"We've told him. He went to get Omri's birth certificate. We're expecting him back any moment."

"Birth certificate?" Ralph was back to puzzlement. "He knew about this?"

"Oh, yes." Francis enjoyed having knowledge others didn't, whether it was about skating, or the father of their dead daughter's child. "He knows all about it. He tried to convince us that Allison had agreed he should raise the baby while she left town."

The sunburn on Ralph's neck crept up to coat his lips, cheek, and forehead. He practically spit as he raged, "Bastard lied to me. He told me he didn't know where she went! No. Better. He actually had the nerve to call me and ask if maybe I knew where Allison had gone. I felt bad for him, can you believe it? He was practically crying over the phone, swearing he didn't know why Allie broke up with him, why she disappeared, what did he do wrong? He kept begging me to forgive him. I told him it wasn't his fault. That it was mine. Because of what I'd said to Allie."

"What did you say, sir?"

His face of rage blushed even more crimson with embarrassment. "I shouldn't have said it. I knew it as soon as I heard the words. But I was so angry."

"What did you say?" Bex was in Diana country now, asking because she really wanted to know, no altruistic motive implied.

Ralph looked at the floor, sighed, cleared his throat, then went back to pulling on his lone tuft of hair. "I told Allison . . . I told her I expected every penny that I'd spent on her skating, reimbursed. I told her I would take her to court, I would garnish any future wages, and if she didn't pay up, I would have her arrested. She was terrified. That's why she ran away. She ran away because she thought I would put her in jail. None of you can imagine how guilty I've felt this past year. I called all of her friends, looking for her. Unfortunately, her only friends were people at the rink, and she'd made it very clear she wasn't going back there. Every time the phone rang, I'd hope it was her. So I could tell her I didn't mean it. So I could ask her to come home."

"Did you try to find her? Did you call the police?"

"Allison is nineteen years old. I didn't think they'd be willing to help me."

"So then you didn't try to find her?"

"I . . ." He stuffed both hands in his pockets. "No," he said. "I guess I didn't."

"So you've had no contact with Allison for the past year?"

"No. None. If I did, maybe she'd have told me . . ."

"Told you what?"

"About the baby. I'd have helped her, you know; taken care of her. I didn't mean what I'd said to her, about the money. I wouldn't have turned her away. Maybe, if she'd come to me, she wouldn't have . . . she wouldn't have felt she needed . . . to do . . . this."

"Do you have any idea, sir, why your daughter might have committed suicide?"

"Well, it's obvious, isn't it?"

"What is, sir?"

"The baby." Ralph suddenly refused to make eye contact with the child. "Allie couldn't handle it. She was so young, after all. And all alone. She'd never lived on her own before. I'd always taken care of her. My God, now that I think about it . . . did Allie even know how to rent an apartment or open a checking account? She never had to do anything on her own. It must have been horrible for her, trying to survive alone."

"Was she? Alone, that is?"

"What do you mean?"

"We got the impression that the father was very much

involved. Surely he could have helped out with the apartment and the checking account and anything else Allison might have needed while she was pregnant. Especially since, as your Mr. Howarth here blurted out earlier, he did expect to assume custody of the boy. He might have thought providing for Allie was the least he could do."

"Then why call me crying, asking if I knew where she was? It doesn't make any sense. Was he messing with me? What kind of a game was Coop Devaney playing?"

Three

Bex had expected as much. Idan Ben-Golan as the father of Allison's baby made a certain amount of sense. After all, Idan was Allie and Sebastian's coach, they spent an incredible amount of time together, and he certainly would not have been the first man in history to seduce—or, to be fair, be seduced by—a barely legal pupil, married or not.

But, Cooper Devaney, Allison's boyfriend up until a year ago, made even better sense. Plus, there was the fact that Bex could imagine Coop sobbing on the telephone to Allie's father a lot easier than she could picture a former Army sergeant doing the same.

"Cooper Devaney?" Francis and Diana's synch was as perfect on their shock as it had once been on their side-by-side stroking.

"Cooper Devaney?" Officer Ho, amateur that he was, proved a beat behind. "Mr. Adler, the person who claimed to be the father of Allison's baby is Mr. Idan Ben-Golan. He is Allison's former coach, is he not?"

"Idan?" Ralph repeated. "He's . . . he's not interested in Allison. He's married."

No one felt the need to comment on the latter.

Ho said, "Be that as it may, Mr. Ben-Golan has claimed to be the father. He is the one getting the birth certificate. He says he and Allison agreed that Mr. Ben-Golan and, I presume, his wife, would raise the baby, and that Allison was planning to leave town."

"It's Devaney," Ralph insisted. "It has to be."

"Why do you say that, sir?"

"Because he and Allie were inseparable. Sebi Vama, he is—was—Allie's dance partner, he used to joke that he felt like he was skating with two people. Cooper came to Allison's practices, and as soon as she got off the ice, she was in his lap, him rubbing her hands to warm them up. He was at our house practically every night. He picked Allie up in the morning for practice. Idan Ben-Golan . . . he was just the coach. Coop and Allie . . . it has to be Coop."

"Then why would Mr. Ben-Golan claim otherwise?"

"I don't know." It should have been a confession or an admission. Instead, it came out like a roar. "I don't know anything, okay? An hour ago I got a call from the police saying my daughter hung herself and she left behind a baby and did I know anything about this and I don't. I didn't know, damn it. I didn't know."

Bex was afraid he might start crying himself now, but anger had finally yanked Ralph Adler out of his confusion. He railed, "I never trusted that kid. Coop. What the hell kind of a name is Coop? All the other parents at the rink, they told me how lucky I was that Allison was with such a nice boy. That Coop, he's so polite, so respectful, just the perfect, All-American Golden Boy, and so talented to boot! Well, no one is perfect, are they? So why is he trying too hard to act like he is? What's he hiding? Why all the 'Yes, sir,' and 'No, sir,' and, 'Of course, I respect Allison, sir—

you can trust me'? And then those goddamn phone calls of his! 'I hope Allison is okay. Please tell me if you hear from her, sir.' Little bastard. Look what he did to her! And now Allie is dead!"

And now Ralph Adler actually did break down and cry.

Which was when Bex realized she'd had enough. A few weeks ago, she might have been thrilled with the development, believing—accurately—that Gil Cahill would want every last detail for his broadcast. And she, eager to prove herself the very bestest researcher ever, would have swindled widows and knocked down orphans in her quest to get the inside story and present it to Gil like the human sacrifice that it, in fact, was. But that was before Bex's 24/7-inspired snooping got a child kidnapped and a woman killed. Since then, Bex was trying hard to be more sensitive and remember that what Gil saw as a surefire rating-grabbing story was somebody else's very real tragedy. And that maybe there were times when Bex simply didn't belong on the scene.

Ralph Adler had lost all semblance of control. His shoulders shook so hard, it sounded like his neck bones were scraping against each other to produce the agonized hack that was gagging his throat until Bex was afraid he might vomit. For the time being he was clearly incapable of offering any useful information, which meant that the only decent thing to do would be to leave the man alone. Bex locked eyes with Francis and Diana, summoning up every molecule of authority her body was capable of bleeding, and with one sharp jerk of the head, indicated that it was time for them to go.

Much to her surprise, the command seemed to do the trick. Francis and Diana did as she ordered. Either Bex was better at taking charge than she thought, or Mr. and Mrs. Howarth were also adept at recognizing the fine lines among fun curiosity, professional necessity, and utterly needless humiliation.

However, they were barely out the door when Francis said, "I don't believe him."

"Of course not," Diana agreed.

Bex, who hadn't seen anything particularly jarring enough to tweak her bullshit detector, was nevertheless willing to listen to her elders. She asked, "Why? What part of his story doesn't add up?"

"Allie and Idan," Francis and Diana said in near unison.

"A parent who is that involved in his child's skating career—" Diana began.

"But aren't they all?" Francis interjected.

Apparently, even when seemingly in synch about a subject, America's first-ever Olympic Gold Medalists in Pairs had to find some tiny slivers in which one could try to best the other.

"No, they are not," Diana snapped, visibly eager to get back to her original point, but unable to let an unqualified assertion of Francis's go unchallenged. "Look at Craig Hunt, for instance."

Craig Hunt was the man Bex had been thinking of earlier. The one who, thanks to Bex's overzealous researching several months ago, ended up with his thirteen-year-old son kidnapped and his wife murdered. Diana may have wanted to discuss Craig Hunt, but Bex was actually doing her best to avoid it.

"Craig Hunt," Diana reminded, "is not involved in his son's skating career at all. In fact, if it weren't for our Bex here, the boy wouldn't even be at Nationals."

Yes. And his mother would still be alive. Hooray for Bex.

"Craig Hunt is an abnormal example." Francis's tone suggested that any fool, even his ninny of a wife, should be able to recognize that. "He had valid reasons for wanting his boy out of the skating spotlight."

Reasons that Bex completely and selfishly ignored when she went after Craig and his son, Jeremy's, story.

"Your Ralph Adler, on the other hand—" Francis continued.

"He is hardly my anything, Franny. The only albatross around my neck these days is—oh, lucky, lucky me—you."

Francis sighed. "Goodness, Diana, how many Ralph Adlers do we see a year? They are all the same. Possessed, deluded, lacking even a modicum of self-awareness. Take the Adler fellow, for instance. Lamenting over the money he's spent to keep his daughter skating. As if poor Allison's happiness were his sole driving force. Any still semicognizant person would realize that if he truly resented the expense and subsequent sacrifice, he needed merely to pull the plug on his child's extracurricular activities. No one, after all, is forcing him to pay out hundreds of thousands of dollars in skating-related paraphernalia. The fact that he never even considered such a thing testifies to the obvious: Allison's skating was as much—perhaps even more so— his endeavor as it was hers. No wonder her abrupt abandonment of the sport was such a self-described slap in the face. It was not only a rejection of everything he believed he'd so selflessly sacrificed to provide her with all these years, it was also the end of a dream—his dream."

"But that was my point exactly, Franny! Goodness, the senility is really kicking up today, isn't it, Precious? My point exactly about Ralph Adler's claim that he had no idea Allison and Idan Ben-Golan were screwing like bunnies." Diana took a deep breath, then picked up where she'd left off prior to Francis's interruption. "When a parent is that involved in their child's skating career, it is simply not possible for him to be unaware of a lecherous coach's intention. Unless, of course, he wants to be."

"What do you mean?" Bex asked.

"I mean, Mr. Adler could have been willing to look away, he could even, on some level, have convinced himself that he truly did not see what was going on with Allison and Idan, if he believed that Ben-Golan was Allison's only chance for skating success."

"He pimped out his daughter in exchange for a National title," Francis translated, in case Bex was having trouble following.

Unfortunately, she wasn't. And she wasn't having much trouble believing that version of events, either. Bex had seen too many parents willing to pretend they didn't notice coaches verbally and even physically abusing their children because they thought the abuse was vital to achieve on-ice results. It wasn't too much of a stretch to suppose that sexual coercion might also end up on the table of acceptable trade-offs.

"Otherwise, why all the protestations?" Diana reasonably asked. "Why all the insistence that Idan couldn't possibly be the father, that it had to be Coop Devaney?"

"Maybe because he really believes it?" Bex was willing to consider Francis and Diana's theory. But that didn't mean she also had to disregard the obvious. She'd done that in the past, and it didn't always turn out well. Occam's razor, after all, asserted that when multiple explanations are available for a phenomenon, the simplest was most likely correct. Even in the skating world.

"Well, I have no fear, Bex." Francis slapped her collegially on the shoulder. "I'm confident you'll get to the bottom of this matter for us. You always do."

Bex smiled weakly as she watched both the Howarths wander away, toasty secure in their knowledge that when it came time for broadcast, a tidy, efficient, and fact-checked document would somehow magically appear in their research binders, outlining the story, listing all of the players, and explaining who'd done what to whom and why. A few days later, 24/7 would be flooded with letters praising Francis and Diana's journalistic skills, and a Sports Emmy nomination would follow shortly after. Bex wasn't projecting. The above had already happened twice on her watch (once after Francis and Diana unmasked Silvana Potenza's killer live on the air, and the second time after 24/7 showed exclusive taped footage of Igor Marchenko's murderer getting arrested while the Howarths narrated his story). Bex had no doubts about history repeating itself.

As long as she held up her part of the bargain and actually did the research.

To that end, Bex headed for the practice arena where, according to her schedule, Coop Devaney was scheduled to be running through his Short Program. Bex figured the U.S. Men's Champion might also have an opinion on who little Omri's daddy was.

As promised, Coop was indeed on the ice. Bex noticed that his coach, the very popular Idan Ben-Golan, was nowhere to be seen, so Idan's assistant, Sebastian Vama, was doing the honors. Not that Coop needed too much last-minute coaching. There was a reason he was the reigning champion and the other five men on the ice, talented as they may have been, were not. On the surface, all six appeared to be doing the same tricks—triple jumps, a quad here and there, combination spins and intricate footwork. But, in Cooper's case, the triples were a bit higher, the quads a tad more consistent, the spins that much quicker, the footwork more jazzy. Bundled together with the undeniable charisma Bex's predecessor noted in twelve-year old Coop, the U.S. Men's crown didn't appear to be in much danger of changing hands. This season, anyway.

A few years down the line, however, Bex could easily imagine a different story. Because, while of the six Senior Men on the ice, five were over the age of eighteen and making at least their second, if not fourth appearance at Nationals, the one whose skills appeared likeliest to someday catch up with Coop belonged to a first-time competitor—thirteen-year-old Jeremy Hunt.

To everyone else at the competition, he would be a complete surprise. Outside of his local, sectional championship, no one had heard of the boy. The fans, Bex felt certain, would go crazy over him. Not only could Jeremy land two different quadruple jumps—the Salchow and the Toe Loop—but also his fundamental skating skills were the kind that old-timers claimed, "They just don't teach to kids anymore." Jeremy didn't so much skate on the ice as float above it. And he had a smile that could melt . . . well, ice.

Jeremy Hunt was destined to be dubbed the discovery of the competition.

But he and Bex had met before.

A few months earlier, Jeremy's coach, Antonia Wright, had convinced Bex to do a story on her prize pupil, predicting that he would be making a splash at Nationals. Bex agreed, even though Jeremy's father, Craig, had made it clear that his son would not be *going* to Nationals, much less headlining an up-close-and-personal television fluff piece. Toni wanted Bex to ferret out why. And Bex did (after she'd convinced Gil to let her by promising him an exclusive). But only after her digging got Jeremy's mother killed.

As a result, Bex was not exactly Craig Hunt's favorite person.

Which was why, seeing him approach her from his seat in the stands made her want to turn around and walk briskly for the nearest exit. But that would be childish, and Bex's New Year's resolution had been to grow up—no matter how unpleasant that might eventually turn out to be.

She forced herself to stay as she was, leaning against the

railing that led from the mezzanine level toward the front-row seats. She hugged her research binder to her chest and wondered why, all of a sudden, she was feeling so self-conscious about her raggedy hat and bulky 24/7 jacket. As Craig got closer, Bex remembered why. Because, while she may not have been his favorite person and their past few encounters had been tense at best, borderline violent at worst, Craig Hunt was nevertheless a very attractive man.

He barely seemed old enough to be the father of a thirteen-year-old, and, in fact, had only been twenty when Jeremy was born. Unlike his blond, blue-eyed son, Craig was dark, with olive skin, chestnut hair, and oval, ginger eyes that looked as if they had been chiseled out of bronze. He wore blue jeans, a white shirt with no tie, and a black, suede jacket. He also, Bex noticed, still wore his wedding ring.

"Bex!" Once he'd called out her name, there went Bex's last chance to pretend she didn't realize he was coming for her and take advantage of an escape option.

Bex looked up, feigning surprise to see him there. She offered a cautious, "Hi, Craig," wondering what sort of tone was appropriately respectful when addressing a man you'd inadvertently widowed.

"What do you think?" He indicated Jeremy on the practice ice.

Bex glanced where he'd pointed and couldn't help a sincere smile. "He looks absolutely thrilled to be here."

"What gave it away? The ear-to-ear grin, or the way he keeps staring at Cooper Devaney like he's in the presence of a god?"

For a moment, Craig looked like your average, doting skating dad. A mellower—and better-looking—Ralph Adler. But Bex knew that was far from the case. Unable to continue without clearing the air first, she instinctively lowered her voice and awkwardly asked, "How is he? Handling everything, I mean?"

Craig shrugged. He continued watching his son and avoided meeting Bex's gaze. Which was okay with her. Really. "He's still trying to process everything, I think. It's one thing to lose your mother. It's another to find out you're adopted, and it's a third to meet your biological parents. All three in one week . . . that could bring a linebacker to his knees."

"Plus, the Nationals." Bex swore she didn't consciously mean to, but she caught herself instinctively shifting the topic from the hell of the past to the more benign present. "I mean, all the stress of being here for the first time—"

"Believe it or not," Craig, along with the half-dozen handfuls of hard-core fans in the stands, applauded as Jeremy landed a triple Axel in the center of the ice. "Nationals has actually been good for him." He turned to face Bex, and she was relieved not to see laser beams incinerating her from each eyeball. "It's given him something to focus on that isn't our ongoing family drama. I guess I have you to thank for that."

"Excuse me?" Bex blurted. She'd been expecting, at best, grudging politeness. Gratitude wasn't even on the agenda.

"You're the one who talked me into allowing Jeremy to compete at Nationals."

"Well, yes, but—"

"And you're the one"—he cleared his throat by tapping his fist against his chest—"you're the one who found him when the police couldn't. I never thanked you for that one, either."

"I'm the one who got Jeremy kidnapped in the first place."

"You didn't know. My God, if someone had told you Jeremy's story without you seeing it for yourself, would you have even believed it?"

"Not without a scorecard to keep track of the players, no."

Craig nodded, indicating he'd expected as much. "Anyway, I owe you a thanks."

"You're . . . uhm . . . welcome." Never in a million years did Bex imagine she'd be having this conversation.

"And now, actually, I'd like to ask you for a favor."

"Sure. Name it. It's the least I can do. Anything."

"The piece 24/7 is doing on Jeremy and—and everything that's happened. Is that still scheduled to run during this Nationals?"

Bex thought she might throw up. She suspected what was going to happen next. "You want me to kill it."

It wasn't fair. The piece on Jeremy Hunt's kidnapping and the untangling of his very twisted skating lineage was going to be Bex's first producer credit for the network. She'd had to beg Gil for permission to research it; she'd even paid her own expenses to prove how serious she was. When she screened the footage of Jeremy's homecoming and showed Gil all the other information she'd dug up, he'd grudgingly agreed that it was worth airing during the Nationals broadcast—even if he did assign a more experienced producer to go over Bex's efforts and physically put the segment together. But it was enough of a start, and Bex had been so eager to finally see her work, at least a part of it, make air. Of course, if Craig, with good reason, asked her not to do it, if he claimed that it would be too damaging to Jeremy to see his parents' past turned into a four-minute reality show, Bex would be obligated to acquiesce. It would be the right thing to do.

Even if it broke her heart.

"No," Craig said. "No, it's not that. Frankly, I figure it'll be good to finally get the whole sordid story out there. Maybe it will open some eyes to the kind of abuses that young women face in this sport. Might even bring about some changes."

Bex realized that Craig was referring to his late wife, Rachel, a once-promising pairs skater who'd quit the sport at what seemed to be the top of her game because she refused to put up with the violence of her partner, and their coach's tacit approval of it. But, at his words, she couldn't help but think of Allison Adler, and her eyes drifted to the ice. Where Allie's ex-boyfriend was putting on a show for the older women in the front row, her former partner was instructing him in the finer points of holding an ending pose, and her coach was ostensibly off procuring a birth certificate to prove he was the father of his ex-pupil's infant.

"Yes." Bex nodded, partially in agreement with Craig, partly at her own thoughts. "People don't realize half of what goes on behind the scenes."

"I think Rachel would have been pleased," Craig hoped. "To know that her story might help somebody else. She wouldn't have minded it being talked about. She wasn't ashamed about what was done to her. She never felt guilty. She knew who the really bad guys were. She was really strong that way."

He cleared his throat again and tugged on his wedding ring so hard, he cracked his knuckle, giving Bex a hint of just how raw his memories still had to be. Cautiously, she asked him, "So what's the favor you wanted to ask me?"

"Oh. Yes. Right, the favor." Craig guiltily stuck his ring hand in his pocket and swiftly looked away. "It's about Jeremy's interview. Some woman named Mollie called and asked to interview Jeremy. She said it was for the piece on Rachel."

"Mollie Vazquez. She's the senior feature producer for this event. Gil thought I needed a little help, so Mollie took my research and the video I shot, and she's actually cutting the feature and putting everything together."

"I'd rather you did the interview," Craig said.

"Me?"

"Jeremy liked you and, frankly, I think he'd be more comfortable with a familiar face over a total stranger. I know I certainly would be."

"Craig, I'm not a producer. Gil loves to remind me of that—sometimes twice a day. Usually when I make a suggestion. Especially if I say, 'I think . . .' And then Gil tells me, 'You're not being paid to think.' And that's when he also reminds me that I'm not a producer. But, uhm, I guess that's my issue. Anyway, that's why I don't usually do the serious interviews, just the prep stuff. Off-camera."

"Please, Bex," he said. "Look, I know I made it sound like Jeremy is doing fine. And he is, up to a point. But he's still only thirteen years old. And his life's been turned upside down. How many people is he supposed to spill his guts to? It's like being in the hospital when, every half hour, a new med student comes to take the same case history. I would like to spare him that. Please. I'm okay with him granting the interview. But I want you to conduct it."

She didn't know what to say. It was a vote of confidence, if not an outright act of absolution. Bex desperately wanted to accept it. But she knew it wasn't all up to her.

She said, "I'll ask Gil if it's okay with him. I don't know what he'll say."

"Great, thanks. Let me know, Bex. I appreciate it." And Craig moved away with a relieved smile, heading down the steps to stand rinkside with Jeremy and his coach.

On the ice, Coop skated up to Jeremy, bent his head, and whispered something in confidence that made Jeremy's usual million-dollar smile beam into the billions. The boy nodded enthusiastically, then turned around, glided backward for half the rink's length, picked up speed, and, just as he got to the center, flung both legs in the air so that his body, for a moment, appeared suspended parallel to the ice in a move the skating world called, rather ominously, a Death Drop. When he finished, he skated back over to Coop, who nodded his head, then made a scissoring movement with his fingers. Jeremy cocked his head to the side and watched Coop's fingers. Coop did it again. Jeremy nodded, and repeated his preparation for the Death Drop. This time, when he leaped into the air, his legs appeared to fly over his head, creating a much more dramatic effect. Coop clapped enthusiastically, and the audience joined him. Even from the top of the stands, Bex could see Jeremy blush and simultaneously drink in the adulation.

That Coop Devaney, he sure did seem like a nice guy, didn't he? The kind of nice guy who would never abandon his pregnant girlfriend, driving her to kill herself. But, then again, Bex supposed even nice guys had their breaking points. And discovering that your girlfriend was pregnant by your coach would probably qualify as reason for one.

Bex checked her schedule, noting that the men's practice was scheduled to go on for another fifteen minutes. She resolved to wait and talk to Coop right after. As far as she knew, no one had told him yet about Allison—at least that's what Bex presumed. She didn't suppose a man could learn that his long-missing ex was lying dead a few feet away, leaving a baby behind, then proceed to step on the ice and commence practicing as if nothing had happened. On the other hand, only yesterday during the Pairs session, Bex had seen a boy drop his partner from an overhead lift. The girl crumpled to the ice, landing on her head, and then lay there, conscious but immobile. A paramedic rushed onto the surface, warned her not to move in case her neck was broken, then ran to call 911. The other pairs skaters watched the commotion for a moment, then proceeded with their practice, skating around the injured girl until a stretcher was brought to carry her off. And then they skated around the stretcher. So, really, even if he did know about

Allison, Coop's disregard wouldn't be completely unprecedented.

Considering that gossip about Allie, Coop, Idan, and Omri was already so thick within the arena Bex felt like she could open her mouth and take a taffy-textured bite, it would have appeared unlikely for Coop not to have heard. Except that the bulk of the commotion began after he'd stepped onto the ice. And most skaters, when practicing, were hard pressed to hear anything beyond the ache of their bones, the whine of their muscles, and the deafening roar of their ambition.

Bex decided to head down toward ice level, meaning to stand by the exit and be the first to grab Cooper as he got off. She was hoping to catch his initial, uncensored reaction to the news, and chart the rest of her investigation accordingly.

Bex only got as far as the second tier of seats before she noticed a figure heading in her direction, zipping along the row just underneath, so that she was primed to cut Bex off from going any farther.

Lian Reilly pressed one arm against the last seat in the row, and another along the barrier, and hopped up to land right in Bex's path. She looked more mature than the last time Bex dealt with her, a few weeks earlier, at the "U.S. vs Russia" invitational cheesefest in Moscow. Gone was the waist-length, ebony pigtail Lian had been neatly winding into a bun atop her head since Juvenile Girls days. She'd cut her hair short, so the ends softly brushed her cheeks and covered her ears, making Lian's face look rounder. It was a nice change from the pinched scowl the pigtail created by yanking Lian' s face into a furrowed oval. She'd also updated her wardrobe. Out went the cutesy denim jeans with pink and white flowers embroidered along the hems and pockets, along with the pastel Peter Pan collar shirts. This morning Lian was wearing low-riding hip-huggers that showed off her flat stomach and just the very edge of a lacy black thong, plus a green cashmere sweater that may have technically been a modest turtleneck, but stretched just enough across the bustline to flaunt two perky, jiggling nipples.

What a difference a boy makes, Bex thought.

"Is it true?" Lian demanded. Unfortunately, despite the cosmetic changes, her tone of voice remained the same. Somewhere between a demand and a whine, it told the world that Lian Reilly refused to be denied, while at the same time making everyone around her want to, on principle, refuse whatever it was she was currently requesting.

"Is what true?" Bex stalled. She told herself it was for reasons of confidentiality. But frankly, it was mostly to mess with her.

"About Allie Adler? Did she really hang herself in the wardrobe room?"

"It seems that way."

"And was there really a baby?"

"That also seems to be the case."

"Is it Allie's baby?"

Bex hesitated. The fact was, no DNA testing had been done. Idan, as far as she knew, hadn't even turned up with Omri's birth certificate yet. So, really, the evidence was still all circumstantial up to this point. Bex wasn't obligated to tell Lian anything.

Not that Lian cared. She had her own agenda, and Bex's actually confirming her assumptions was a mere technicality. Lian said, "I bet you think it's Coop's baby, too."

Bex told the truth. "Allie's dad said so, yes."

"Well, he's not. He's not, Bex." She may have been wearing a thong, but Lian also could stomp her foot like somebody wrapped in a diaper. "I'm Coop Devancy's girlfriend, and I'm telling you, there's no way he could be the father of Allie's baby."

Four

"What makes you say that?" Bex asked, keeping her voice neutral. The better not to blurt out even one of the many sentiments currently coursing through her brain.

"Because"—Lian looked quite pleased to be the one telling Bex something she didn't know, for a change—"Coop doesn't believe in premarital sex!"

"Really?" Bex stayed in neutral. And thought of all the girls she'd heard swear differently.

"Yes. He thinks it's morally wrong. We both do. That's why we're going to have a purity ceremony."

"A purity ceremony," Bex repeated.

"We're going to pledge not to have sex before marriage. And we're going to exchange purity rings. Here, look." Lian, with great effort, managed to squeeze one hand into the pocket of her skintight jeans and tugged out a shiny ring that she proudly displayed to Bex atop her palm. "This is the Unblossomed Rose model. See the rose on the front? It's real gold. Fourteen karats. Coop is getting the Rugged

Cross model. Also in gold. It's more masculine. We thought about getting matching ones, you know? But I didn't want one like his, and Coop didn't really want to wear a rose—I don't blame him or anything. It would have been nice to match, but it's the thought that counts. We're going to do it right here, during the Nationals. After the Ladies' Short Program and the Men's Long."

Bex may not have been to a lot of weddings, and she'd certainly never been to a purity ceremony. But she was, nevertheless, amused by the image of an invitation with the words *TIME—After the Ladies' Short Program* handwritten in calligraphy.

"Maybe 24/7 can cover the ceremony!" Lian piped up. "That way, Coop and I can be role models, you know? For other young people who might not have values as good as us."

Bex asked, "This purity ceremony, whose idea was it? Yours or Coop's?"

"Both of ours," Lian said proudly. "But he's totally into it. Really. That's how I know Coop can't be Allie's baby's father. He's not like that."

"Lian is right, Bex." Amanda Reilly materialized on the steps beside them and beamed at her little girl. "Cooper Devaney is a lovely boy. He has excellent values. I can't imagine a more proper young man to court my daughter. I'm thrilled."

To be honest, Amanda really did look thrilled. Bex guessed it was because Lian was finally doing something normal for a change. Nevertheless, Bex also couldn't help wondering if Lian's passionate defense of her and Cooper's mutual virginity had been as much for Bex's benefit as it had been for her mother's. What if Lian spotted Amanda lurking (wasn't she always, where Lian was concerned?) and decided to put on a little show to keep Mommy off her back, with Bex as a witness. Not to mention the even more obvious fact—just because Coop allegedly wasn't having sex with Lian didn't mean he hadn't had it with Allison. At least once. Which was all it took. In fact, it made sense that Coop would be so proabstinence now, if he'd already learned—say, nine months or so ago—the consequences of his last, nonpure relationship.

A few feet away, the referee got on his microphone and called men's practice over, ordering the ice cleared.

"Excuse me," Bex said to Lian and Amanda, heading toward the ground level and Coop. Much to her displeasure, Mother and Daughter Reilly followed her.

Even worse, as soon as they got within hearing distance, Lian pushed ahead of Bex and called out, for the whole arena to hear, "Coop! Coop! Did you hear? Isn't it awful? Did they tell you?"

Her shrieks attracted not only Coop's attention but also that of Sebastian Vama and half the arena, including Jeremy and Craig Hunt. Since, by Bex's best estimate, the only people in the place who currently didn't know what Lian was yelling about were Coop and Sebastian, it made sense that the rest of the crowd stopped what they were doing to watch how the two would react to the bombshell. Which was exactly what Bex had been planning to do. Only she hadn't been planning on an audience.

Bex picked up the pace, hoping to be standing close enough when Lian spilled the beans to accurately gauge Coop and Sebastian's responses. At the moment, however, the pair resembled nothing so much as a pair of befuddled photo negatives. Both stood close to six feet tall, limbs, shoulders, abdomens, and butts as encased in a sheath of glistening muscle as butterflies in a tight cocoon. Both wore tight-fitting, navy, Lycra pants with a plain white T-shirt, though Coop had already shed his USA World Team jacket in the heat of practice, while Sebastian, coaching from the side, still wore his. The main difference however, was in their coloring. Coop with his sandy hair, hazel eyes, and dimpled chin stood in direct contrast to Sebastian, who, despite being only half Indian on his father's side, nevertheless sported jet-black hair, mocha latte skin, eyes so dark it was impossible to discern iris from pupil, thick brows that jutted menacingly over those eyes as if they might swallow them, and an overall visage that appeared to have been forged by a boulder being repeatedly sharpened against the side of a cliff.

Upon Lian's hollering, Coop and Sebastian turned around to face her. Sebastian raised a well-rehearsed eyebrow to indicate he found her outburst most unseemly. Coop looked equally displeased, but also resigned.

"What is it?" he asked Lian. "What are you yelling about?"

Anyone else would have run out of breath from the effort of zipping down two flights of stairs while spewing gossip like rose petals at a wedding, but Lian was, in the end, a world-class athlete, and she was barely winded. She leaped over the final barrier separating spectators from skaters and landed smack in front of her boyfriend, looking even more pleased with herself than she usually did at the end of a six-triple program.

She beamed and said, "Allison Adler," presenting the name like a triumph.

Both Coop and Sebastian jerked at the declaration.

"Allie?"

"What about Allie?"

"Did you hear from her?"

"Is she here?"

"What's she doing here?"

"Where is she?"

The questions clanked like javelins colliding in midflight. It was impossible to figure out who said what, although, even from a distance, it was obvious how shocked both men were by the mere mention of Allison's name.

Bex arrived in time to hear Lian gleefully announce, "She's dead!"

No one said a word. Even the spectators were frozen in place. Sebastian and Coop looked at each other. They both looked back at Lian.

Finally Coop said, "What are you talking about, baby?"

"It's true," she insisted. "The police were here and everything. Allie hung herself right in the costume room this morning."

Coop looked sick. Sebastian just looked furious. "That's not a funny joke, Lian."

"I'm not joking! Ask anyone! Ask Bex!"

They turned to look at her. Bex could only nod her head awkwardly. When the gesture failed to illicit a reaction, she swallowed hard and admitted, "It is true. I spoke with the policeman in charge of the investigation. They found Allison in the costume room, she had a belt around her neck, and she was dead."

"But that's not all!" Lian had ceded the spotlight long enough, and now it was time for everyone to look at her again. "There was a baby!"

"A . . . what?" Sebastian asked.

Meanwhile Coop, whose sickness seemed to be progressing from a minor flu to the bubonic kind, couldn't take it any longer. Still recovering from an intense workout, his legs gave out from under him and he fell to the floor with a thud more awkward than anything they'd ever seen from him on the ice. Coop landed smack on his tailbone, but didn't even seem to register the expected pain. He hadn't had a chance to put his skateguards on yet, which meant his exposed blades sliced and sunk into the padded walkway from the impact, leaving him sitting at an

DEATH DROP

impossibly uncomfortable angle, knees sticking straight up. He didn't appear to notice.

He looked up at Lian as if pleading for her to correct him. "A baby? Allie had a baby?"

Lian nodded eagerly, her boyfriend sprawled devastated on the ground not a great concern. "And you'll never guess who the dad is!" She turned to face Sebastian, knowing the revelation would be an equally big deal to him. "Idan Ben-Golan!"

"You're lying," Sebastian replied, as far away from normal on the eerily calm spectrum as Coop was on the distraught. "That's impossible."

"Uh-ha! Idan told the police so."

Bex gently agreed. "He says he has a birth certificate to prove it."

Sebastian shook his head. "No," he said. "I'd have known. Allie would have told me. The three of us—me, Allie, and Idan—we were constantly together. On the ice, six hours a day, every day. And when she wasn't with us, she was with . . ." Sebastian trailed off and turned his head in Coop's direction. "No," he repeated. "I'd have known. *We'd* have known."

Coop said, "Allie never said a word. I kept asking her what was wrong. And she never said a word."

"Well, she probably felt so guilty," Lian reasoned. "I mean, you two were dating, and she knew how you felt about premarital sex, and there she goes cheating on you and having sex, and with Idan, too, and he's married!"

Coop shook his head. "Last year, at Nationals, I knew something was wrong. I thought she was going to break up with me. But she didn't. She just disappeared. She never said a word to me. She just took off. I couldn't figure it out."

"She didn't want you to realize how promiscuous she'd been," Lian asserted.

Coop asked Bex, "What kind of baby is it?"

"What?"

"I mean"—he waved an arm in front of his face as if desperately trying to chase off a mental fog—"is it a boy or a girl?"

"A boy," Bex said.

"A boy," Coop repeated. He looked up. "Can I see him?"

Bex wasn't sure when it became her place to grant visitation rights, but TV did have that effect on people. She said, "He's in the waiting lounge upstairs. Come on. I'll take you. I know where it is."

Coop struggled to get up. Bex wondered how far he intended to get with skates still on his feet, but he appeared oblivious.

Lian grabbed Coop's arm. He thought she was helping him up, but she actually merely wanted to tug aggressively on his sleeve and demand, "Where are you going? What are you doing? Coop! Answer me!"

"Lian." The way he said her name made it obvious Coop had forgotten she was even there. And the way her nose crinkled made it equally obvious that Lian realized it. "Lian, please, I need to go."

"Why?" she asked. Bex had a fleeting impulse to play schoolteacher, turn to the crowd still watching them, and ask, "Class, who would like to explain for Lian why it is that Cooper wishes to see Allison's baby?"

"Lian . . ." he tried to shake her off, but she'd already let go of his arm in disgust.

"You son of a bitch!" Lian shouted.

"Not now, Lian."

"Son! Of! A! Bitch!" Lian gave each word its own personal explanation point. "So what was all that purity crap about, huh? You said premarital sex was wrong. That you loved me too much to disrespect me. Here I thought you were being the gentleman, not putting moves on me. You weren't a gentleman! You were just exhausted!"

At this, Amanda Reilly squeezed her way past the seats to stand next to Lian at ground level. She wrapped her arms around Lian's shoulders, practically rocking her, and soothed, "It's okay, honey, it's all right. Calm down, angel. Let Coop go. We can talk about this later. Just us girls. Don't get upset, sweetie."

From the shelter of her mother's unconditional adoration, with Amanda's crossed forearms tucked under her chin and Lian's hands clutching her mom's elbows like a life preserver, Lian glared at Coop. He sighed and, for a moment, looked like he might try to explain. But the audience discouraged him. Coop looked around, finally comprehending just how many people had witnessed his personal scene and blushed almost as crimson as his gloves. Quickly, he yanked off his skates, dropping them where he stood, and pulled on his sneakers without bothering to tie the laces. Coop ducked his head so that his eyes only met Bex's. He jerked his chin to indicate that they should go.

She followed by leading.

The two headed for the arena tunnel. Much to Bex's surprise, nobody followed them. Maybe Bex wasn't the only one coming to realize that no story was worth another person's suffering. Maybe the entire skating world was growing up.

She and Coop walked in silence for a few minutes, the monotonous gray tunnels hardly inspiring small talk. His strides were so long, Bex had to double-time to keep up, but since she was the one who knew where they were going, he was forced to stop every few feet and wait for her to catch up. He would bounce in place, nervous energy panting to escape from every pore. Finally, unable to bear the silence, Coop asked Bex, "So, what happened, again? Lian said—"

"Lian got the bulk of it right."

"So Idan really said he . . . and Allie?"

"Yes. I was there for that. For what it's worth, he seemed very anxious about the baby. I don't think it was an act."

"I don't believe it. Idan, he wasn't like that. Some coaches, you can see it right away. I mean, everybody knows you don't need to put your hands on a girl's boobs to show her how to hold her position in a lift. But there are coaches who do it all the time. Boobs, ass, right between her legs with practically the whole rink watching. Some of them like girls and some of them like boys, but you can always tell who the perverts are."

"And Idan never—"

"Never!" Coop turned his palms up toward the ceiling. "I thought he was a good guy. That's why I switched to him, you know, two years ago, before I won Nationals. I used to take from Gary Gold all the way across the country, over in Connecticut. Do you know him?"

"Yes," Bex said. And added sincerely, "He may not be the cuddliest person, but he's one of the most decent human beings in the sport."

"Yeah, I liked him, too. My mom and him, they disagreed on some stuff, so that was a pain. There were things about him personally, nothing to do with skating, that she didn't like. She wanted me to switch over to Igor Marchenko—well, obviously before he died—'cause they were in the same rink and we wouldn't have to move then. But, I told her, if I had to leave Gary, Idan was the only coach I wanted. He'd choreographed my Short and Long the year before, and we just got along really great. Nobody thought he could do the technical coaching, they thought he was for artistic stuff only, but I really liked how he'd look at a move and take it apart, then put it back together better. I thought he'd make an awesome technical coach, and he did."

"And did your mother not have as many issues with him as she did with Gary?" Bex felt kind of silly asking a twenty-two-year-old how his mommy liked a colleague, but Coop had brought the issue up.

"Oh, yes. Mom and Idan get along fine. She thought he was a good role model for me. Well, not about everything. She was a little disturbed about him having been in the army. Mom's a serious liberal—you know, *War is dangerous for children and other living things.* That poster was on my wall long as I can remember. But she got over it when she saw that Idan didn't, like, teach with an Uzi over his shoulder or anything. The thing I liked best about Idan, though, was how he didn't treat his students like babies. A lot of the other coaches, it doesn't matter how old you really are, they act like you're five. They make all your decisions for you. Not just your music and your costumes, but what you should eat and when you should sleep and who your friends should be. Idan, he's all, 'Hey, man, you're an adult. I'm just here to teach you some skating. Do whatever you want on your own time.' Gary was a little like that, too. He didn't like to get into your personal business. But if you asked him for advice, he'd give it. I used to do it all the time. Gary is a really smart guy. But that's what my mom didn't like. She didn't agree with some things he believed in and practiced, and she didn't want him influencing me."

Bex could imagine. Gary Gold was one of the most conservative men in figure skating. He wore a perfectly pressed suit and tie not only to competitions, but to practice as well. He tolerated no backtalk or swearing, made his students address him as "Sir," and thank him after every session, and had no qualms about punishing a child for breaking any of his rules by stopping their lesson midway and refusing to continue, no matter how much the parents pleaded. Pairing him with a "serious liberal" mom seemed like a recipe for conflict.

"Did Allison like Idan?" Bex asked.

"Yeah. She and Sebi were the first serious contenders to have him as a full-time coach. He choreographed some gorgeous programs for them—international judges loved them. But, see, that's what I mean about Idan being cool. A lot of other coaches, they'd have objected to Allie and me dating. They'd say it was distracting us from training, or they'd say, we skate in the same rink, if we broke up it would make things awkward. But Idan just said, 'Go ahead, have a good time, guys.' He seemed chill with us going out."

"After Allison quit skating last year and just took off, did Idan say anything? Did he have any ideas why she did it?"

They were standing side by side, waiting for the elevator that would take them to the upper level, giving Coop time to really think about her question. He crossed his arms and rubbed his neck thoughtfully, pinching the skin so hard little tufts of red poof from his gloves remained embedded in the crease. "I don't . . . I don't remember exactly. He sure seemed as surprised as the rest of us. And pissed, too. I mean, Allie and Sebi had just won Nationals, he was dying to take them to Worlds and show them off. Allie really let him down in that respect. Sebi, too. He was furious. But neither one of us suspected anything like . . . like . . ."

Bex asked, "You didn't?"

"I didn't what?" They got on the elevator.

"You didn't suspect Allison might be pregnant? You seem pretty certain her baby is yours. Which means you two must have been having unprotected sex."

"Not that often. We tried to be careful. Sometimes, though, well . . ."

"But you never thought she might be pregnant?"

"I . . . it was because, if Allie was pregnant, there was no reason for her not to tell me. I'd have definitely stood by her, no doubt about it. I'd have married her and taken care of her and the baby, too. She had no reason not to tell me, Bex. And she certainly had no reason to kill herself!"

Bex and Coop got off the elevator and headed for the lounge.

"But if Idan was the father . . ." she pointed out.

"You really think Allie was cheating on me with Idan?"

"I only have Idan's word for it. But, then again, I only have your word that your relationship with Allie was what you say it was."

"This is messed up." Coop sighed.

Bex agreed with him.

They arrived at the lounge and, as soon as she opened the door, Bex realized they wouldn't be alone. Omri was still there, this time without his ad hoc guardian, but so was Officer Ho. He was standing next to Ralph Adler, helping him fill out some paperwork.

Ralph was hunched over a desk, pen in his hand, and Ho was leaning over him, so that neither saw the door open. Bex considered suggesting to Coop that they come back later, now probably wasn't a good time, but she never had the chance. Coop pushed the door open the rest of the way, and the squeak got both Ralph and Ho's attention.

L.A.'s finest clearly had no idea who the young man with Bex was. Ralph, on the other hand, looked like he'd been waiting specifically for his arrival.

Despite being, by Bex's estimate, a good fifty pounds overweight, and probably thirty years older that his target, Ralph didn't hesitate in dropping the pen and, with a roar, tearing across the room to smack both fleshy palms against Coop's chest.

Unprepared for the blow, Coop staggered, accidentally stepping on the loose lace of his left shoe with his right foot and going down completely.

Pleased, Ralph raised his leg and aimed a kick at Coop's head. Coop, employing the same catlike stealth that had saved many a seemingly doomed triple jump at the last minute, managed to roll out of the way and hop back onto his feet, raising his own leg to deflect the blow and nearly knocking Ralph off-balance instead.

"Little shit!" Ralph screamed as he grabbed a table to keep from toppling over. "You killed my daughter!"

Five

Officer Ho pounced on Ralph, squeezing his wrists and yanking both arms behind his back. The older man howled in protest and tried to squeeze his way out, but Ho held on, pinning his elbows for good measure. Ralph's hat fell off his head as he struggled and screamed at Ho, "Let go of me, damn it! Don't you know who this little punk is?"

Realizing that words weren't going to do the trick here, Ralph attempted to slip out of his raincoat sleeves, but this wasn't Officer Ho's first time at the human rodeo, and Ralph had barely gotten his shoulders loose before Ho stuck a knee in Ralph's lower back, driving his shoulder blades closer together and making the escape impossible.

Bex felt like she should be taking notes, but everything happened so quickly she had barely registered one event before the next took place.

Coop, back up on his feet, instinctively raised his fists—Bex recalled from his bio that in addition to running, cycling, biking, weight lifting, and, for all she knew, leaping tall buildings in a single bound, Coop also boxed to cross-train. He looked for a moment like he might take a retaliatory swing at the jutting gut that was now so tantalizingly wide open in his direction, but a stern bark of "Step down, kid!" from Ho kept Coop's clenched palms by his sides, even as he refused to relax his fight stance, legs wide apart, bounding on his toes, every muscle hyperalert.

Instead, Coop merely screamed back, "What are you talking about? No one killed Allie! She committed suicide. Right?" Suddenly unsure, Coop dropped his stance, heels on the floor, fingers loose, and swiveled his head to look at Bex for confirmation.

She, in turn, looked to Ho, who—in a move so fleeting, Bex was left wondering if maybe she'd imagined seeing it—shook his head, "No."

Now, what in the world did *that* mean?

Did it mean, "No, don't tell him anything"? Or did it mean, "No, I told her father something else since you've been gone"? Or did it mean, "No, she didn't commit suicide"?

In any case, it was a response Bex was desperate to pursue, although she was certain that, should she choose to do so now, the answer from Ho would, without a doubt, be a not-at-all cryptic "No." Obviously Officer Ho had something he wanted to tell her. Equally obvious was that he didn't want to do it at the present time, surrounded by the present people. So Bex would just have to wait. And tread carefully.

Strapped now for how to respond, Bex was saved from deciding between a lie she was once positive about and an inflammatory truth she only suspected, by Ralph—still pinned and so forced to make up the frustration through sheer volume—spitting out, "And who drove her to it, huh, boy? Who made my little girl put a noose around her neck?"

The choice of words made Coop, instinctively, raise a hand to his own throat. He quickly realized what he was doing and flung down his hand as if it had touched something particularly foul.

"I—" He clearly meant to answer, but in that moment, Coop's eyes were once again drawn to Omri in his car seat. Was he looking for a resemblance? Bex wondered. It was a pretty tough call. About the only thing six-foot-tall Coop and sixteen-inch Omri had in common was that they were both Caucasian, with two eyes, a nose, a mouth, the usual number of limbs. The baby might have had a cleft in his chin, but it was hard to see what was natural skin and what was a dent from the front of his jacket poking his jaw. The tufts of hair sprouting atop his head might have been a familiar, sandy color, but there were too few of them to really tell. There were no telling birthmarks, no hereditary red lines shaped like stork bites on the back of the neck that Bex could see. And, as far as anyone knew, the boy had yet to display so much as a hint of talent for landing triple jumps. But that, she supposed, would come with time.

At this point, if asked to comment under oath, Bex would have to say that Omri looked about as much like Cooper Devaney as he did like Idan Ben-Golan as he did like the late Allison Adler. He was an identifiable baby human being. But that was about all.

In the silence of Coop gazing at Omri, Ralph's accusatory question hung in the air like the smell of tuna days after the last can was digested. Coop, as if possessed to do it, took a hesitant step in the infant's direction.

"Don't you even think about it, you son of a bitch," Ralph threatened.

Coop froze. Or at least the bulk of his body did. His eyes shifted nervously from Omri to Ralph and back again. He knew there was really nothing Ralph could do to stop him. Even if he weren't being held down and wanted to take another swing at him, the whole room knew his first blow had been a lucky shot. Coop was more agile, fitter, and don't forget, younger. He could easily take Ralph Adler if he really wanted to.

But Cooper Devaney was also, as far as Bex knew, one other thing. He was a decent kid who really didn't enjoy having anyone mad at him, much less filled with as much hate as Ralph seemed to be.

Yes, he wanted to see his son up close. But he also wanted to settle the situation before it went any further.

To that end, Coop dropped his attempt to approach Omri and pleaded with Ralph, "I didn't know Allie was pregnant. I swear to God, I didn't know."

"Oh, yeah?" Ralph's tone did not ring with newly converted belief. "Well, what did you think might happen after you screwed around with my daughter?"

"Allie and me . . . we were careful." Bex hoped the stuttered denial sounded more convincing to Ralph than it did to her, because she just wasn't buying.

"Tell him that." Ralph managed to pull out one arm from Ho's grip so he could jerk a thumb in Omri's direction.

As his tone now was merely sarcastic, no longer homicidal, Ho cautiously relaxed his hold. Ralph rubbed his sore shoulders with both hands, practically hugging himself, and glared, but he validated Ho's evaluation by making no move to launch another assault. Instead, he walked over to Omri, so that Ralph was blocking Coop's view.

Feeling like maybe he'd made some progress in trying to get across his point of view, Coop, somewhat encouraged, continued attempting to reason with his presumed son's grandfather. "Mr. Adler," he said, "you have to believe me. Allison never told me she was pregnant. I was as stunned as you were when she announced she wasn't going to Worlds and then disappeared. I was devastated. I didn't understand what'd happened, what I'd done. Don't you remember how I kept calling you, asking if you'd heard anything?"

"I remember," Ralph said with a grunt, suggesting the groveling had hardly worked in Coop's favor. Then or now.

"I loved Allison. I would have married her."

"She didn't want to get married!" Ralph thundered so loudly, the baby, who'd already endured more than his share of yelling, finally broke down and, after an endless, silent moment wherein his mouth was wide open but no sound came out, burst into pitiful, tearless shrieks. His face folded into itself, the sides of his mouth drooping into a U, eyes squeezing into dry slashes, chubby cheeks quivering, then turning purple.

There were three men in the room. Two of them were presumably the little guy's family. At the first shriek, all three turned to look at Bex, each radiating a variation on, "You're a woman. Do something."

Bex wasn't a parent. She'd grown up an only child. But she had babysat a lot during her teens, so she figured that did make her the most qualified temporary guardian. (Although hadn't Ho mentioned something earlier about having a daughter? But maybe he was the traditional sex-roles type.) Bex stepped around Ralph, unbuckled Omri from his car seat, and picked the baby up. She rested his face against her chest and bounced him up and down in place for a few moments while soothingly humming, "Shhh . . ." After a few moments he settled down, stuck a fist in his mouth, and proceeded to chew it lustily while staring at the whiteness of the wall.

Ralph, Coop, and Ho stared at Bex not unlike she imagined the Ancient Greeks once gazed upon Prometheus bringing fire to his tribe. It was a very nice feeling, but neither here nor there at the moment.

Ralph realized as much, and opened his mouth to continue the howl that had once been so rudely interrupted.

However, before he could reach full volume, Bex hissed "Shhh!" and indicated the temporarily content baby with her chin. She narrowed her eyes and shook her head for good measure. That seemed to do the trick.

Instead of yelling, Ralph lowered his voice to an angry stage whisper as he hissed at Coop, "Allison didn't want to get married, you idiot. You claim you loved her. Did you ever listen to her? What did Allison want more than anything in the world?"

Coop stared at him blankly, suspecting a trick question and stymied as to what reply might not earn him another kick to the head.

"Well, it wasn't to get married, that's for sure! And it wasn't to get knocked up!" Ralph mocked in disgust. "Allie wanted to be a champion, that's what she wanted. Why else would she have put up with the three A.M. wake-up calls, and the bleeding sores on her feet, and the starvation diets, and the endless, endless rejections? She wanted to be a champion! She wanted to be a star. And you took that all away from her."

"Me?" Coop didn't know whether to be angry or condescending. "I encouraged Allie. I was behind her all the way. If anyone knows what it's like to get up at three A.M. to go skating, or to be just sitting around, reading a book, and feel the front of your ankles burst and gush blood, it's me. That's why Allie and I were so tremendous together. We understood where the other was coming from."

"And did you also understand that while you were having sex, if anything went wrong, Allie's career would be the one to suffer, not yours? Did you both understand that little piece of reality?"

Coop actually blushed, which was sweet to see, but

didn't carry much weight with Ralph. "We tried to be careful. Honestly we did."

"You made more effort putting guards on your skates to keep them from rusting."

At that, Bex did have to smirk. She hid it by burying her face in Omri's hair. It was an excellent analogy, both thematically and visually. Even if it meant she'd never be able to look at skate guards in the same way again.

"You ruined any chance Allie had of ever becoming a World champion," Ralph went back to his original aria. "Even if she'd made up her mind early enough to get rid of the baby—"

"No," Coop said. "I wouldn't have asked her to—"

"She still would have had to miss the Worlds. We would have had to make up a reason, I suppose. An injury of some sort, maybe another flare-up of the bruised hip she had a season before—she and Sebastian were training the Killian so hard, he actually left handprints on her skin, and she had to take several weeks off to keep from getting a more serious hematoma. We might have said it happened again." For a moment, Bex could see Ralph slipping into his alternate timeline, the one where Allie's little . . . problem was still fixable and her precious skating career intact. "But no. No, that wouldn't have done any good in the end. Allie and Sebi were the National champions. If they missed their first Worlds as champs, they'd have dropped too far down in the standings. Heck, they might even have lost the National title next year. Judges hate recurrent injuries. They lose faith in you. Move on to someone else. Someone younger. We had enough of an obstacle with Sebi's age. Even if Allie took only one season off, it would have ruined everything. You," he told Coop, "ruined everything."

"I loved Allie," Coop reiterated. "Her problem would have been my problem."

"Would you have skipped Worlds last year to stay home

and hold her hand? Huh? Would you have skipped Nationals this year to change diapers? Tell the truth, boy. It doesn't really matter much now."

"Allie and I would have worked it out. I'm sure of it."

Ralph snorted. "Sure sounds like a big-ass no to me. How 'bout the rest of you?"

Though it wasn't Bex's place to judge—she merely reported the facts and left the judging to the folks watching at home—she did have to admit that yeah, it kinda sounded like a big-ass no to her, too.

It must have sounded like one to Coop, too, because, he admitted, "I don't know what I would have done." Then, somewhat defensively, he added, "Allie never gave me the chance to find out."

"Oh, that's cute. That's real, real cute. Now you're the victim in all this? Now, you're the one we're supposed to feel sorry for?"

"I didn't say you should feel sorry for me, I just said that I also—"

"How do you think it was for Allison, sitting wherever she ended up after she left home? I can only imagine what sort of place a young, pregnant girl with no money ends up—turning the television on and watching you skate at Worlds. How do you think she felt, watching you win your first World medal?"

Coop didn't reply, so Ralph helped out: "It should have been her! She should have been winning that medal. Instead, she was all alone, no one to turn to, stuck with a baby she didn't want and, worst of all, off the ice!"

Yes, Bex thought, considering the world this little drama was unfolding in, *the latter really would be considered the worst fate of all.*

"Are you surprised she killed herself? What else could she do? She had nothing to look forward to, no future at all." Ralph zeroed in. "Because of you."

It was the third or fourth time since they'd come in that Ralph had lobbed that particular charge in Coop's direction. And even though he hadn't seen the slightest of twitches in Ho's chin that suggested maybe Allison hadn't committed suicide after all, Coop nevertheless decided he wasn't about to stand for any more accusations.

He waved his hand dismissively in Ralph's direction, turned decisively around, and approached Bex. He held out his arms and requested, "May I have my son, please?"

Bex didn't immediately respond. She wasn't sure how she should. For one thing, Bex had been in this very room when Idan Ben-Golan had made the same demand just as compellingly, and been rebuffed for presenting no evidence of paternity. As far as Bex could see, Coop's claim was equally as dubious. The only difference was that Ralph—quite loudly and clearly and violently—believed Coop's assertion over Ben-Golan's, but they didn't decide DNA tests by majority vote.

Bex didn't want to just hand Omri over indiscriminately. Fortunately, she was spared having to make a decision by Ralph bellowing, "That boy is coming home with me. I'm just getting the paperwork taken care of now. I don't care how many of you sons of bitches come out of the woodwork claiming he's your bastard. He's my grandson, and I'll be taking responsibility for him, thank you very much."

"That isn't fair," Coop pointed out to Ho, to Bex, to anyone who he thought had jurisdiction. "Ralph isn't even Allison's real father. He's not a blood relative. I am."

"I adopted Allie. Maybe I'll adopt this little guy, too. What do you think, boy? How do you like that idea?"

"You have no right!" Some people hated to see a grown man cry. Personally, Bex had a lot more issues with seeing grown men whine. "He's my son. If he's going home with anyone right now, it should be with me."

"Oh, you'd like that, wouldn't you? That would just make the sweet-sweetest up-close-and-personal TV profile for the Nationals broadcast, wouldn't it? Brave Champion Juggles Daddyhood and Death Drops! Oh, my eyes are already tearing up just thinking about it. You didn't think I had your number, did you, boy? You didn't think I got what you are really after. It's the publicity. It's always the publicity angle with you. You and that mother of yours are whores for it. You think I didn't figure out why you first started sniffing around Allison? It's because two champs make better copy than one, that's why. Everyone assumes that our boy skaters are fags, so you got to make sure the whole world knows you're different. You have a girlfriend, la dee dah! The skating magazines loved you for that. Hell, even *People* ran a story, and you know there's no way in hell you'd have gotten that kind of action alone. This whole mess started because you were after the publicity. Well, there's no way in hell I'm letting you use Allie's baby to get more of it."

"You're insane," Coop said politely.

"Yes. He is." A voice in the doorway made everyone turn around as Idan Ben-Golan strode in, as graceful as he'd been going out and, if it were possible, even more self-confident. "With all due respect, Mr. Adler, you are insane if you believe that Coop will be using that child for publicity purposes. He has no grounds. The boy is my son, not his."

Ralph looked like he wanted to snort in disdain again. But Idan Ben-Golan was not a twenty-two-year-old lad wearing skating sweats and struggling to tell his side of a romance gone bad. Idan was (1) a grown man; (2) a grown man who'd been taught to kill other grown men; and (3) a grown man uninterested in being understood or forgiven. Just obeyed. He clearly wasn't about to be intimidated by an irate father, a confused and guilty ex, or a lowly researcher turned babysitter.

When Idan held out his arms expectantly for Omri, it was all Bex could do not to instantly acquiesce.

The only person Idan seemed willing to have a semblance of a conversation with was Officer Ho. He said, "I believe this is what you requested of me," and handed Ho an original—stamped and everything—document.

Bex wasn't the only one curious about what it said. She just had the farthest distance to cross and so was the last to huddle with the group that instantly surrounded it. She craned her head for a complete view.

The document in question appeared to be a legitimate, State of California birth certificate for a little dude named Omri.

Listing one Allison Adler, age nineteen, as his mother.

And Idan Ben-Golan as the father.

Six

If Idan Ben-Golan had been in the room with Bex when Ralph first charged Coop, he might have been a bit more anxious about the cavalier way he thrust his official proof of paternity in Allie's definitely unstable father's face. But as things stood, even though Ralph's face tightened into a knot until he was practically inhaling his lips and his eyes all but smashed into each other above the bridge of his nose as he tried to swallow and digest the document whole, Idan made no move to protect himself from what the rest of them presumed would be an imminent assault.

Officer Ho seemed so certain one was coming that he took a step closer to Ralph and even put both arms out, in case he needed to block another wild swing. But Idan simply stayed where he was, hands on his hips, eyes glaring impatiently at the crowd inspecting Omri's birth certificate. He willed them to hurry up and grant him his son, the implication being that he was a busy man and there was only so much time he could afford to waste on this nonsense.

"I should have known," Ralph mumbled. Was this when he would charge again? Judging from the way he moved out of the way to give Ralph a clear shot, Coop certainly thought so. And, in Bex's opinion, he looked rather delighted by the possibility.

But Ralph, either already spent from his encounter with the last daddy candidate, or finally realizing that if he stood no chance against Coop, taking on Idan was out of the question, just shook his head and repeated, "I should have known. You!"

There was no way Idan could have misunderstood who the "you" was directed at, but his facial expression refused to flicker.

Ralph said, "I used to joke that Allie thought you not only hung the moon, you came up with the idea for it in the first place. All I heard day and night was, 'Idan thinks this,' and 'Idan thinks that.' I should have known you had some sick hold on her."

Idan turned to Officer Ho. He asked, "Is the documentation you hold in your hand adequate for me to take my son?"

Ralph may have been the one Idan was ignoring, but it was Coop who couldn't take it. Deciding that the role of angry lunatic needed to be played by someone, and if Ralph refused to fill it, Coop might as well give it a shot, he slammed one hand on Idan's shoulder from behind and attempted to spin him around, demanding, "How can you just stand there like that? Don't you have anything to say for yourself?"

The slow and steady manner with which he pivoted to face Coop was Idan's way of making clear that he was turning of his own volition, rather than in response to being either manhandled or chastised. Without raising his voice he said, "This has nothing to do with you, Coop."

"Allie was my girlfriend!"

"That relationship ended almost a year ago."

"But it was still going on when you and she—"

"It is over now, Coop. That is the only relevant fact."

"The baby could be mine," Coop asserted, puffing out his chest as if to suggest that his entire body was filled with viable, virile, manly sperm cells.

"He isn't."

"That birth certificate doesn't prove anything."

"It proves that I am Omri's legal father."

Ralph asked, "How could you do it?" Unlike the angry accusations he'd lobbed at Coop, Ralph seemed truly puzzled now. "How could you do that to yourself?"

"To himself?" Officer Ho was completely lost. He glanced at Bex for guidance, and she sighed to indicate that yes, unfortunately, she knew exactly where this was going. Ho would see in a minute.

Ralph said to Idan, "Allie and Sebi were finally National champions. You'd been waiting for four years for this moment. You were dying to take them to Worlds as the U.S. champs. You knew what that would do for their ranking. You wanted that as much as we all did. We had a plan. National title. World. Olympic Gold. How could you throw that all away by getting Allie pregnant?"

Ho looked at Bex again, wondering if Ralph was serious. Bex nodded. He was dead serious.

Idan said, "That is no longer relevant. Ralph, I am truly sorry for your loss. I cared for Allison, too—"

"What about your wife?" Now that he was in the position of getting to make a self-righteous accusation, Coop was warming up to this whole loud discussion culture. "Did you care for Pandora as much as you did for Allison when you were cheating on her with a teenager?"

"Calm down, Coop." Idan was using his coaching voice, steady and strong with no options for backtalk.

"Why should I?"

"Because," Idan said, "you are making an imbecile of yourself."

"Oh, yeah? So what's wrong with that?" Coop was unspooling in front of them, and it was not pleasant to watch. His California surfer-dude, "Whatever, it's all good," demeanor cracked and fell away like an eggshell, exposing a wet, unformed tangle of confusion and blind fury. Coop, Bex realized, could act as if nothing bothered him and he didn't care who was in control as long as he knew that he actually was. The minute that was taken away from him, Coop crumbled. "Are you the only one allowed to make me look like an idiot? Stealing my girl right in front of my face? I bet you thought it was really funny, didn't you?"

"Coop," Idan wouldn't be baited, "this matter has nothing to do with you."

"Were you jealous, is that it? Jealous that I was going to be the champion you never could be? Hell, I can get from one end of the rink to the other without falling on my face—that's more than you managed at the Olympics. Were you trying to get back at me by stealing Allie? Did that make you feel like a big man?"

For Idan, the conversation was definitely over. He turned to Bex and held out his arms again for Omri. "My son," he requested politely.

"No way, José!" Ralph interrupted. "I've got papers right here saying I'm taking that boy home with me."

Idan informed Officer Ho, "You have no right to grant him guardianship—(a) it is outside of your jurisdiction, and (b) my documentation trumps his. Now that Allison is dead, I am the recognized, legal guardian."

Now that Allison is dead . . . Somehow, in all the commotion, they all seemed to have forgotten that. Even Bex, who only a moment ago had been wondering what Ho's cryptic nod in her direction meant, had gotten so caught up in the pissing contest among Coop, Idan, and Ralph that she'd forgotten what set off this melee in the first place. The guilt was not a pleasant sensation. Bex wondered how Idan's memory jog was affecting the men who'd claimed to love her.

Ralph told Idan, "You killed my daughter. You drove Allie to commit suicide. You think I'm going to reward you by giving up her boy?"

"I am the legal guardian," Idan repeated. Then he asked Officer Ho, "Would you care to speak to my lawyer about it? He is standing by at his office, waiting for your call."

"Actually," Ho said, "I think I'd like to do that."

Idan handed over a card with, Bex presumed, the lawyer's name and number, and added, "After you finish speaking to him, make sure you call the Department of Family Services. He has been on the phone with them as well."

Not looking happy about receiving orders from a civilian, Ho nevertheless took the card, pulled out his cell phone, and retreated to a quieter corner to make the call.

That left Idan, Coop, and Ralph to stare at Omri. And, by extension, Bex, because the little guy had fallen asleep curled up against her chest. And she was the only one still awake to encounter their combined gaze.

Ralph said, "You make sure 24/7 tells the whole story. You make sure the whole world knows what these two did to my little girl." To Coop he said with a smirk, "Let's see how you and your mommy can spin that one for the media." To Idan he said, "Pedophilia's a good reason for deportation back to where you came from, wouldn't you say? Especially when your rich wife doesn't feel like standing up for your sorry ass."

"Allison," Idan reminded, "was eighteen years old. No crime was committed."

"What about a moral crime?" Coop challenged. "How many parents you think are going to send their kids to you for lessons after they find out what you did?"

"Not every parent," Idan replied pointedly, "withdraws their child away from a winning coach simply because they do not like certain aspects of their personal life."

"You're going to tell the whole story, aren't you?" Ralph had only one tune to sing where Bex was concerned and like a player piano, he was on infinite loop with it. "When Golden Boy here is out there skating his Long Program live in prime time, you'll make sure Francis and Diana have all the facts."

Bex was about to reply that she wasn't certain she had all the facts yet, but then remembered that her presence was token. If Bex hadn't been here, the three would have been sniping at each other over any available intermediary, including the chairs.

"The baby might still be mine," Coop insisted, apropos of nothing.

"I thought you and Allie were always careful," Ralph said, mocking Coop's tone from before. He managed to capture the equal parts of defensiveness and self-pity perfectly.

"Accidents happen."

"You are not Omri's father," Idan said, and Bex feared they were about to launch on another round of "next verse, same as the first."

Thank God, at that moment Officer Ho returned from the corner, cell phone still in hand, a look of resignation dotting his features.

"All right," he said. "This is what we're going to do."

Three faces looked at him expectantly. Bex made the fourth, because while she had enjoyed rocking little Omri to sleep—it made a pleasant change to her usual day and it *had* been fun to figure out how to calm him while the men ran helpless, not to mention the fact that, as long as she was Official Keeper of Omri, it gave Bex an excuse to eavesdrop on a fight that otherwise would have been none of her business—Bex's arms were getting tired. Ten pounds could be a lot when you had to stand with them for close to a half hour. Not to mention the fact that the little guy was drooling a hole into the center of her shirt that had started out the size of a dime and now was more of a saucer. She was ready to hand the baby dude over. She just needed to know to whom.

"Mr. Ben-Golan"—Ho assumed the mantle of Solomon—"you do seem to have the superseding claim here. You may take the infant with you."

"Thank you, Officer." Ben-Golan's face betrayed no expression. But Bex did notice his hands shaking ever so slightly as he reached for his son. She handed Omri over, careful not to wake him. "And thank you, Bex," he said.

"You're welcome. He's adorable."

"Wait a damn minute—" Ralph began, only to be interrupted by Coop's by now familiar, "But what if the baby is mine?"

Obviously expecting the protest, Ho went right into, "And here's what both of you gentlemen can do if you're unhappy with my decision. Go to Family Court, file a petition for custody. One for each of you. Let a judge decide where that boy belongs."

Ho had barely completed his invective before Idan had gathered up Omri's car seat and was headed for the door. He didn't say good-bye or even indicate that anything had happened. He simply strapped in his son and walked out.

"Son of a bitch," Ralph swore.

"It isn't fair," Coop stomped.

DEATH DROP

Neither made any attempt to leave. They just stood there, as if waiting for further instructions.

Eventually Ho took pity and gave them some. "You're free to go," he said. "Mr. Adler, we have your identification of Allison's body. Thank you very much, sir, for your cooperation. And Mr. Devaney, someone will contact you if the police have any further questions about your relationship with Miss Adler."

"I loved her," Coop said.

"That's nice," Ho said. "Now you two are both free to go."

Bex noticed he didn't ask her to do the same.

She waited until Ralph and Coop had taken their leave. Allison's father shuffled out as if kicking Coop had been his last attempt at actually lifting a leg and now he was magnetically tethered to the floor. He put on his baseball cap, straightened his coat, and tucked the shirt that had gotten loose during one scuffle or another into his pants. He hitched up his belt with his thumbs, stuck the remaining fingers in the loops, and looked around the room again, as if afraid he'd forgotten something. He had forgotten nothing, because he'd come in already having lost everything.

Coop followed a few steps behind. He didn't shuffle, his shoulders didn't sag, his jaw remained set. He was too athletic to be anything but graceful. But his hands told the story. Coop peeled off his gloves as if it were the first time he'd done such a thing. Each gesture was suddenly new and unfamiliar. He acted as if he were being directed, step by step, in how to complete the task by someone speaking a different language. His hands no longer belonged to him, his fingers no longer obeyed him, because he was no longer the same person he'd been when he came in.

Once out the door, Coop and Ralph headed in different directions—not because either had a reason for going that way, but simply because they were desperate to get away from each other.

Bex wanted to feel sorry for them, but there were too many loose, unanswered questions to this story. And Bex had long ago made a point of refusing to feel sorry for anyone until she'd gotten—and confirmed—the whole story. She'd made the mistake of feeling sympathy for, and thus trusting, the wrong people before.

"Close the door, would you, please, Bex?" Officer Ho asked, and she obeyed.

He sat down on the couch previously occupied by Omri's car seat and gestured for Bex to do the same. Once she was settled across from him, Ho sighed, exhausted, and rubbed his eyes. He said, "I hate domestic issues. They're always the worst."

"Is it true more policemen are killed responding to domestic calls than any other kind of crime?" Bex asked. Because that, alas, was what she did in stressful situations. She spouted facts.

Ho seemed surprised by her inquiry.

Bex shrugged and apologized. "I'm a researcher. I make my living learning useless trivia on the off chance it might be useful one day."

"Sounds a lot like being a cop."

Bex was going to quip, "But with less bloodshed" until she recalled her last few months on the job and realized that wasn't exactly true.

"But yes," Ho said, "domestic disputes are the most dangerous for police officers. Everyone's emotions are so raw." He asked, "What did you think of what we saw here today? You know the players better than I do."

Bex said, "It's hard to say. I've certainly heard of coaches seducing their students—and students younger than eighteen, believe me. So it's not like Idan's version is out of the question. On the other hand, I worked Nationals last year, and Coop and Allie were certainly acting like a couple of kids in love. I mean, they sat together in the stands, they held hands walking around the arena, he came to all her practices, she came to his—"

"Is that the figure skating equivalent of going steady?"

"More or less."

"What about the dad?"

"He's pretty standard issue, too. I can believe that he didn't know Allison was cheating on Coop with Idan, and I can believe that he knew it damn well and looked the other way because Idan was going to turn his baby into a champion."

"So the kid could be anyone's?"

"I suppose . . . but does it really matter?" Bex tread carefully now, realizing that one wrong move could get her locked out of the information cycle for good. She had thought that Ho was on her side, even slipping her advance information. But what if that was a misinterpretation on her part? She couldn't presume to know anything. "If Allison committed suicide"—Bex chose each word as if the fate of her job depended on it—"what difference does the identity of her baby's father make to the police?"

Ho finished rubbing his eyes and looked Bex right in the eye, so there could be no misunderstanding between them. He said, "Allison Adler didn't commit suicide. She was murdered. And in that case, the identity of her baby's father matters a hell of a lot."

Seven

"Murdered?" Bex repeated. She wasn't all that surprised. Ho had insinuated as much earlier. All she really wanted to know was, "How can you be certain?"

"Well, the final autopsy report hasn't come in yet, obviously. But I've done this before. I know the signs." Ho explained, "If a person hangs himself—or herself, as the case may be—the knot of the loop will rise upward in direct opposition to gravity, so the marks will appear high up on the neck in a rising fashion. On the other hand, if a person is, let's say, strangled first, then strung up to make it look like they hung themselves, the marks will be more level or even straight across because most likely the killer is pushing down with balanced force, either with his bare hands or some kind of ligature."

"And the marks on Allison's neck—"

"Like they were made by a ruler."

Bex sighed. "So you think she was strangled, then hung."

"I'd testify to it in court."

"Let's hope you get the chance to."

"And there was one more thing. Allison was wearing a black turtleneck sweater, one of those fluffy things that's like a sheep gone bad. My daughter loves them, but they attract all sorts of garbage—hair, lint, bits of food; like flypaper. When I brought Allison down, there were bright red fibers practically ground into her neck, plus a couple pressed under her left armpit and on her opposite hip. She put up a fight."

"Against someone wearing red."

"Yeah . . ."

Bex took a wild guess, but she had the feeling Ho had been leading her there all along. "Was it the same texture and shade of red as the gloves Coop Devaney wears?"

Ho tipped his head at her ability to follow his lead. She suspected he might even have smiled, except where he had led her was too depressing. "Yup."

"Well, that sucks, doesn't it?"

"Yup."

"Those gloves were part of the official World Team uniform this season. Half the arena has identical pairs."

"Yup," Ho agreed.

Bex asked, "Why are you telling me this?"

She'd been meaning to inquire since he'd first allowed her to sit in on Harris Knox's statement, not to mention Idan, Ralph, and Coop's respective outbursts. Most police officers would have long ago asked her politely to leave; then, when she dawdled (Bex never flat out refused, but she'd concentrated the act of obeying very slowly down to a fine art), thrown her out. But Ho was different. And Bex doubted that her reputation for solving other skating-related messes had preceded her.

"Because," he said, "I'd like to ask for your help."

"I'll tell you everything I know."

"No. More than that. The fact is, yes, I have a forensics teams in the costume room right now, but I don't hold out much hope for them finding anything. How many people go through that room in a single day? Tens? Dozens?"

"Could be hundreds."

"So any DNA or fingerprint evidence we might find is useless. As for Allie's autopsy, it will determine the cause of death was strangulation. They'll take out the red threads and analyze them. But, like you said, half the arena is wearing those gloves—skaters, coaches, officials, even fans probably, since those same gloves are sold on the USFSA website, right?"

Bex said, "You've done your homework."

"I'm a thorough guy. Because I never expect to get lucky. Especially here. Even if, by some divine providence, the ME is able to extract a skin cell or two from the red threads that we then match to an actual person—God only knows how, I hardly have the authority to ask everyone who happened to be on the premises to submit to a DNA test—any semicompetent attorney could point out that there were a million ways those threads might have gotten on Allie. The most obvious one being, she'd been gone from skating for a long time. The minute an old friend saw her, he gave her a big hug. End of story."

"You said 'he,'" Bex noted. "You think Allie was killed by a man?"

"Suffocation is a pretty grueling way to kill someone. You need to be relatively strong, especially if the victim is fighting back." Ho reasoned. "But, why? Do you think there's a woman I should be questioning?"

"Lian Reilly is the only one I can think of with a motive. She's Coop's current girlfriend. She might not have been too happy to find out his ex had given birth to his baby. This is Lian's first relationship, and she's not the most mature specimen around. I wouldn't put it past her to snap."

"Coop claims he didn't know anything about the kid— or Allie, for that matter."

"In my business," Bex said, "people lie to me all the time. How about yours?"

Ho grinned and conceded, "Once in a while."

"Furthermore, Coop's not knowing doesn't mean Lian didn't. The skating grapevine is a terrifying thing in its efficiency. Lian could have heard from someone else and acted completely on her own. She could have called Allie and lured her to the rink, led her to the costume room, and killed her. That's one way to make sure your guy doesn't go back to his ex. Baby or no baby."

"It's not the worst motive I've ever heard."

"Except for one thing."

"What's that?"

"Lian Reilly is a tiny little thing. She's about a head shorter than Allison. I don't really see her overpowering Allie, element of surprise or not."

"So why the jealous girlfriend scenario?"

"Because Lian's mother isn't tiny at all."

"She was dating Devaney, too?"

"No. But she lives for Lian's happiness. And there's one more thing. Amanda Reilly would love for her daughter to quit skating and live a normal life. Coop was the closest Lian had ever come to that. What if Amanda was more concerned about Lian losing her boyfriend to his son and ex than Lian was?"

"So her mother knocked off the competition?"

Bex blushed. "Is that the worst motive you've ever heard?"

"Nope," Ho said.

Emboldened and downright giddy at being listened to,

Bex volunteered, "There's also Pandora Westby, Idan Ben-Golan's wife."

"We're moving on to Daddy Candidate Number Two?"

"Pandora could not have been happy about Allie and Idan. And she didn't have to do the dirty work herself. She's loaded. She could have hired someone to do it."

"She hired someone who just happened to be wearing USFSA gloves?"

"Maybe our killer does his homework, too. And has access to the Internet."

Ho chuckled. "Touché."

"And what's to say she didn't hire a member of the World Team? Pandora has sponsored a lot of athletes over the years. Maybe she finally called in a favor." That didn't involve a bare-chested boy following her around adoringly.

"Who are some of her protégés?"

"Well, Coop, for one. Sebastian Vama, Allie's old partner, for another."

"So we could be looking at some group effort here. Sounds like a lot of people wanted this poor kid dead."

"What about her dad?" Bex asked. "You interviewed him. Did he have an alibi for the time Allison was killed?"

"Home. Sleeping. It was five A.M. Hard to argue with that."

"It's just the way he kept talking about how much money Allie's skating cost him. Like that loss was more important than she was."

"Killing her wouldn't have gotten him his money back."

"No. But it might have made him feel better about the whole thing. And it would give him custody of her baby—or so he thought, anyway, until Idan stepped up. Maybe he saw Allie's son as a second chance. And he was willing to sacrifice her for it."

"Except Mr. Ben-Golan threw a monkey wrench into those plans."

"Ralph Adler sounded positive that Coop was the father. Allie might have even told him that."

"Why? Assuming Ralph knew about the pregnancy, why lie to her dad?"

"To keep Idan from finding out?" Bex guessed.

"His name is on the birth certificate."

"But we don't know how it got there. Allie might have been meaning to keep the baby a secret from him, but he found out somehow—again, don't underestimate skating's grapevine—and coerced her into admitting he was the father and putting his name on the birth certificate. You saw how crazy Idan acted when he burst in here the first time. This isn't some guy unhappy to be a father. He wanted that boy. What if Allie knew just how badly Idan wanted him, and was afraid he would try to take Omri away from her?"

"Why go to court when you can just kill the mother?" Ho articulated what they were both thinking.

"Idan is certainly big enough and strong enough to overpower Allie. And he's got a set of those gloves, too, I'm sure of it."

"So we're right back where we started from."

Bex bit down on her thumbnail. "Sorry. I guess I wasn't much help."

"That's all right," Ho said. "This wasn't what I was talking about, anyway."

"It's not?" Bex wondered what else he could possibly ask of her.

"No. When I said I needed your help, I meant 24/7's."

"Oh." Suddenly Bex felt a lot less important than her previous several minutes of conversation had suggested. Her swelled head shrunk like a snail curling into itself.

"Here's the thing: I have permission from my department to go public with details about Allie's murder. We have so little to go on, we need to ask anyone who might have seen something suspicious this morning to step forward and let us know. And we'd like 24/7 to announce that on the air. Who knows? Someone who may have come here just to watch the practices with no intention of coming back might hear about it and offer a tip. Heck, maybe even someone with no connection to skating but just driving by the arena on their way to work has something we could use."

So Ho only wanted Bex for her television connections. Oh, well, what else was new? Here she'd actually thought someone had realized that her research might be a key element to solving a crime; but no, he was just buttering her up for the big request.

"Uhm, I could ask." Bex resolved to sound professional, even if that snail of her ego was now as shriveled as after a salt shower. "But, to be honest, I think my producer, Gil Cahill, will hate the idea."

"I love the idea!" Gil thundered.

At this particular championship, he'd set up his office in the twenty-foot-long, five-foot-wide production trailer parked in a lot right next to the arena. Which meant that Bex was attempting to have this conversation while, all around them, sound technicians were checking audio levels, technical directors were monitoring camera placement in the arena, and the four assistant directors were assisting the director by furiously scribbling notes around hasty pen-and-ink diagrams of every skater's program.

Bex could barely hear what she herself was asking, much less feel certain about Gil's answer.

"Really?" she shouted while, at the same time, ducking a crew member walking by with a camera on his shoulder, right at Bex's nose level. "But I thought you hated giving away 24/7 airtime for any cause. Remember when those former Olympians put on a benefit show for their old coach who had lung cancer and couldn't afford the treatment? Gary Gold wanted to mention the American Cancer Society and how people could donate on the air, and you told him he could do good on his own time, 24/7 wasn't a nonprofit."

"This isn't do-gooding," Gil explained. "This is good business. The viewers will tune in to get all the latest salacious details—even people who otherwise never watch a skating show. We could even do a call-in poll about who they think did it. Like one of those reality programs. This is great. Tell your cops 24/7 is at their service."

"Uhm . . . okay," Bex said and turned to leave, knowing that she should feel like she'd won, but having a tough time summoning the motivation.

"Except, Bex?"

"Yes?"

"One little thing."

"Okay. What?"

"We can't have Coop Devaney being guilty."

Bex just stared at Gil, unable to think of a single thing to say. Did Gil think this was a script Bex was writing? Or did he expect her to cover up evidence? Tamper with forensic results? Did he expect her to will the results he wanted into being?

"Come to the parking lot with me, Bex," Gil said.

They stepped out of the trailer, Gil suddenly discovering chivalry and holding the door open for her. Which was really less chivalrous than it seemed at first glance.

The problem with production trailers—besides the fact that they were narrow and crowded and noisy and always had multicolored M&M's ground into the carpet even if everyone inside was on a low-carb diet—was that the only way to climb in and out of one was by a barely foot-wide metallic ladder, each step the dimension and sturdiness of your average kid's ruler. Going up wasn't so bad because you could hold on to the sides and sort of vault yourself, leaping over several wobbly steps as you went. The biggest danger to going up was that someone would open the door from the inside out and wallop you sprawling to the ground again. But the risk there was low, because people did tend to at least look through the window before swinging the door open. (The old showbiz adage "Be nice to the people you meet on the way up because you'll see them again on the way down" was reimagined for life in a production trailer as "Be careful going out, because someday you might be the one coming in.")

Going down, on the other hand, was a different story. Trying to skip all the stairs entirely by jumping seemed tempting—until the first time you landed from a height of two feet on concrete while wearing high heels, or even any sort of street shoes. And while, by taking it easy, it was possible to ease your way down the swaying contraption while clinging to both guardrails, it was almost impossible to do so comfortably when someone else was behind you, stepping on your heels every inch of the way and shaking the steps even more with his own weight.

By acting chivalrous and offering Bex an "After you," Gil had ensured that he'd be the second person on the steps rather than the first.

And he didn't even wait for Bex to maneuver her way down to the bottom before he launched in with, "This isn't public knowledge yet—we're planning to make the announcement after he wins the National title again—but Coop Devaney is going to do a reality show for us."

"A *what*?" As soon as Bex reached terra firma, she spun around, facing Gil. He was so shocked by her abruptness that he actually stumbled on the final step and had to grab Bex's shoulder for support.

"A reality show. You know, they're all the rage now. Turns out viewers can't get enough of sticking their noses in other people's private business. Singers, celebrities, lousy parents, desperate single people, ugly chicks, dirty islanders—I thought, why not a skater? Well, actually, the mother, What's-her-name Devaney, first pitched me the idea. But I saw its potential right away, which is what matters in the end. And Coop is perfect. He's good-looking, he's built, he's got that All-American boy thing happening, and best of all, he's no fag. We'll get teenage girls watching by the millions. Do you know what kinds of rates advertisers pay for the teenage girl demo? The 24/7 brass has been on me for the last year, bitching that our audience is mostly old guys. Bring us some girls, they keep telling me. Well, Coop Devaney is going to bring us a shitload of girls."

"But not if he's in jail for killing his baby's Mama." Once again, Bex had no trouble comprehending the obvious. "That wouldn't be quite as hot and hunky."

"This show only works if Cooper Devaney is every twelve-year-old's pinup. We need that boy's face on teenybopper centerfolds and magazines, not wanted posters. You make sure Coop comes off looking good."

"And if he's the killer?"

"Oh, he's not the killer." Gil waved dismissively. "Are you kidding me? Cooper Devaney may have pecs coming out of his ass, but he's a mama's boy if I ever saw one. She makes the decisions, he nods and shuffles his feet. Not to mention, this Adler girl just dumps him without a word, pops out his kid, and he's standing around playing with himself, no idea what's going on. Guys like that don't kill, Bex. Give me some credit. You think it's by accident that I'm marketing him to the ten-fourteen demo? No. I'm selling him to the precious tween market, because any high school girl can see there's no real there, there. He's a wuss, Bex, a weenie. For the ten-fourteen, that translates as being safe and unthreatening. The perfect dream boy without any of that icky adult sexuality. Now you make sure he comes off that way on camera during this sting of yours. You make certain he comes off so squeaky clean no one can even imagine him being Allison's killer."

Eight

With such concrete marching orders, Bex felt ready to go forth and ensure Cooper Devaney came off as a lovable and harmless imp, whether or not he happened to have choked a young woman to death a few hours earlier. Sounded simple.

But there was one other issue she needed to take care of first.

"Gil?"

"What?" He'd been ready to spring up the steps, and her query stopped him with one leg awkwardly in the air.

"You know that other murder-based piece we were planning to run? Rachel Rose, Robby Sharpton, Jeremy Hunt, that whole scandal?"

"Oh, that piece."

Only this morning at their production meeting, Gil had been raving about how awesome the story was and how they were going to whip the competition with it when it aired during the Men's Long Program on Friday night.

Now it was, "Oh, that piece." In Gil's world the motto was "Who have you killed for me lately?"

"Jeremy Hunt's dad, Craig, asked if I could interview Jeremy instead of Mollie doing it. Jeremy knows me, and his dad thinks he might be more comfortable."

Gil just stared at Bex blankly.

And so Bex reacted the way she always did when stared upon blankly. She began to talk faster. Bex didn't know why this happened every time, and she didn't know why, knowing that this happened every time, she had yet to think of something to do about it. All she knew was, when Bex couldn't assess what another person was thinking by either their words or body language, her own verbal language went into overdrive. She guessed that it might be in the hope that if she kept talking quickly she would sooner rather than later stumble upon a topic that would prompt the person to respond, which would, in turn, put her out of her misery and give her something to base her subsequent babbling on. But all Bex knew for sure was that it was an annoying habit, for both her and the listener.

Not that the knowledge kept her from rambling. She blathered. "Look, Gil, I—I know I'm not a real producer and I've never actually produced a piece before. But I did research this story and I shot some of the footage and Mollie was going to work off my notes anyway, and she's still the one putting it together in the edit room, so it probably doesn't matter who does the actual sit-down, right?"

Gil continued staring blankly.

Bex had run out of things to say.

Finally he shrugged and told her, "Yeah, sure, fine, whatever. It's not like it's an important piece. I'm running it during the Dance Event. No one watches that, anyway."

• • •

Bex decided not to tell the Hunts that they'd been demoted from the Men's Long Program broadcast to the Ice Dance Final. Even if they didn't realize it was a demotion. After all, officially, the 24/7 network swore that they covered each of the events equally, with no favoritism. There was another reason—one that nobody could quite think of at the moment—for why the Ladies had their short and long programs broadcast in their entirety, the Men and Pairs got complete long program and short program highlights, and the dancers were a ten-minute-long, "And among the other events taking place here this weekend . . ." wherein the top three couples were melded together into a pastiche of ruffles, lip gloss, and cha-cha.

Besides, Bex got the feeling that neither Craig nor Jeremy cared particularly about the fame that could or could not be garnered from appearing in a four-minute segment on 24/7. She believed Craig when he professed that he was allowing Jeremy to participate and Rachel's story to be told in the hope that it might help other skaters trapped in an abusive situation. She also believed her gut feeling that said Craig would never pimp Jeremy out to a reality show.

Craig and Jeremy arrived on time in the room Bex had set aside for their interview. At every venue, 24/7 was perennially challenged with the task of finding a room that was both aesthetically pleasing and soundproof enough to serve as a backdrop for their up-close-and-personal feature. Most of the time their choices fell between either a gray, windowless, barrackslike office deep in the bowels of the arena, or a garishly decorated hotel room right next door to (a) the ice machine, (b) a filled-to-capacity banquet hall, or (c) the restaurant kitchen. Once, Bex had the pleasure of conducting an interview just as, on the other side of the flimsy wall between them, the master of ceremonies began handing out trophies for a very happy and very rowdy high school football team. With the camera set on "record," Bex would ask the skater in question about the crippling year she'd spent battling depression. The skater would be just at the part where she'd sit for hours in the bathroom, staring at razor blades and trying to think of one reason not to slit her wrists, when a round of applause accompanied by "Woof, woof, woof" would make it impossible to hear anything, and they'd have to start all over again.

Hoping to avoid a rerun of that experience, Bex went with the ugly but quiet cave of a room, intending to dress it up for the camera. She'd managed to borrow a bolt of shimmering, silvery cloth from the costume area—now that she thought about it, Bex bet the forensics team would find her fingerprints among the others at the scene of the crime; a kind of creepy notion—and with the cameraman and soundman's help managed to hang it from the ceiling. Now it no longer looked like she was interviewing Jeremy in a bunker. It looked like she was interviewing him in a disco.

Bex told herself the shimmering silver was a metaphor for the ice. And that it was the only material she'd been able to score.

While her technical crew set up their equipment, Bex popped over to the arena's bar and, using her natural charm, wit, and a folded ten-dollar bill, convinced the manager to let her take one of the hand-carved wooden stools into the interview room for Jeremy to sit on, and several of his different-colored, empty liquor bottles so they could reflect light against the back of the silver cloth. The rainbow, dancing images would lighten up their fundamentally static shot of a talking head.

Although, Bex had to admit, there was nothing static about Jeremy. He bounded into the room, several feet ahead of Craig, so full of energy Bex thought she could see the equipment start to quiver with it. He walked over to introduce himself to the tech crew, then proceeded to question them about every piece of hardware, from the camera to the microphone to the sandbags used to weigh them down.

Meeting Craig's eyes, Bex noted, "Shy and retiring fellow, isn't he?"

"Oh, yeah." Craig smiled. "We're thinking of getting him some therapy."

Craig looked good. Was there another, less forthright way to put it? A softening adjective, maybe? Sure. Craig looked damn good.

Craig had replaced the suede jacket he'd worn that morning at the arena with a rich, green V-neck sweater that emphasized his tan. He'd casually pushed his sleeves up nearly to the elbow and, for reasons that would only be known to her therapist—if Bex ever obeyed frequently given advice and got one—she found herself mesmerized by his bare forearms.

Objectively speaking, they were rather ordinary forearms. Okay, a little browner than those of the average rink dweller, and with a fine down of ebony hair tapering off just above the wrists. But nothing to write the Forearm Hall of Fame about.

Nevertheless, as he wrapped one arm playfully around Jeremy's neck and circled the other to clutch his own opposite elbow, jokingly pinning the boy and bending over to whisper, "Give 'em a rest, Jer, they've got work to do. You can ask your questions after they're done," Bex found she couldn't look away. There was just such a combination of strength and gentleness in his arms. Such a sense of both power and kindness. For a split second she was reminded of the way Idan Ben-Golan had cradled Allison's son. Another example of liquid force.

"All right, dude, you're on." Craig released Jeremy from

his mock hold and gave him an encouraging smack on the back as the boy headed for his allotted interview chair. Bex took a seat across from him, her eyes level with the camera's so that when Jeremy was answering her questions it would look like he was addressing the viewer at home.

Craig looked for a spot where he could be out of the way, and finally settled for sitting right on the floor, his back against the wall, knees up, elbows resting on his thighs, fingers linked in front of him, wrists bobbing gently up and down. He'd made a logical choice. From their vantage points, neither the camera nor Jeremy could see him. There was no likelihood of him accidentally ending up in the shot or of Jeremy being distracted by the sight of his dad and either clamming up or sneaking furtive glances, looking for his approval. Because the only person whose field of vision Craig sat in was Bex.

And there was no danger of Bex being distracted.

Because she was a professional.

Bex peered down at the clipboard on her lap where, on a yellow notepad, she'd neatly written all her questions for Jeremy. She reviewed them one final time before getting started. Out of the corner of her eye she saw Craig's forearms again. They were bobbing in the absent-minded manner of a bored fellow killing time. But for Bex, Craig may as well have been waving frantically, as if trying to get her attention from across the street or flagging down a departing bus.

It was a good thing Bex was a professional.

And it was a good thing she'd at least written down Jeremy's questions. Because even as Bex was shaking both Hunts's hands and thanking them for coming to do the interview, she realized that she couldn't recall a single answer the boy had given.

"We'll see you around, Bex," Craig said.

"Yeah . . ." was all she managed in reply.

• • •

After Craig and Jeremy departed, Bex took her time returning the cloth and the stool and the bottles to their respective home bases. She wanted a quiet moment to think over what just happened. Alas, her only thought proved, *What the hell just happened?*

It wasn't very productive.

She was, ironically enough, in the costume room, looking for signs that the police had been through while rotating the borrowed silver cloth this way and that to convince the seamstress that no damage had been done—"Scout's honor!"—when Bex heard the beep of her cell phone.

By the time she was able to neatly roll up the unwieldy bolt and finally answer, there was nothing but a message.

Tess Devaney, Cooper Devaney's mother, needed to see Bex right away.

They were at the hotel. They'd be expecting her.

From a distance, Coop Devaney's mother could pass for his sister. Or his girlfriend.

A research binder tucked under one arm, hat off, parka unzipped and thinking subzero thoughts to combat the fact that Bex had dressed for an ice rink but was now dealing with L.A. weather, she crossed the parking lot that separated arena from hotel. In the distance, reclining at one of the outdoor tables set up by the hotel's café, Bex spotted two figures, both lean and long-limbed, both sandy-haired, both wearing blue jeans, T-shirts, and flip-flops. Facing each other, their profiles matched up so perfectly, they might have been two halves of the same face. Only the shoulder-length hair versus a tidy trim suggested that one visage was male and the other female. Brother and sister—that would be the logical assumption. Except that the absolute way they were focused on each other, unaware of and uninterested in anyone else, the way their eyes locked and held, and the way Tess was clutching Coop's hand, her palm curling his cramped fingers and pinning his thumb down with her own, bespoke an intimacy beyond the simple, sibling bond.

They were so engrossed in each other, Bex felt awkward interrupting. But then she recalled that they'd called this meeting, not her. She used the memory to beat down her concerns and walk right up to their table.

"Ms. Devaney?" she said. "You wanted to meet with me?"

Considering that Bex was dressed like an Eskimo who'd accidentally stepped into a black hole and come out on the wrong end of the equator, complete with three layers of winter wear, Bex couldn't imagine that anyone's peripheral vision might have missed her waddling by. Yet Tess, when she managed to tear herself away from the instructions she seemed to be grinding into her son's conscious both verbally and telepathically, appeared stunned to see her there. She blinked several times, as if at a bright light, until Coop stood—ever the gentleman—and exclaimed, "Bex!" Tess didn't seem to recognize who Bex was, even thought they'd interacted several times previously.

"Bex," she repeated slowly, visibly shifting gears from the conversation she'd been having to the one she intended to have. Bex could see her mentally tucking one file into a virtual filing cabinet and efficiently searching the drawer until she found the next one on her agenda. The process took only a second, but in that second, Tess managed to let go of Coop's hand, turn her back to him, and, with a tight smile, indicate the remaining free chair by their table.

"Have a seat, Bex. Thank you for coming." She reached into the bag by her side for a notepad. "We have a lot to discuss. Let's get started."

Bex sat down. She took off her coat. Then she peeled off the sweater she'd been wearing underneath and tugged on her turtleneck, holding it as far away from her skin as possible, desperate for a whiff of cool air. Her fake-fur-lined boots slowly baked her feet like a pair of similarly shaped crullers, but she doubted that yanking them off to air out her socks would be perceived as particularly professional. Oh, well. She'd had her feet held to the fire before, in the metaphorical sense. Might as well experience the literal.

Tess looked up from a sheet of notes that she pointedly tilted away from Bex's view and observed, "Gil Cahill tells me you'll be supervising coverage of the Allison Adler tragedy."

Gil did, did he? How interesting that he should mention this to Tess and not actually to Bex herself. But also, how terribly Gil. He would never, in a million years, allow Bex to believe she might actually be granted some responsibility or an assignment beyond typing up and alphabetizing the biographical questionnaires they sent out to the athletes at the beginning of every season. Because that would require Gil admitting that a researcher was actually a valuable part of their team, rather than just a pest the 24/7 crew dragged around the world out of the goodness of their hearts. On the other hand, he had no problem telling outsiders that someone else was in charge, because it kept him from having to deal with the problem.

"Okay," Bex agreed. Because, until she knew exactly what was going on, it was always best to agree.

"Good." Tess gestured for Coop to quit standing and sit back down, but her focus remained on Bex. "Because this will need to be handled very carefully."

"I agree," Bex . . . agreed.

"A situation like this could be deadly to Coop's image."

"Not to mention Allison Adler's life," Bex most definitely did not say.

"However, handled carefully, it also has the potential to reap great benefits."

Bex said, "Hmmm..."

"Gil told me the police believe Allison was murdered."

Gil certainly was chatty, wasn't he? Bex cursed silently. She'd wanted to spring the news on Coop herself and gauge his reaction. If he believed he committed the perfect crime, only to get tripped up, Bex wanted to be there when he realized it.

Except it was too late now. The best Bex got when she sneaked a peek in Coop's direction was the sight of him staring intently into space, fascinated by the sun umbrella above their heads, either counting the spokes or taking a nap with his eyes open. Bex and Tess might as well have been discussing next year's hem lengths rather than the murder of his child's mother, for all the interest Coop was taking.

"This could be very bad for Coop," Tess said. "I know how the public thinks. I've worked in advertising and marketing for years. The fact is, complex messages just don't penetrate. And innocent until proven guilty is definitely too complex for the average consumer. They'll see Coop, they'll hear the girl was murdered, and bam! It could take years to untangle the two facts, if then. Coop could win the Olympics from now until the end of time, and they all will still think Cooper Devaney equals killer."

The girl. Allie Adler was presumably the mother of Tess Devaney's grandchild, and she was calling her "the girl," like it was a supporting role that needed to be filled in a movie. Or a television commercial.

"It does no good to try and change the public's mind. Once they have made the association, it's in there for eternity. And since I suppose there is no way to keep Coop's name completely out of this scandal . . ." Tess's eyes tiptoed cautiously in Bex's direction, blatantly suggesting that if there was a way to keep Coop's name completely out of this scandal, now would be a good time for her to bring it up so they could talk turkey. But when Bex simply shook her head in a nonanswer to the nonquestion, Tess proceeded, "Then our only option is to try to supplant the inevitable killer correlation with another equally powerful impression."

Bex noted that the word "killer" rolled off Tess's tongue in conjunction with her son as easily as "the girl" did in reference to Allison. Obviously, Tess's advertising and marketing background stressed turning everything into a product. And an object.

"What do you have in mind?" Bex asked politely, figuring that if Tess was willing to do her whole job for her, Bex might as well take advantage. Maybe Tess even wanted to do the whole write-up, leaving Bex free to sneak a little free time.

"The single-father angle," Tess announced triumphantly. "It's perfect. It's visual. Women love to see a man nurturing a small child. It's programmed into their genes from the cavemen days. Women find a man who is good with children very appealing. If we can always cover up any talk of Cooper possibly being a suspect in Allison's murder with images of him with the baby, that should be enough to counter the negative effects. The public remembers what they see much better than what they hear, and they remember the visceral a thousand percent better than the intellectual. So Bex, I realize you have to talk about Coop and Allie's past involvement—otherwise it would seem like a cover-up and we certainly don't need that on top of all our other problems. But I do think that as long as you pair the visual of Coop and the baby with the audio, we'll be okay."

Bex said, "How do you intend to do that?"

"Excuse me?" Tess was already putting her notes away, presuming the meeting to be over. Apparently none of her notes said anything about follow-up questions.

"How do you plan to get video of Coop with Omri? The baby's name is Omri, by the way."

Tess said, "No. No, I don't like it. It's too foreign. People will have a hard time pronouncing it. We'll think of something else. Allan was what I had in mind. To show how we're honoring his mother's memory."

Bex said, "Idan Ben-Golan showed the police a birth certificate listing the baby's name as Omri, and his name as the father. How do you intend to get around that for these shots of Coop with Baby Allan?"

"It's ridiculous," Tess said. "Ask anyone. Coop and Allie were dating when that child was conceived. Everybody knew it."

"Then why is Idan's name on the birth certificate?"

"How should I know? Allison was obviously a disturbed girl. She killed herself, for goodness' sake!"

"She was murdered."

"That's just a theory. The police have no evidence or clues; that's why they came to you. They expect the public to do their work for them. Isn't that just like the LAPD? Maybe they can beat a confession out of some poor, non-English-speaking janitor who had the misfortune to be in the vicinity. That'll solve their case."

"As of right now, Idan was awarded temporary custody of Omri."

"I know. But we're challenging it. I have my lawyer drawing up the papers now. We're asking for an emergency session with the Family Court."

Bex turned to Coop, figuring he might want to contribute to the discussion at this time. She asked him, "Are you really ready to be a single dad? I mean, you're so young. And you've got your career. The Olympics are next year. How will you handle it?"

"My mom will help," Coop said. He was still counting umbrella spokes.

"Coop will manage," she reassured. "And, like I said, it will make a fantastic human interest story. The baby will be old enough to travel to the Olympics by next year. He can wave to his daddy from the stands. It'll look great."

Coop suddenly sat up, elbows on the table, fingers jutting in Bex's direction as he struggled to make his point. "It's my responsibility," he stressed. "It's a sign, I think. A sign that none of this would have happened if only I'd been honest with everyone from the beginning and—"

"Coop." Tess did not raise her voice. She didn't snap and she didn't bark. She simply said her son's name. And he promptly closed his mouth and sat back deeper in the chair, arms crossed against his chest. Tess told Bex, "As you can see, Coop is very, very ready and willing to accept his responsibilities as a father." Then, in a conspiratorial tone, Tess added, "Am I happy about this development? Of course not. You said it yourself, it's going to be excruciatingly hard for him to raise a child while continuing with his training. I was nineteen and single myself when I had Coop. I know the drill. I suppose I should have been more vigilant, considering my own experience. But what can you do? Boys will be boys. And normal boys like girls. To which, unfortunately, there are sometimes consequences. Yes, the simple thing for us to have done would have been to say, 'Great! Idan Ben-Golan wants to take responsibility for Cooper's child? Terrific! Boy, we really dodged a bullet there, didn't we?' and go on with his training as if nothing had happened. But that's not who my son is. He is a decent, responsible person. And he will be a wonderful father."

"If," Bex pointed out, "the court grants him custody."

"Of course they will," Tess said. "I have a block-long line of people who will testify to that, including an unimpeachable witness that I guarantee you will make this an open-and-shut case."

While Bex liked surprises as much as the next person, she couldn't help asking, "Why go to all that trouble, though? Why doesn't Coop just take a paternity test and—"

"Absolutely not!" Tess smacked the table with her open palm for emphasis, then lowered her voice to hiss, "There is absolutely no way in hell I am letting Coop submit to a paternity test. I won't allow it."

Nine

Bex pointed out, "But if you're certain he's the father—"

"Of course he's the father. Why would I go through all this if I wasn't certain that Coop was the father?"

"Because you need a photo-op with a cute baby to cover up the fact that your son may have killed a girl," Bex also did not say. She had this habit. It wasn't a very good one and it had never served her well, but Bex had this habit of making up theories as she went along. She could go through three, four during a single conversation. For instance, in the one Bex was mulling now, Coop killed Allison specifically because he found out he wasn't Omri's father, meaning Allie cheated on him with his coach. Tess knew it and was trying to distract everyone with the paternity and custody issue so that no one would guess Coop's true motive. Well, that and the cute-baby photo-op.

"Obviously, a blood test would be the quickest way to prove Coop's claim. But there is absolutely no way that I am letting the Los Angeles Police Department obtain any physical samples. And that includes blood, tissue, hair. You know how they are. They say they're just taking it for a paternity test, and next thing you know they've suddenly found physical evidence to link Coop to the crime scene."

"So you do think that Allison was murdered," Bex followed up.

Tess shrugged. "I have no idea. It's a violent world we live in these days, isn't it? That Hunt boy—the little one in Coop's practice group, didn't I hear something about his mother being murdered a few months back? So I suppose it could happen to anyone. You never know."

"He's a good kid," Coop piped up. "Jeremy Hunt. I talked to him. It's rough, being at your first Nationals. And he's the youngest in the whole group, too. I remember what that's like. I gave him some pointers today. Told him to have fun, not worry about placing. Well, not worry about it yet. In a few years—"

"You see?" Tess crowed. "Coop is great with kids."

Bex said to Tess, "You must have known Allison pretty well. Who do you think killed her?"

Tess looked surprised to be asked. Surprised, and somewhat embarrassed. She stammered, "Well, I wouldn't say I knew Allie well. Coop isn't a child, you understand. I don't drive him to the rink or sit in the stands during his practices. He's an adult. He's in charge of his skating. My role is really more as a manager. A consultant. I work on his PR opportunities, media appearances, that sort of thing. I don't run his life. And, in the past few years, I've been so busy trying to get this reality show off the ground . . . well, I'm afraid I didn't get a chance to know Allison as well as I might have liked."

And yet she had no trouble calling Allison unstable earlier. Interesting.

Coop said, "I've been thinking and thinking about this

ever since I found out. I don't know who would want to kill Allie."

"What about her father?" Tess postulated.

Coop hesitated. Then he said, "Mr. Adler was really mad when Allie quit skating. He would practically lose his mind and go on and on about it to me whenever I called. I remember thinking once that I was afraid of what he would do to Allie when he finally did find her."

Tess said, "You want to talk about unstable . . . I actually knew Ralph better than Allison in some ways. I remember when they first started coming to the rink. She was just a little girl then, and I thought it was . . . disturbing, the way he stuck to her side. If Allie was on the ice, he was out there watching. If Allie came into the snack bar, there he was, hovering, asking her if she wanted something. The poor child would get off the ice to go to the bathroom, and he would follow her as far as the ladies' room door, standing outside, waiting to walk her back out. That behavior always seemed rather . . . odd. But when I found out he was only the stepfather, well . . . well, I guess I thought the obvious. Anyone would have."

If anyone included Bex, then she thought she had a pretty good idea of what Tess was hinting at.

"Coop," Bex asked, "did Allie ever say anything to you about her father being, well, I guess . . . inappropriate to her?"

Coop shook his head. "She thought he was too into her skating and stuff. She used to say he got so nervous before competitions that he made her nervous even when she didn't start out that way. She used to say that he wanted her to win more than she did. That he would always pour over the protocol, looking at her marks, comparing them to other people's, coming up with these strategies that he'd take to Idan—"

"Oh, but it wasn't just that," Tess interrupted. "Ralph

approved all her costumes. And I don't mean just "yay" or "nay" on whether there should be a red flower or a yellow one in the ruffle of her skirt. I mean, he went with her to fittings. And this is when Allie had to be, what, already fifteen, sixteen years old? It wasn't too long ago, that's for sure. If you ask me, a father, most especially a stepfather, has no business seeing his teenage daughter half dressed. It's sick."

Bex nodded thoughtfully, not liking where the insinuations were leading. She had enough candidates for the Daddy pool as it was without adding a truly disturbing entrant. "So you really think Ralph Adler was capable of strangling his own child in cold blood?"

"Not in cold blood," Tess pointed out. "In a rage. When Ralph saw Allison with her baby and realized what had happened, he snapped."

"That is possible," Bex conceded. "But what doesn't make sense is, why would Allison, her baby, and Ralph all be at the rink this morning? Neither of them had a good reason for being here."

Judging by Tess and Coop's matching faces, yup, that was a stumper, all right.

Of course, Bex had a theory. If Idan was to be believed and Allison really was dropping off Omri with him before leaving town for good, maybe she called her father, asked him to meet her at the arena so they could clear the air before she started a new life. Conversely, maybe Allie, after giving up her baby, turned to her father for support, asked to come home, told him what had happened, and begged for sympathetic understanding. But instead of embracing his prodigal child, an incensed Ralph strangled her.

"You know how fathers are," Tess prompted. "They can't stand the idea of their little girl being sexually active. Becoming pregnant, well, there's no way you can avoid the truth then, can you? Ralph was so obsessed with Allie, the idea of her being a little slut, excuse my language—"

"She wasn't a slut." Coop didn't raise his voice, either. But just like his mother's warning earlier, there was something in Coop's tone that made Tess reconsider and quiet down. "If Allie was a slut, Mom, what does that make me?"

"Coop, honey—"

"What, Mom, what? Slut? That sure sounds like a double standard to me. What happened to that stuff you taught me growing up, about how men were always allowed to sow their wild oats in whatever fashion they could afford and how twentieth-century, liberated, and enlightened women should be accorded the same rights and not be judged but treated with respect and dignity? Does having a kid out of wedlock make you a slut, too, Mom?"

Tess bristled, "I didn't have a line of men thinking they could be your father."

"There's no line! None of you get it!" Coop rose from his chair. "Allie wasn't cheating on me. She wasn't like that. I would have known. She loved me, and I loved her. I don't know why Idan is claiming the baby is his, but it's not possible."

"What about Idan's wife?" Tess's response to Coop's tantrum—not to mention his suggestion that perhaps her proud, liberal values might not be quite as egalitarian as she'd raised her son to believe—was to ignore the outburst completely. She literally turned her back to Coop and addressed Bex as if no other question had been raised two feet to the left of them. She said, "Even though we all know that Coop is the father, Idan's name was on the baby's birth certificate. For all we know, he told Pandora Westby the same story he told the police, that he is the biological father. Surely she couldn't have taken that well."

"Probably not," Bex agreed.

"Pan didn't like Idan coaching girls," Coop offered.

Bex turned to him in surprise. A minute ago he'd appeared primed to engage his mother in public debate about the role of women in modern society and how many Daddy candidates constituted a "slut" versus a liberated woman reveling in her hard-won sexual freedom. But apparently Tess's out-of-sight, out-of-mind approach had calmed him quicker than a bucket of ice chips dumped over his head. Coop was no longer standing, but sitting tranquilly in his chair, palms turned up, as he quietly and rationally proposed a pertinent observation.

"Most of Idan's students were guys. Which actually made sense, because more than half of them—us—were on scholarship from Pan, and she only sponsored guys. She liked men's Singles skating, she said, because we pushed the technical envelope more than anybody else. It was Sebi, actually, who I think convinced her to sponsor him and Allie. They were her only dance team, and Allie was the only girl she ever sponsored. Idan had a few girls who competed in Singles—Novice, Junior; he just did their choreography, but Pan didn't pay for them. And she didn't like that he had them. I think she was jealous."

"It's a pretty old story, isn't it," Tess tried to sound sympathetic but didn't quite make it. "Older, wealthy woman marries much younger, very attractive man..." Her sigh made it clear that an independent, modern woman like Tess would never lower herself to such an arrangement. Though Bex did have to wonder, whatever happened to "men were always allowed to sow their wild oats in whatever fashion they could afford and liberated and enlightened women should be accorded the same rights and not be judged"?

"How do you know Pandora was jealous?" Bex asked, figuring she should gather some actual evidence before taking a hardly disinterested party's word for motive.

"Well..." Put on the spot, Coop didn't act nearly as

positive as when frolicking in the land of generalities. "Like I said, she didn't like Idan coaching girls."

"How do you know?"

"She never sponsored any. No one until Allie, and that was as part of a team."

"But that just proves she preferred Men's Singles as a general discipline, not that she didn't like Idan working with girls."

"Coop," Tess prompted, "didn't Pan refuse to let Idan work with Lian?"

"Oh. Yes, right." He nodded. "Mrs. Reilly wanted Idan to choreograph Lian's programs this year, but Pan walked right up to her, I remember, and she said, 'Amanda, that would not be a very good idea. And you and I both know why.' Mrs. Reilly seemed scared. She never mentioned it again."

Which could mean absolutely anything.

Including the obvious fact that Bex needed to have a little chat with Mrs. Pandora Westby Ben-Golan.

After assuring Tess and Coop that she would get back to them to talk further about their "packaging" of Coop's newfound paternity for air, Bex intended to take the hotel elevator up to her room, dump the research binder, change from thermal rink clothes into more appropriate L.A.-in-winter clothes, and without so much as a deep breath or a real meal, head out again for more research-type fun. She got as far as the hotel lobby, this time wearing blue jeans, sneakers, and a short-sleeved, bright yellow blouse that, Bex realized, made her look like a nuclear-assisted lemon drop, but nevertheless provided indescribable cheer at the end of an exhausting day, when she spotted Craig Hunt. He was sitting in the overstuffed, olive chair closest to the revolving doors, his tailbone uncomfortably sunk below thigh level, making him look like a tipped-over letter Z. He was watching the doors go round and round while sporting an expression equal parts fascination, boredom, and disgust that anyone could be so bored that they might actually find the activity fascinating. In any case, he appeared unnaturally delighted to see Bex.

He called her name loudly enough to make a few other hotel patrons turn around in surprise. He enthusiastically waved her over.

"Hi . . ." she said cautiously, finding it weird to be meeting Craig in this practically civilian capacity. Every time in the past that they'd run into each other—whether the encounters ended up friendly or not—Bex had been working on a story about Jeremy or, like earlier that morning at the rink, still working. So even when Craig was railing at her for destroying his family, it was professional. Now, even though she was technically on her way to do more work, it had nothing to do with Craig. And suddenly she didn't know what to say to him. Not to mention that she felt alien dressed like a regular person. It was almost as if, out of her parka, gloves, and hat, Craig were seeing her naked.

"Why didn't anyone tell me?" Craig asked.

Oh. God. Did Gil call him, too? What had he promised on her behalf this time?

"Tell you what?"

"How boring Nationals was!"

"Uhm, Craig? The competition hasn't started yet."

"I'm not talking about the competition. I'm talking about the hours between eight and eleven P.M., when skaters with a five A.M. practice time tomorrow are sleeping, leaving their chaperone and father—who does not, as a rule, go to bed while the sun is still out—to wander the hotel halls looking for something to do."

"Oh," Bex said. "That."

"Is it always like this?"

"Pretty much."

"I mean, it's bad enough that the only folks I know here are Jeremy, who's sound asleep; Toni Wright, who is a lovely, lovely woman and a terrific coach, but also over sixty and maybe not up to or interested in hanging out with me; and several other parents from the rink back home, whose notion of a scintillating conversation is how the new Code of Points will affect their child's chances to make the World Team."

"Not your cup of tea?"

"There isn't enough in China."

Bex nodded, sympathetic, but at a loss about what Craig wanted her to do about it, when he answered her unspoken question.

"I know you, Bex," he said. "Want to join me for a drink?"

She blinked in surprise. Was Craig Hunt asking her *out*?

Misinterpreting her hesitation, Craig backtracked, "Uhm, you are old enough to drink, aren't you?"

She nodded fervently. "Three years over, as a matter of fact."

That seemed to set his mind at ease. "How about it, then?"

She really needed to speak to Pandora, and Idan, too, if Bex expected to have copy ready for Francis and Diana by the next day.

She said, "Sure."

A hotel bar in the heat of Nationals is always an interesting animal. Unlike at the World Championships, where even drunken louts can sound charming while railing in a delightful and incomprehensible foreign tongue, Nationals is a homegrown affair. There are actually more American journalists in attendance than at the Worlds (few newspapers have the budget to send a reporter overseas in a non-Olympic year). But at Nationals, the bar is crowded with representatives of everything from *Sports Illustrated*, the *Los Angeles Times*, and the *Boston Globe* to each contender's hometown paper. And 97 percent of them (not all, Bex had to admit) have one thing in common. They are "real sports reporters." And "real sports reporters" think figure skating is for sissies.

That's why, year after year, "real sports reporters" file stories that only focus on the Ladies' event and inevitably begin with a joke about Zambonis, proceed to mock the costumes ("She looks like she escaped from a whorehouse after being mauled by a lion!"), and wrap up by explaining how the results are fixed from the beginning, that the audience clapped louder for the girl who came in seventh so obviously she deserved to win, and finally, if they have time, list the top three finishers in the Men's, Pairs, and Dance events. The "real sports reporters" were easily identified as the ones who stayed late in the hotel bar because no way were they getting up early to watch practices the next morning. They were also easily identified as the ones yakking at the tops of their lungs about where they could have been right now, if only their lousy editor weren't out to get them.

In contrast, the other group of Nationals hotel-bar regulars rarely spoke above a whisper. Though they, in actuality, did have to get up early and attend practice the next morning, they also knew that a big part of their job took place off the ice. These were the coaches. And they were in the bar to talk up their students. To anyone who would listen.

Those lucky enough to possess an actual medal contender sidled up to the mostly indifferent press corps to wax poetic about how their protégé was the next big thing. They figured if it was printed and televised and repeated enough, judges would get the message and mark accordingly. Those with students more likely to end up in the bottom half of the standings saved their powers of persuasion for the few judges who also happened to be in the bar. It wasn't that they told them how to vote, exactly. No one could do that. What they did was more along the lines of planting subliminal suggestions, such as, "A well-done spiral really should be worth as much as a spin," or vice versa, depending on their skater's particular expertise. They also, should the subject come up—and somehow it always did—pointed out, "You know, I was watching the Hunt boy's quad this morning. And it's the darndest thing, really, but when you look closely, you realize it's not a quadruple Toe at all! It's just a triple Axel taking off backward. He cheats the first half a revolution on the ice; oh, and he cheats the landing, too."

Bex and Craig, on their way to a booth, he with a Scotch in his hand, she with a Tequila Sunrise, managed to overhear that exact exchange. The speaker was Lucian Pryce, a coach Bex recognized as attending this Nationals with a boy who spun like a piece of film loose in a projector, emoted like a silent-film star, but couldn't jump more than three revolutions if his life—or National ranking—depended on it.

It was the judge who spotted Craig first. Lucian followed his gaze and realized that the father of the skater he'd just maligned was standing a foot away. And Craig was several inches taller than Lucian. And about two decades younger.

A normal person might have felt somewhat threatened under the circumstances. The judge certainly looked terrified at the possibility of fisticuffs breaking out. Lucian, on the other hand, stared back defiantly, as if daring Craig to say or do anything in reply. He cocked his head to one side and raised a palm in a gesture of, "Give it your best shot."

Craig, for his part, turned around slowly and, most

politely, handed his drink to Bex. He pushed one sweater sleeve up past the elbow, then the other.

Bex wished any of the reporters who so regularly smirked their way through a column about what a sissy sport skating was, would turn around and check out the off-ice pissing contest. She wasn't sure if Craig were going to deck Lucian or blow him off.

As it turned out, he did neither. Craig simply smiled sympathetically. And then he told Lucian, "Don't worry, Mr. Pryce. Jeremy may have twice your boy's jumps, but he's also half his age. At this rate, I figure your kid should catch up with mine . . . never?"

At that, he retrieved his drink from Bex, waved cheerily, and kept walking.

Dazed, Lucian stared at Craig's retreating back in stunned silence. The judge stared at Craig's retreating back in stunned silence. Bex stared at Craig's retreating back in stunned silence—until she remembered that they were supposedly together, and trotted off to join him.

He was already sitting at their booth, sipping his Scotch, when Bex caught up. He was staring straight ahead, seemingly lost in thought, making Bex, all of a sudden, feel as if she were interrupting. She'd been intending to just plop down across from him, but now that felt weirdly intrusive. Craig didn't even appear to realize that she was there, and Bex wondered how she should make her presence known, short of waving a hand in front of his face, or loudly clearing her throat several times.

She was still flipping mental coins to decide which option made her look less pathetic when Craig snapped out of the reverie he'd been in, noticed Bex standing there awkwardly, and stared at her, puzzled as to why she wasn't taking a seat.

So Bex took a seat. And she told him, "Smooth smackdown."

"You mean Lucian?"

"I don't think he's used to being talked to like that."

"Lucian does prefer to be the one verbally assaulting, of that we're all aware."

Bex felt like an idiot. Here she was, 24/7's head and/or only researcher, and she'd totally missed the subtext of the altercation. It wasn't all about Jeremy. Fifteen years ago, Lucian Pryce had been the coach who allowed Craig's future wife, Rachel Rose, to be abused by her Pairs partner, Robby Sharpton. A relationship that, after over a decade of lies and deception, culminated with Rachel's murder the previous fall.

She said, "I forgot you and Lucian met before."

Craig raised his glass to his lips and paused to clarify, "I wouldn't say we exactly met. Rachel didn't like me coming to the rink when she was practicing, so most of our relationship is hearsay. But I saw the effects of Lucian's tutelage on Rachel. And hell, on Robby, too. You'd think, knowing I was married to Rachel, Lucian wouldn't have the balls to actually pick up a phone and offer to train Jeremy. And yet he did."

"Lucian offered to coach Jeremy? When?"

"About a month ago. He was at our rink, supposedly to consult with Toni about something—they used to be Pairs partners, can you believe it? Two of the most different people on the planet. . . . Anyway, he watched Jeremy practice, and that evening he called me. Said he'd been thinking about it, and even though he was severely busy, had all the students he could handle, future champions each and every one, he was willing to allow me to beg him to take on Jeremy. When I said no, thank you, Toni had gotten Jeremy this far and we were committed to her, plus, well, there's that whole thing where he's the Antichrist—"

Bex had to gulp the sip in her mouth to demand, "You actually said that to him?"

"Maybe I said Antichrist, maybe I said the devil himself, but yes, that was the sentiment I attempted to convey."

"How did he respond?"

"He told me I was a fool. That Toni Wright had never trained a champion and that she never would. She was a loser—a lovely thing to say about a woman he earlier publicly claimed was his oldest and dearest friend. And that if I stayed with her, I would be a loser, too."

"And you said?"

"That if Robby Sharpton was his shining example of a winner, I'd pass."

Bex said, "You're a brave man. Lucian can destroy Jeremy politically."

"Better than some other way." Craig shrugged, finished his drink, and signaled the wandering waiter to bring him another one. "I didn't, of course, tell Jeremy about any of this. I can get pretty brave with geriatrics over the phone. My kid, on the other hand . . . I don't relish hearing from Jeremy how I ruined his potential career before it even got started. So let's just keep the details of me pissing off one of the most influential men in skating between the two of us for now. Deal?"

Bex said, "You're a good dad."

"I've tried to be. Best anyone can do, really. Just try."

"It's funny," Bex mused. "You always hear about deadbeat dads and paternity suits and Peter Pan guys who won't take responsibility. But then there are men like you. And this thing with Allison Adler's baby. Rather than denying they were even in town at the time, we've got two men fighting for the right to be declared Omri's father. They both can't be right, but they're both dying to be."

"Ego," Craig suggested. "That whole call-of-the-wild/caveman compulsion to reproduce yourself. It makes some guys absolutely crazy."

"Not you," Bex pointed out. "You raised—you're still raising—another man's child. A man you hated, to boot."

"Primordial ooze hardwiring on the fritz, I guess." Craig accepted his refill.

"Everything about Allison's murder, it somehow comes down to fatherhood." Bex finally articulated what had been nagging her ever since she dove into the mystery. "Not just Idan and Coop both claiming to be Omri's dad, but even Allison's dad, Ralph Adler, he's her stepfather, and some people think he was way too involved in her life for a non-biological parent. It's like, everywhere you turn, you hit a paternity puzzle. Craig"—Bex figured she had an expert in front of her, might as well pick his brain—"you must have some insight on this. What would make a man claim someone else's child as his own?"

It was an intensely personal question, and Bex knew that she should have been sorry for asking it the minute the words were out of her mouth. Except that she wasn't sorry. Because, even if it hadn't been connected with Allison Adler's murder, Bex still would have wanted to know the answer. Because of what it would tell her about Craig.

The question, of course, was: Would he want to tell her? Especially considering that Bex was more or less a total stranger. And had been indirectly responsible for the murder of his wife. Because, other than that, they were cool.

Bex figured Craig would need a moment to think about his answer. God knows she'd needed more than a moment to think about the question, and that was after she'd already asked it.

"In my case, it was because I was in love with Rachel." Or maybe he would just blurt it out as soon as she inquired. It really could go either way.

"That's it?" Bex asked.

"That's it." He shrugged. "She wanted us to raise Jeremy. So I went along."

"And you didn't care that you weren't Jeremy's biological father?"

"Not really."

"So could that mean that in Omri's case, one of the guys could know that he's not the biological father and could still be fighting for him, anyway?"

"Bex"—Craig leaned forward conspiratorially—"I genuinely have no idea."

"Why would they do that?"

"Still drawing a blank."

"Because they were in love with Allie?"

"And that would have to be my strike three."

"You're not helping here, Craig."

"I invited you out for a drink, Bex, not a game of Clue."

He was absolutely right. But unfortunately, at the moment Bex happened to be paddling in the middle of the latter. And she realized that try as she might, there would be no kicking back and enjoying the former—much as she may have wanted to—until she was able to tell Gil and the Howarths and the perennially voyeuristic viewing public *It was Colonel Mustard in the costume room with a shiny, sharpened sequin* and be able to prove it. Not just to 24/7's Legal Department's satisfaction, but to her own as well.

She looked at Craig, who was leaning back in their booth, one thumb rubbing the mist off his drink, the other tapping it playfully against the glass's rim. He was smiling at her in a manner more relaxed and welcoming than Bex had ever seen him before. He had admitted to inviting her out for a drink, which was not truly the same as a real date. But it was most certainly an arrow wiggle into the friendly and/or nonprofessional portion of the "Where do we stand?" pie chart. Bex took all of these developments in.

And she asked Craig, "Could I have a rain check?"

Ten

Bex did not, as a rule, leave the immediate area during a competition. There was usually no need to. All the information she was required to collect was available either at the rink or at the competitors' official hotel, often a short walk from the rink. Sometimes a feature producer might take a skater off-site to videotape them strolling through some local, easily recognizable landmark (plug in the Eiffel Tower, St. Basil's Cathedral, the Great Wall of China, or a canal, Venetian or Dutch) to prove to the viewers at home that see, we are, too, on location; this all isn't being phoned in from a studio back in the States.

But as a mere researcher, even though she was the one who generated the list of potentially photogenic sites, Bex did not get to actually join the excursions. Her route was arena, hotel, production truck. Rinse. Repeat. Regret.

Which was why, when confronted with getting into her rental car and driving out to Idan and Pandora Westby Ben-Golan's presumed mansion in Beverly Hills, Bex felt at a disadvantage. For one thing, this was Los Angeles, where all of the streets followed logical patterns, until they didn't. What kind of a city, Bex wondered, would have Sunset and Hollywood running parallel to each other for miles and miles, only to suddenly make them become perpendicular? It wasn't normal.

And it was only one of the reasons why it took Bex close to two hours to locate the Ben-Golans's residence, despite the many gas stations she'd been forced to pull into, to ask for directions only to be reassured that it "should be like, fifteen minutes, tops."

Fortunately, once she finally turned onto the correct street, Bex had no problem identifying which particular abode belonged to the Ben-Golans. On a cul-de-sac where every house appeared engaged in a game of "Can You Top This?" with perfectly manicured lawns, swooping arches, and never installing one window when you could instead boast a series, Bex still guessed that Pandora Westby was the proud owner of the mirrored, oval-shaped koi pond with the granite, layback-spin figure fountain twirling in the center, and a front porch displaying marble columns in the shape of three male pair skaters lifting their females. Who were then holding up the rest of the roof.

The doorbell played "The Skater's Waltz."

The knocker was in the shape of an antique, brass skate blade.

The woman who answered the door was not happy to see her.

She was dressed much more casually than Bex was used to. Instead of the silver fur, chandelier earrings, and suede gloves that matched her lipstick exactly, Pandora was wearing black Capri pants and a lavender cotton fitted T-shirt with short sleeves. Seeing the pale skin quivering above her elbow in a manner Pandora would certainly never allow to protrude in public was as embarrassing to

Bex as if she'd stumbled in on the dowager naked. Or, even worse, having sex with her shockingly fit husband.

Pandora did not appear any more thrilled by the potential encounter. She hugged her arms across her chest. Bex couldn't tell if it was a generally defensive gesture, or one specific to hiding the loose flesh. In any case, it screamed: Keep Out!

Bex, to the surprise of no one, did not.

She said, "Could I have a few words with you, Mrs. Ben-Golan? I'm—"

"I know who you are."

"You do?" As far as Bex could recollect, they'd never officially met. Pandora wasn't a skater or a coach or a judge. She had no actual standing in the skating community, at least not as far as television was concerned. They rarely interviewed sponsors, preferring instead to tell the tale of the spunky, struggling athlete subsisting on sheer . . . spunk. "Cash of the Pan," as she was so politely called outside of earshot, may have been someone everybody on the inside of the sport was well acquainted with, but to the general audience, she was a nonentity. Which meant Bex never had a need to bother her until now.

"You're all the same," Pandora snapped.

"We are?" Bex asked the obvious question, despite not knowing what she was asking. "We who?"

"Like little moles," Pandora said. "All of you production assistants. P.A.s, is that the correct abbreviation? Who can keep track? Year after year, you're the same. Just out of college and desperate to make your terribly distinctive mark. Always running around, trying to look busy, hoping someone will notice how talented and industrious you are. I suppose it's possible. Look at Gil Cahill, after all."

"Gil?" Gil as a P.A.? Hard to imagine. As far as Bex knew, he'd gotten his start in radio—hence his ability to project obscenities over distances that might daunt others—

and moved from producing his own sports broadcasts to working in television.

"Oh, yes. He was the worst of them. He wanted to prove how much smarter he was than everybody else in his position. He ended up miscounting how many seconds were left until the end of the broadcast and called time early. The entire network went to black for ten seconds because little Gilbert Cahill was too good to use a stopwatch."

Bex wanted to giggle. But it was hard to do with your mouth hanging open.

"They fired him, of course," Pandora added. "I remember because it was the talk of the other P.A.s for a while. At Nationals that year, the joke was 'What time is it?' 'Oh, Cahill to one,' that sort of thing. I was shocked to see him again sixteen years later. And a producer, no less. I guess life really is full of second chances."

Bex said, "I'm not a P.A." She'd been meaning to bring that up for a while, but the moment never seemed right. It wasn't any righter now, but Bex also had nothing else to say. "I'm a researcher."

"What's the difference?"

Mainly that the P.A.s had to share hotel rooms while Bex got one of her own.

"I'm gathering information about Allison Adler's murder."

"I know." Pandora indicated some undisclosed location with the upward tilt of her chin. "Idan told me you were there this morning."

"Idan is here?" Bex double-checked. "With Omri?"

"Where else would he be?"

"Uhm . . ." This really was not a chat to be having on the front stoop, even if the neighborhood was deserted at this time of night. "Can I come in?"

"What would happen if I refused?"

"I would make things up."

Pandora sighed. She opened her door a bit broader. "Come in."

Bex stepped inside a foyer and, though she knew it was bad manners, had to gasp. The entire far wall facing the front door had been removed and in its place was an at least ten-by-ten-feet stained glass window featuring a painstakingly detailed competition scene, complete with skaters on the ice, colorfully dressed spectators in the stands, and national flags billowing in the breeze.

"When the sun comes through the window," Pandora said, "you can also see the tableau sparkling across the floor."

"Wow," Bex said. But by the time she got to the second "w," her attention was captured by a round, wooden, eight-story display case at the center of the sunken living room, each shelf holding half a dozen or so glass figurines, ranging in shape from a rose small enough to fit in the palm of a hand, to a carving of a young girl sitting on a bench, tying her skates, that had to weigh at least fifty pounds from the looks of it.

"Lalique," Pandora explained. "One-of-a-kind items all. I commissioned them. It's the least I could do. They've been so supportive of figure skating."

Bex would have said "wow" again, but she figured she'd better pace herself.

She also figured she'd better get to the point of her visit.

"Mrs. Ben-Golan," she said, "you have a lovely home; really, you do. But I'm here to talk—"

"I know what you're here to talk about, Miss . . ."

"Levy. Bex Levy."

"I'm not a fool."

"I'm not suggesting—"

"I watched television discover skating. Yes, believe it or not, we did exist before the cameras were turned on. My father and mother skated at Nationals back when all our competitions were still held outside. Back when compulsory figures were still actually a part of figure skating. One stiff wind at the wrong time, and you could watch an entire year's worth of practice go down the drain. My grandparents were founding members of the California Skating Club. It was more of a social club then. People competed, but it was a gentleman's sport. Why do you think those early skaters competed in white dinner jackets and pressed slacks? It was part of the uniform. Television changed things. You wanted to make it more accessible to the viewing public, you said. Something people can relate to, a story they could follow, heroes they could root for. You said the compulsory figures were too complicated. There should be more free skating. So television created the Short Program. And then you got rid of figures altogether."

Bex felt like pointing out that she had barely been born when most of the offenses Pandora was listing were committed, but the lady was on a roll. And a rambling subject was always preferable to a hostile one.

"I watched skating evolve. Well, *devolve* would be more accurate. We're no different now than any other sport. No more ladies and gentlemen. No more manners. Television made the sport popular, the champions international stars, and the governing body wealthy. All we had to give up in return was the last vestiges of class, decorum, and privacy."

Bex figured this was her cue to get crass.

She asked, "Mrs. Ben-Golan, about your husband—"

"Neither of us had anything to do with Allison's death."

Well. Talk about getting right to the point.

"Again, I didn't mean to suggest—"

"Of course you did. Miss Levy, I told you before, I'm not a fool. I know what kind of ratings 24/7 got from exposing Silvana Potenza's killer live on the air last season. I have no doubt Gil Cahill is hoping for a repeat at this championship. And I do look like such a promising suspect."

"It's just that—"

"My husband fathered a child with the dead girl. Yes, thank you, I realize what it looks like."

"You sound like you're okay with this. The affair, I mean, not being a suspect."

"If I were not, as you put it, 'okay with this,' Miss Levy, would the situation change in any way? Would the little bastard disappear?"

She had a valid point. "So you're certain that Idan is Omri's father?"

"If I wasn't, would I have agreed to pay Allison Adler's living expenses for the past seven months?"

"You did?"

Pandora waved for Bex to follow her up the stairs. She opened the first door on the second-floor hallway, revealing a home office complete with a desk, computer, bookshelves, and framed antique, Olympic posters on the walls. Pandora unlocked a drawer and pulled out a folder, but at that moment Bex's attention was captured by the room directly across from the study. A nursery.

Without asking permission. Bex stepped out of the office and poked her head into the junior bedroom. The wallpaper was a soothing blue. The truck and race car sheets on the crib matched the drapes and the ruffles on the changing table. A stuffed bear wearing a sailor cap perched on a rocking chair. Idan Ben-Golan, army vet, choreographer, rebel, was standing by a *Blue's Clues* mobile, dressed only in cut-off shorts, a burp cloth over his shoulder, a baby pressed to his bare chest.

Bex could not imagine a more disorienting rabbit hole than the one she had fallen down through. She was about to say "hi" when Pandora materialized, glaring at Bex and Idan in turn but making no move to drag her out of there.

"Pretty nursery," Bex observed, skipping the salutations.

"Thank you." Idan shifted the baby so that Omri rested horizontally in his arms, covering more of Idan's chest, in a gesture not unlike the one Pandora employed before.

"You went to a lot of trouble. It must have taken you a couple of months."

"More like a few weeks. Pan is an excellent decorator. She decorated this entire house."

Bex nodded, making the mental note that Idan claiming Omri had clearly not been an impulsive or last-minute deal. He obviously had everything ready in advance.

As if reading Bex's mind, Pandora said, "You might be interested in these, Miss Levy." She handed Bex a manila folder and then, without waiting for Bex to explore for herself, identified, "Canceled checks. Made out to Allison Adler. Each endorsed by the recipient herself. Allie took our money."

"Why?" Bex asked.

"She needed to live somehow. Her father threw her out of the house. She had nowhere to go."

"No. I mean, why did you support Allison?"

"What choice did we have?" To Idan, Pandora said, "Miss Levy here wondered how I could be certain you're the father. I thought seeing it in black, white, and green might prove helpful."

"We went over everything this morning, Bex," Idan reminded. "My name is on Omri's birth certificate. I'm his father."

"Coop Devaney thinks—"

"Coop Devaney is missing key pieces of information."

"Such as your affair with Allie?" Though Bex addressed Idan, she snuck a peek at Pandora to gauge her reaction. For better or for worse, Idan's wife winced at the words and looked away, focusing on the nautical bear leaning precariously to the right and in danger of falling off his rocker.

"Such as that, yes."

"Allie was your student."

"She was over eighteen. I did nothing illegal."

"Yes, but as her coach, you were in a position of power. You could manipulate her to act against her best interests and her will."

"I did no such thing."

"You're married."

"Which is not really a concern of yours."

"How did you get Allie to agree to give up her baby?" Bex asked.

Pandora interjected, "It was her idea. Well, her blackmail, actually."

"Pan—"

"No, Idan. No, let's tell the truth. It will make a nice change from the last year, won't it, darling?" She turned to face Bex, hands on her hips. "Why don't you put this down in your report for Gil Cahill? This is a story the viewing public should be able to relate to. Allison Adler's father threw her out of their home for being a little tramp."

"Ralph Adler says she ran away."

"Well, Ralph Adler is lying. Ralph threw her out of the house with nothing. She had barely forty dollars in her wallet and an ATM card for an account her father closed the next day. She came to us and told Idan that she would abort his baby unless we paid up. She looked around my home and she told me, 'Look at all this crap. You guys are loaded. Shouldn't hurt a bit.'"

"And you agreed?"

Pandora hesitated. She and Idan exchanged charged looks, during which an entire conversation Bex wasn't privy to passed in the set of a jaw, the lift of an eyebrow, and the flare of a nostril. Finally Pandora replied, "We agreed. We agreed to cover her expenses and find her a place to live and handle the medical bills."

"In exchange for her leaving Omri with you?"

"Allison didn't want him!" Idan exploded. "She told us she didn't want to be a mother. She just wanted to have the baby—'get it over with,' that's what she called it—and forget it happened. She didn't want him. And I didn't want him going to strangers."

"Which, believe me," Pandora drawled, "cost us extra."

"Why did you go along with this?" Bex asked. In all the time she'd stood in the nursery, Pandora hadn't so much as looked at Omri or even faced in his direction. Her body language was not screaming "Stepmother of the Year."

"He's Idan's child." Pandora shrugged. "Idan is my husband. I decided to look at it as if I had married a man who already had a child. It's a little game I play with myself. To stay sane."

Bex wondered if a trained professional would concur with Mrs. Ben-Golan's assessment of her mental state. But she doubted now would be a good time to ask.

Instead Bex told Idan, "You know that Coop is going to challenge your custody."

"He can try all he likes. I am Omri's legal father. Coop has no standing." Idan sighed and elaborated, "With Coop, it is about the image. You don't know him well. I do. He cares what the people think of him. He takes care to present his best side. His mother, she has him convinced his entire future depends on projecting the right image."

Bex took a gamble.

"Coop is going to demand a paternity test to prove who Omri's father really is," she lied, wondering if the news would please Idan or unnerve him.

"Very well then." His expression didn't change. Bex had no idea what he really thought. "Let him do it."

"Oh, yes," Pan agreed. "Let the dear boy do it. Maybe

we will get a wonderful surprise and solve the problem once and for all."

Bex looked from Idan to Pandora and suddenly had a flash-forward of little Omri on a therapist's coach, trying to explain his complicated family situation... not to mention household decor, and being disbelieved on both counts. For a moment, Bex was tempted to just grab the little guy and run. But she figured there were enough people fighting over him at the moment. Besides, no matter how interesting the true story of Omri's paternity might turn out to be, Bex had to remember that her only stake in the predicament had to be in how it related to Allison's murder.

Which was why her next question was, "Do either of you have any thoughts about who might have wanted Allie dead?"

"No," Pandora drawled. "But since you're here, talking to the two of us, I simply have to assume that you do."

"Where were you the morning Allie was strangled?"

Idan smirked. "This is the American idea of interrogation? Are you deliberately playing stupid, or have you honestly not explored this all in advance? You know where I was. Everyone knows where I was. Allison was killed during the Dance practice. The Men's practice was next. Obviously I was on my way to the rink. However, I cannot prove that I did not arrive ahead of time to strangle Allie. Then again, neither can Coop."

"Doesn't Coop need to warm up before his practice?"

"Yes."

"But you weren't with him."

"Coop is not a child. It is not necessary for me to hold his hand."

"It's a shame," Bex said. "You could have alibied each other."

"The next time I plan a murder, I will make certain to call you first, Bex."

That sounded like a cue to change topics if she'd ever heard one. Bex had gotten much better at recognizing them over the years.

"And what about you, Mrs. Ben-Golan? Where were you?"

"Perhaps I was 'warming up' with Coop." Pandora did not need to wiggle her fingers to form air quotes. They were right there in her tone.

"I'm sorry?"

"I'm Cooper Devaney's sponsor. I was also at the rink, waiting to observe his practice. He and I spend a great deal of time together, pondering his future."

"So were you with Coop that morning?"

"What did he say?"

"He didn't mention it."

"There is your answer then."

Under normal circumstances Bex would have wondered if these people were deliberately trying to make her job more difficult. But in this case, she didn't have to ask. She knew. Idan and Pandora Ben-Golan were deliberately trying to make her job more difficult.

The only question was: Why?

Bex spent the night trying out various theories: Did Coop kill Allie because she'd cheated on him with their coach, or because she was planning to keep him away from his child? Did Idan kill Allie to get their son, or did Pandora commit the murder in a jealous rage? And if either Coop or Idan were knowingly lying about being Omri's father, what could possibly be their respective motives? Plus there were Ralph and Sebastian, both furious over Allie's abandonment of her skating career and, by extension, them. Did they get angry enough to kill? All Bex knew for sure was that no one had a sound alibi for the time of Allie's death. And that the physical evidence of bruises and crimson glove fibers implicated all of them. Which means it implicated none of them.

If Bex were going to get to the bottom of this case, she couldn't count on forensic science. She would have to keep talking to people until somebody made a mistake. And hope like heck that when it happened, Bex would be smart enough to catch it.

Oh, and that said, the recognizable mistake should take place before the final day of the U.S. Championship. Because if it happened afterward, well, no one—i.e., TV—would really care.

Hoping to get some insight into both Idan and Coop (not to mention Pandora and Ralph), Bex decided her next stop needed to be the one person who'd had a relationship with them all: Sebastian Vama. As Idan's assistant, Coop's trainer, one of Pandora's charity cases, and Allison's partner, Sebastian had not only enjoyed a unique relationship with each of Bex's suspects, but he was also privy to their relationships among each other. He knew everyone from a distinctive perspective. Which made him an invaluable interview for Bex.

She got up bright and early the next morning, gambling that Sebastian would be putting Coop on the ice for his subsequent practice session. Somehow she had a hard time imagining Coop and Idan having a very productive workout at this particular point in time. Bex got to the arena a few minutes before his Senior Men group was announced to take the ice. But before she had the chance to corner Sebastian, Bex was waylaid by Craig. He called her name and waved her over. She really should have been tracking down Sebastian. So, of course, she walked right over when Craig called.

"Listen," he said, "I know you're busy, but I have a quick question to ask."

"Sure," Bex said, all the while wondering if he'd found someone else to share that drink with after Bex had to scamper off to annoy people.

"Do you know Pandora Westby?"

Bex nodded, suddenly very alert and vaguely uncomfortable.

"She called me last night. She said she was watching Jeremy at the practice, and she would like to sponsor him. I guess she does this kind of thing all the time. I don't really know much about it. Do you think I should accept?"

Eleven

"Pandora Westby," Bex repeated. Mostly because the simultaneous thoughts shooting through her brain were too nebulous and scattered to produce actual words.

"Yes. She said she's been sponsoring skaters for years. Do you know anything about her? Is she on the level?"

"Well"—Bex stuck to the facts she was certain of, despite the suspicions and rumors jostling her tongue for equal time—"she is a big philanthropist. I've heard a lot of champions say they wouldn't have been able to continue skating if it weren't for her."

"Yeah. The numbers she mentioned on the phone were rather substantial. I won't lie to you, Bex, I could use the help. When Jeremy was just skating recreationally, I was barely affording the boots and the blades and the ice time and the coaching. Now that he's decided to seriously compete, I don't know how I'm going to swing the costumes and the travel and the hotels, not to mention the extra lessons. Pandora Westby could really make our lives easier.

But I want to know what I'm getting into. I figured you'd be the go-to person for the straight scoop. You tell me: What should I do?"

When Bex first started working in television, she'd been blown away by how she could scribble something down on a piece of paper, hand it to Francis and Diana, and they would, more often than not, read it on the air for millions of people to hear. It was mind-boggling to think that little Bex Levy, small, meek, and unimportant, unchecked by anyone greater and, well, more important, could just write something off the top of her head and hear it be pronounced, coast to coast, as fact.

The responsibility was heady and intimidating. But it was nothing compared to the panic that seized her when Craig basically asked her to decide the future course of his son's life.

Of course, being a mature young woman, Bex replied to the request in a mature manner. She said, "Uhm . . . why don't I talk to a few people and get back to you, k?"

As Bex suspected, Idan did not attend Coop Devaney's practice session. As she would have suspected, if Bex had given the matter any thought, the local and syndicated press was out in full force, gathering at the entryway to the ice and sticking microphones in Coop's face, demanding details about Allie's death and Coop's petition for custody of the baby she left behind.

His mother on one side, Sebastian on the other, Coop appeared pleased to greet the cameras. In fact, in her report for Gil, Bex actually noted that Coop Devaney looked more tense before entering the arena, as he feared *not* being swamped by a media circus, than he did once he realized that, thank goodness, they were there and interested in him.

DEATH DROP

Smiling the same cocky, flirtatious smile that prompted his ten-fourteen demographic to shriek "Super Cooper!" every time he took the ice, Coop waited until every cameraman had him perfectly centered and lit before launching into his letter-perfect statement about how devastated Coop was by Allie's death.

"I only wish she'd come to me and we could have dealt with this issue together. I can't bring Allie back to life. She's in God's hands now. And I can't help identify or dispense justice to her killer. The Los Angeles Police Department is on the case about that. What I can do, however, is raise our child to be the kind of boy who would be a credit to his mother. Oh, and I also plan to do some volunteer work with other pregnant teenagers. Maybe hearing Allie's story will help them see that they're not alone, and that there are people out there who would like to help them. You can get all the details on my website, *www.Super Cooper.com*. Plus, the photos are cleared for publication."

Coop smiled, excused himself, and stepped onto the ice. Sebastian took his place by the boards. Tess Devaney stayed around to answer any additional questions and hand out Coop's press kit for those who didn't get one in the media room.

Bex settled in the front row, close enough to hear Coop and Sebastian's on-ice conversation if she really strained her ears and watched their lips. Unfortunately, at least one of her eyes kept being distracted by the sight of Craig, sitting a dozen seats over in the same row, monitoring Jeremy's practice with Toni.

He was visibly unhappy with Jeremy's behavior, and Bex couldn't blame him. The boy seemed to be fighting every word Toni said. He trudged around the ice, arms limply by his sides, falling out of jumps instead of trying to save them, and signifying the spot where a spin would go in his program by twirling his finger above his head,

Yahoo-style, instead of actually executing it. When Toni reprimanded him, Jeremy crossed his arms and sulked. When she grabbed him by both shoulders and forced him to look her in the eye, Jeremy yanked away and slammed the back of his blade into the ice, creating a crater. At that Craig leaped out of his seat, jumped over the barrier separating spectators from skaters, and seized his son's elbow.

Bex wondered if Craig realized that such outbursts were simply not done at the Nationals. And then remembered that he probably didn't give a damn.

"Apologize to Toni," Craig ordered.

"Screw you," Jeremy said.

"Get off the ice." Craig let go of Jeremy's elbow and pointed to the exit. "Now."

"Whatever . . ." Jeremy rolled his eyes, made a dramatic show of turning around, then, as slowly as possible without actually coming to a standstill, glided in the general direction of the exit. If taking the long way—three quarters of the way around the rink—could be considered the general direction. He stopped at one point to exchange a few words with Coop, who whispered something in Jeremy's ear. The younger boy glared defiantly at his father the whole time, knowing Craig could hardly step onto the ice and drag him off. Looking calm, though Bex couldn't imagine he wasn't fuming, Craig jerked his thumb toward the exit. Jeremy continued his leisurely pace.

Craig met him on the way out and, without a word, pulled Jeremy away from the ice. Toni followed. A few members of the press took note of the altercations, but seeing as how Jeremy was a nobody, continued their monitoring of Coop without investigating further. After all, if the combined Fourth Estate could pretend not to notice when the Novice champion's mother beat her with a filled water bottle or the Junior Pairs champ cut herself with a razor in the corner after falling on a throw in the Short Program, they could certainly overlook a mere tantrum.

Only Bex, who had spent a lot of time with Jeremy and never seen anything even remotely like this, was left wondering what in the world was going on. Unfortunately, at the moment her place was at the arena, with the Coop and Sebastian show.

Unlike Jeremy and Toni, this practice session was all business. Coop ran through his Long Program twice, back to back. The first time he attempted—and landed—all of his triple jumps, as well as a quadruple Toe Loop. The second time, he left the jumps out but did do his trademark single Axel with arms outstretched (he called it "Flying the Coop"), to the squealing glee of the girls who'd gathered to watch.

Sebastian followed each move with a critical eye, making suggestions about where Coop might want to extend a gesture or take an extra beat in the choreography. It was clear to Bex that all of Sebastian's advice was for the artistic rather than technical portion of the program. Which was well and good for this one practice, but Coop couldn't continue with that sort of coaching indefinitely. In an endeavor where a fraction of a point could mean the difference between going to Worlds and sobbing at home, not to mention Gold and Silver, Coop needed a technical coach like Idan. And he needed one sooner rather than later.

Tess Devaney obviously agreed, because the minute Coop got off the ice, she pulled him away for a quick confab, leaving Sebi standing alone at rinkside. Which was just fine with Bex. She was the only reporter on site who'd actually come specifically to talk to Mr. Vama.

Bex caught up with him as Sebi was heading for the coaches' lounge and asked if she might have a minute of his time.

"Time," Sebastian said. "That black and narrow isthmus between two eternities."

Bex wondered if that meant "yes."

"Charles Caleb Cotton," Sebi enlightened the simple-minded. "He was a British clergyman quite famous for his observations."

"And a fun guy, I'm sure."

They found a spot in the corner, away from ears both human and electronic. Sebi reached into the pocket of his vermilion warm-up suit. Bex thought he was about to offer her a cigarette, but what came out was a PowerBar. A touch of his exotic, multicultured air disappeared with the peeling of the wrapper and a hearty bite. Not that Anglo-Indians shouldn't be allowed to eat great-tasting, high-protein bars that helped you manage your carbohydrate intake and provided you with the energy to be great no matter what the challenge. But it just didn't seem very . . . cool.

Because if there was one word to describe Sebastian Vama, it was cool.

He walked as if he expected the rest of the world to adjust to his pace. He spoke as if everybody should be able to comprehend what he was saying—though he doubted they actually would. And he skated as if the judges wouldn't dare place him and Allison anywhere but first. The two had made a striking competitive pair. Both tall—well, for skaters, not necessarily human beings; Allison was five-foot-five and Sebi an inch short of six feet—long-legged, straight-backed, and dark-haired. They preferred to concentrate on Spanish, Gypsy, Greek, and Middle Eastern programs, where their colorful costumes, imperial attitude, and exotic appearance came together for the perfect image. Sebastian and Allie had more of a problem when it came to dances that required a lighter touch—the fox-trot, the waltz, the polka. This was one team that most definitely did not float on air or convey a spirit of light nonchalance.

They managed to cover up their deficiency by—with Idan—choreographing waltzes or fox-trots so technically difficult, the judges were too busy trying to keep up with all the changes of handholds, twizzles in both directions, and gravity-defying lifts to penalize Sebi and Allison for a lack in conveying the dance's true character (supposedly a requirement). The only part of the competition where Idan's team couldn't get away with their subterfuge was in the compulsories, where no external choreography was allowed outside of the opening and closing poses. To Bex, Sebastian and Allie's scariest compulsory was the Killian. As a march tempo, it did require some intensity. But not nearly as much as they brought to it, seemingly without trying. Both would attempt to smile while they skated it, but considering their extreme demeanors, it came off more as a baring of the teeth. Sebi and Allison's Killian was . . . unnatural. Idan used to complain, "I have them practicing that dance more than any of the others, and still it is the one they always score in the lowest." Bex didn't think they'd ever won a Killian, even at Nationals, much less internationally.

Not that any of it mattered now. The career that had looked so promising only a season ago was definitely over. Bex wondered if, before Allie's death, Sebi had held out some faint hope of her return and their triumphant reunion. She wondered if, as a result, Sebi might be even more motivated to help her find the killer.

He asked Bex, "So, this is a bit of a mess, isn't it?"

She guessed he didn't mean the crumbling PowerBar. "What can you tell me about it?"

"Oh, where, oh, where to begin?" Sebastian sighed. "Did I know Allie was screwing Idan?"

"Did you?"

"I knew she was screwing somebody."

"In addition to Coop?"

"Ah, Coop . . ."

"Was that a yes?"

"Coop is an interesting case."

"How so?"

"He's a very special boy."

"Which means?"

Sebi sighed again and circled his arms in the air dramatically. "Alas, there are no words." Sebastian Vama was also, quite obviously, another very special boy. Only Bex wasn't in the mood to encourage him.

Trying to move the conversation along, she asked, "What about you?"

The arms came crashing down. Obviously, when Sebi wasn't setting the cryptic agenda, his gift for spectacle abandoned him.

"What?" he asked. Neither quote nor allusion in sight. He even mislaid a trace of his English accent. (Bex always found it suspect. Yes, his father was Indian and his mother English, but Sebi had been born and raised in Plano, Texas.)

"How do you feel about what happened to Allison?"

"Crushed. Mortified. Disgusted. Need I go on?"

"Any idea who might have done it?"

"Not a one."

"You were pretty angry when she broke up your partnership."

"Correction: I was incensed. I was enraged. I was livid and irate and most beside myself with rancor."

"Sounds like a motive for murder to me."

"Oh, please. Committing murder, that is so, so banal. My goodness, the crime rates in the country are staggering. I assure you, Bex, I would never perform any task that might lump me in with the common folk."

"Where were you when Allie was killed?"

"Here . . . there . . . everywhere. Wandering about the arena in a carbon-monoxide-induced stupor."

"Why do I get the feeling you're not taking this seriously?"

"Because, my dear Bex, this is all such a joke. Come now—two fathers fighting over a child? It's biblical! And farcical."

"Who do you think the baby's father is?"

"I'm sure I have no idea save a certainty that I am not the culprit."

"But you do think Idan could be the father."

"There is no reason why not. Well, save for Pan possibly cutting his balls off with a sharp blade from her divine crystal collection whilst he slumbers in revenge for the transgression. But you know us lads: The mind often isn't the organ making choices."

"You spent hours on the ice with Allie. You must have known something about her personal life. Do you think she was sleeping with Idan and Coop at the same time?"

"Hmmm . . ." Sebi said.

"Care to clarify?"

"Not really."

"Force yourself."

"Well . . ." Sebi managed to turn four letters, two of which were the same, into four distinct syllables. "You see, the thing about Cooper is . . ."

"Yes?"

"He's not like the other fellows, you see. Cooper has certain . . . inclinations that, according to Mama Tess, at least, the couch-potato people watching back home might not accept from their Wheaties-box Golden Boy. Which is why, no matter how hard I try—and believe me, I've made the effort; I have an inquisitive mind and it most certainly likes to know *everything*—I just cannot picture our Cooper impregnating my little Allie. Sorry, Ms. Levy, better luck next time...."

After dropping that tantalizing tidbit, Sebi, grinning maliciously the entire time, proceeded to play stupid and refused to answer any more follow-up questions, no matter how many times and how many ways Bex found to ask. She finally let him go because it was either that or hit him over the head with *Bartlett's Familiar Quotations.* And Gil frowned on Bex roughing up participants if there was a possibility they might be needed on camera later.

Her next stop was Francis and Diana. Bex found them in the hotel gym, side by side on the treadmills. They wore matching baby blue track suits and Nike sneakers that let out a little swoosh of air with every health-affirming step. In addition, Diana sported her wedding band, her diamond engagement ring, and a sparkling, jeweled clasp to hold up her French Twist. Their treadmill strides were as well matched as their on-ice strokes had once been, and their mutual focus was on the digital readouts analyzing their heart rates, respirations rates, and, for all Bex knew, market rates. She didn't exercise much.

Francis and Diana, on the other hand, took their workouts so seriously, they insisted on staying perpetually in that zone "on the edge of one's breathing." Meaning that going any faster would make them short of breath. Also meaning that conversation was impossible.

Bex supposed any normal person would have waited to come back another time. But she had a very full day ahead of her, including several practices to watch, a meeting with Gil, and with Craig, too, to talk about Jeremy and Pandora Westby. So instead of inquiring when might be a good time to return, Bex told the Howarths, "I'm going to ask you some questions, okay? Just nod your heads when I'm on the right track."

Francis and Diana exchanged glances. Then nodded in unison.

She stepped in the middle of the treadmills so that both could read her lips in case they had trouble making out what she was saying over the metallic noise. Bex said, "You two have known Pandora Westby for a long time, right?"

Nods in the affirmative.

"And she's sponsored a lot of skaters in that time, mostly boys, right?"

More nods, though these also came with more cryptic exchanged looks.

"You don't approve?" Bex asked.

Francis shrugged. Diana shook her head no.

Okay, this was interesting.

"Is it because the rumors are true? Pandora's boys are . . . kept?" Bex couldn't really think of a more tactful word. And she'd heard a lot worse when it came to Cash of the Pan and her harem. People snickered about how Pandora didn't just pay for skating lessons. She bought some of her favorite protégés top-of-the-line wardrobes—"It's so they look good for the draw parties," Pandora explained. "Appearance is so important, after all." Cars—"My boys need to get to the rink somehow." And even put some up in her home long after their competitive careers ended—"Poor fellow. Skating was all he knew. He just needs a little time to get his life together and figure out what to do next. I can't very well throw him to the wolves, now, can I?" When Pandora wed Idan, speculation ran rowdy as to whether he merely refused to put out for all the standard enticements and needed a bigger incentive than the others, or if he was simply so good Pan couldn't risk his getting away.

This time, in response to Bex's question, it was Diana

who shrugged and Francis who nodded. He then wiggled his eyebrows suggestively, should Bex not understand the implications of her own question.

"So Pandora is pretty used to buying anything she wants."

Nod. Nod.

"And if one of her ... purchases ... betrayed her, what would her reaction be? Do you think Pandora is capable of killing Allison over her affair with Idan?"

Shrug.

Double shrug.

"What about Idan? Could he have killed Allie? Either to get Omri away from her, or to keep her quiet about something, or—"

Francis cut her off. Not with a nod, but with a quick release of the treadmill's bar and a disturbingly accurate miming of a rifle being fired. A reminder that Idan Ben-Golan was once a professional sniper. If he did kill Allison, odds are she wouldn't be his first casualty.

"And Coop," Bex asked. "Could he have killed Allie? You know him better than I do. Does he have a temper? When I spoke to him and his mother yesterday"—Diana rolled her eyes at the word "mother"—"he seemed to have somewhat of a temper. My theory is, either he killed Allie because he found out she cheated on him with Idan, or because he didn't want her to tell anyone that they'd had a baby. Everyone keeps saying how important image is to Coop and his mom. They're making the best of it now, but maybe he didn't want word getting out that a clean-cut guy like him could dump his pregnant girlfriend."

Diana raised her arm, palm up, indicating she had no insight on that one. Francis, however, shook his head vehemently.

"You don't think Coop killed Allison?"

Francis shook his head no. And then he mimed rocking a baby.

It took Bex a minute to figure out what he meant. At first she assumed Francis was trying to tell her that Coop wouldn't kill Allie over Omri's existence. But when he shook his head in disgust at her conjecture, Bex finally got it.

"You don't think the baby is Coop's!"

Francis nodded so hard he almost lost his stride and had to grip the bar to regain his balance.

"Why not?"

It wasn't a yes-or-no question, and they both realized it. But obviously, Francis's need to share gossip overruled even the desire for a healthy heart and lungs. He smacked the "pause" button and, as the treadmill ground to a stop, managed to breathlessly croak out, "That's just not what our boy is about these days" before restarting the machine and refusing to elaborate further.

When Bex looked to Diana for confirmation, the older woman feigned great interest in her heart rate and refused to meet Bex's eyes.

She was on to something. Bex didn't just feel it, she also *knew* it now. There was something no one was telling her about Cooper Devaney. Well, not out loud, anyway. They were perfectly happy to drop cryptic hints and giggle at her cluelessness.

Gil had to know. He may have been a screaming nut who'd once gotten fired for putting an entire television network into black for ten seconds (Bex still hadn't found the time to fully process and enjoy that tidbit), but he wasn't dimwitted. He wouldn't have agreed to produce Coop's reality show without fully investigating the boy.

"Of course not," Gil said, agreeing with Bex's assessment. "I know what they're talking about. Coop's mother told me all about it. She knew I wouldn't agree to do the show if Coop was open about his . . . lifestyle choice. But she assured me he'd be keeping it to himself as long as the cameras were rolling. The rest of the time, frankly, I don't give a flying fuck what he does. As long as the press doesn't get whiff of it, naturally."

"How do you expect to keep a secret like that, Gil?"

"Pretty easily." He grinned. "I mean, you're the press. And notice how I'm not telling you . . ."

Bex fumed for the rest of the day. She expended so much energy on the project, she was amazed the ice at the practice arena didn't start melting any time she looked in its direction.

For five hours, Bex sat in the stands, took notes on the practices, wrote up her observations, and continued to fume.

What the hell did Gil think he was doing?

Well, obviously, she knew what he *thought* he was doing. He was protecting the cash that had been sunk into Coop Devaney's reality show, by protecting the truth about Coop Devaney. The gist of which was getting more and more obvious by the moment to anyone paying attention.

According to Gil, Coop's status had no bearing on Allison's murder. Which Bex found impossible to believe on a swarm of levels. As far as she knew, Omri's paternity, not to mention custody, had yet to be settled. In fact, the Family Court of Los Angeles was holding an emergency hearing the following day to decide whether the boy would be allowed to remain with Idan, or handed over to either Coop or Ralph. All of the parties, including character witnesses for both sides, intended to testify. And a 24/7 camera crew would be there to record every sensational, salacious word. For the reality show. Not for the Nationals broadcast. When Bex asked Gil why she hadn't been invited to cover it as well, he informed her that he wanted the footage to be exclusive, and besides, none of it had to do with Allison's murder. Bex should really be focusing her attention on that.

So she continued to fume. And made plans to show up anyway. With luck, the camera guys wouldn't know she'd been banned.

As the last practice session scraped to a close, Bex tidied up her notes, stood, stretched, stomped her feet to restore circulation, and finally allowed herself to remember the appointment that, all day, she'd been telling herself was the least important of the lot. Despite the fact that it was the only one she was actually looking forward to.

She had to see Craig, to tell him what she'd learned about Pandora. Because he'd asked her to. No other reason than that.

Bex thought maybe they could make an evening out of it—she was done with the practices and interviews. She had nothing much to do except write the summary, and Bex could do that any old time, even late at night if she needed to. If Craig was bored again, maybe they could grab dinner. With Jeremy, of course. The three of them could eat at the hotel or they could go out and just hang. Hanging was good. Just a trio of friends killing time in a strange city. Nothing more than that.

When Jeremy opened the door to his hotel room, Bex was so enthused about her plan that she nearly blurted it out without so much as a peremptory hello. All she had to offer instead was an admittedly goofy smile of anticipation. A smile that remained on her visage even after Jeremy, half his face obscured by the door he refused to open all the way, growled, "What the hell do you want?"

The greeting was so unexpected and, frankly, so out of character for the otherwise sunny kid that Bex's first thought was that it was some sort of joke.

But when her idea of a witty retort, "Love, love, and Puppy Chow" (it was a TV commercial from a decade earlier that asked what all dogs want), was greeted by a snort and a "Jesus, you're nuts," Bex realized that this wasn't a game of Simulated Surly Teen. This was the real deal. Apparently developed over the past twenty-four hours.

"It's her," Jeremy snapped over his shoulder in response to Craig asking who was at the door. Bex didn't know whether to be insulted that she no longer had a name, or to feel honored that she was such an important woman in their lives that a mere pronoun was ample identification.

"Bex, hey." Craig scurried to the door, shooing Jeremy deeper inside their room but making no effort to open the door farther.

"Hi." Bex, who'd come skipping in with what she believed was a solid idea of how their first few minutes of conversation might go, felt like she was being blown backward by a huge wind machine and could hardly remain upright, much less pry her words out and in the right direction. "What's going—"

Craig shook his head and, when he spoke, it was in a whisper. "Look, Bex, this isn't a good time. I can't explain right now, but I think you—and I—we made a mistake. Things are not good right now. Let's talk later, okay?"

And he shut the door, if not in her face, then at least in that general direction.

Twelve

"Men just don't make any sense, do they?" Lian Reilly wailed. She stood in the bathroom of her hotel suite, waving a puffing steam iron in the vague direction of a teal competition dress, but mostly just lacerating the air with it for emphasis.

"No," Bex agreed, without a trace of condescension or irony. On any other day, squirming pinned between someone else's toilet and sink while dandelions of hot steam matted not only her bangs but even her eyelashes to her cheeks while listening to Lian rant about the latest universal plot against her, was cause for a postmodern chuckle. But as of today, Bex was down with her sister-woman.

"I thought I didn't have to worry about Coop. I mean, I'd heard he and Allison were dating and, before I knew better, I thought the same thing everybody else did. But once I got to know Coop, I found out we all got it wrong."

"What was all wrong?"

"What people said about him. I mean, about him and Allison. Turned out it was the exact opposite."

"You've lost me," Bex said.

Lian sighed. It made the edges of her newly funkified hair twitch, as if they'd just realized they were on the wrong head. "We all thought Coop and Allie had this really hot and heavy thing going on. They certainly acted like they did. We used to joke that they were going for the first ever side-by-side triple Lip Lock, considering how much time they spent globbed onto each other. That's why, when Coop first asked me to go out, I was kind of nervous. Well, really, really nervous, actually. I'm not . . . Allie was . . . I'm not like Allie, you know what I mean?"

Bex knew exactly what she meant. "And you thought it would bother Coop?"

"Yeah. I figured, a guy like him . . . and he's older, too. He's going to want to . . . you know."

"But he didn't?"

"No. He didn't."

"Not at all?"

"Uh-uh. To be honest, after a couple of dates where he didn't, I started worrying that it was me. That he didn't like me. Stupid, huh? I mean, first I stress that he'll want to, and then I stress when he doesn't. Men can really mess with your mind, can't they?"

"Yes," Bex said. "They can."

"But that was before Coop explained it to me."

"Explained what?"

"About how he's . . . he's not like other guys his age."

"He told you, then?"

"But there's nothing wrong with it. Even if his mother wishes Coop would keep it a secret. That's the part I felt worst about. Having to keep it a secret."

"Coop's mother knows?"

"Oh, yeah. As soon as Coop figured out what he was

really into, he went straight to his mom. He figured she'd be understanding. I mean, she's Ms. Super Liberal, right? Like, when Coop and I first started dating, she practically tripped over herself telling me how interesting she thought the history of China was and what a great culture we have and how she'd love to learn more about it. Bex, I haven't been to China since I was six months old. But Tess just went on and on about it. She's all about multiculturalism and being open-minded and tolerant."

"Except when it came to Coop and his lifestyle choices."

"She said it wasn't that. She said if he wanted to go ahead and experiment, it was okay with her. He was young, that's when you're supposed to try out different things and figure out where you belong. She said her hesitation had to do with what if a couple of months down the road Coop changes his mind. If he told everybody now, the damage would already be done. His public image would be ruined. Tess said she didn't want Coop doing anything foolhardy until he was certain this was what he really wanted. Of course, when Coop actually tried to decide if this was what he really wanted by talking to people who were the same as him, you know, like Gary Gold, my coach? Tess really pulled the plug on that one ASAP."

"That's why Tess had Coop change coaches from Gary to Idan?"

"Yeah . . . and that's when he started dating Allie, too. Or at least we thought they were dating."

"You don't think Coop and Allie were sexually involved?" Bex had gotten tired of euphemisms. Besides, how exactly did you phrase, "You don't think Coop and Allie were . . . you know-ing?"

"It's just hard to imagine. With everything I know now, I mean. When I first heard Coop say he was the baby's dad, I kind of lost it. I thought Coop had been lying to me. But

I've had some time to think about it." Lian flicked off the steam iron and turned to face Bex. "Want to hear what I think really happened there?"

"Absolutely."

"I think, after Tess made Coop switch from Gary to Idan, Coop didn't want his mom on his back anymore. So he pretended to be dating Allison. Meanwhile, Allison was having this secret thing with Idan, and they didn't want Pandora to know. Because that would be seriously scary. So Coop pretended to be dating Allie to keep his mom off the scent, and Allie pretended to be dating Coop to keep Pan in the dark."

Penalty for overusing clichés aside, Bex thought Lian had an excellent theory.

"Then, after Allie got pregnant, maybe Coop didn't want to play along anymore, or Allie just figured they should tell Pandora the truth—it's not like she could ruin Allie's career now, right? Allie took care of that all by herself—and so she took off."

"But why is Coop claiming to be Omri's dad now, if you're sure he couldn't be?"

"His mom. It's got to be his mom. I mean, how many pieces did 24/7 do about Allie and Coop and what a golden couple they are? How's it going to make Coop look if everyone finds out his girlfriend was cheating on him with his coach and he didn't know anything about it? It's going to make Coop look major stupid."

Lian had another great point. If 24/7 was pitching Coop as a heartthrob, *cuckold* was not an image they needed plastered across his forehead.

"And one more thing," Lian said.

"What's that?"

"For Coop to say in public that he's not the baby's father, he'd have to say why he knows that for sure. And no way would Tess let him do that."

"Lian"—Bex phrased the question as tactfully as she could, especially since this question was just a preamble toward what she really wanted to ask—"do you think Tess could have killed Allie, to keep her from saying why Coop couldn't be Omri's father?"

Lian looked horrified by the thought. But she didn't say no.

Emboldened, Bex pressed about as far as she dared to go for now. "What about Coop, Lian? Could he have kill—"

"No! No, absolutely not, no way! You're totally missing my point. I keep telling you, Coop isn't like everybody else. He's a really, really good person. He tries hard to always do the right thing and make everybody happy and not let anyone down. He could never hurt anyone, especially not Allie."

Bex nodded thoughtfully, and, realizing she had reached the end of Lian's value—plus the room had gotten so moist it was like Florida and San Francisco had mated—Bex wedged her thighs out from between the toilet and the sink. But before she left, she did have one more question for Lian. "Okay, so we think we know why Allison went along with the charade of acting like she was Coop's girlfriend. But Lian, why did you do it?"

"Because it wasn't a charade," Lian insisted. "Coop and I are soulmates. Real soulmates. I mean, anyone can just . . . you know. But what Coop and I have is deeper than that. He gets me. And I get him. He loves me. This isn't like him and Allie at all."

Getting an audience with Gary Gold inevitably meant waylaying him on the path to someplace else and trapping him in an inescapable confine. The previous instances when Bex managed to pry useful information out of the notoriously tight-lipped coach, she'd needed to ambush him at the barrier while coaching a student, invite herself along on a constitutional in the middle of a Moscow snowstorm, and physically block him from exiting a restaurant. Because Gary Gold was not what anyone would ever call free with the information. He was a very private person in a very public sphere, and he preferred to keep it that way.

Even during Gary's own competitive days, he refused to answer any personal questions that strayed from the ice. His up-close-and-personal television profile the year that he represented the United States at the 1978 Olympics consisted of Gary practicing at the rink, being interviewed at the rink, and walking from the rink to the bus. He wouldn't let the crew shoot him at home, with his parents, or even reveal which bus he took. He said it had nothing to do with his skating, so what business was it of anyone's?

As a coach, Gary preferred to stand back and let his students absorb all the limelight. He would come to the mandatory press conferences after various events, but only for moral support, not to offer quotes. "Their skating speaks for itself" was the closest anyone could get out of him for a sound bite.

Personally, Bex didn't get the reticent act. What Gary had to hide really wasn't all that interesting. Sure, he was assumed to be gay. But in skating, that was like saying someone was assumed to be chilly.

Nevertheless, Gary never discussed his personal life, and Bex had to believe the gag order extended to the personal lives of his students as well. Which didn't mean she shouldn't try her best to pump him for details about Coop, just that she didn't expect to get anywhere.

This time around, instead of tackling Gary during practice or after a meal, Bex took a chance and went up to his hotel room, knocking meekly on the door and standing back quickly, lest he had a booby trap in place specifically for the nosy.

Gary opened the door dressed in perfectly pressed beige linen slacks and a white shirt that most certainly did not look as if it had arrived courtesy of an overstuffed valise all the way from Connecticut. No matter how distant the competition—Russia, Australia, China—Gary's clothes always looked crisp and stainless.

"Ah, Miss Levy," he said. "I've been expecting you."

"You have?"

"Indeed. I suspected you would be turning up at my door sooner or later. I took the liberty of ordering lunch."

He wasn't kidding. Gary stood back so that Bex could peek inside his hotel room and notice a table set with two silver, room-service trays. He walked over to lift first one lid, then another, and told Bex, "You have a choice, steak or vegetarian lasagna. I wasn't sure which you preferred."

"You really ordered lunch for me?" Bex repeated, incredulous.

"I didn't want you leaving with nothing for your trouble," Gary said, his inference perfectly clear.

"But how did you know I'd be here?"

"My dear Miss Levy, we have met before under similar circumstances, have we not? I know how you operate, by now. You're a bright girl, but rather set in your ways for someone so young. You've spoken to the police, you've spoken to Cooper, to Idan, to Pandora, the Howarths, and to Lian. Where else would you come next but to me? I am certain everyone has given you quite the earful about my coaching Cooper as well as his mother's reasons for severing that relationship."

"Everybody said that Tess and you didn't see eye to eye. On some philosophical issues." Bex stepped into the room and, not needing to be asked twice, headed straight over to the preset table. She chose the steak option. This job required all of her strength.

"A philosophical issue." Gary took the seat across from

Bex while juggling the verbiage and determining if he liked it. "Yes, I suppose that would be one way to put it."

"You'd like to put it another way?"

"Not necessarily."

"Were you surprised by Tess's reaction?"

"Why should I have been?"

"Well, for one thing, because she makes this big show of being liberal and open-minded and accepting."

"Quite a few people, in my experience, are rather liberal and open-minded and accepting. Until the tide reaches their own doorstep."

"Tess thought you were a bad influence on Coop."

"Tess was correct."

"Really?" That brought Bex up short. She even stopped shoveling steak into her mouth.

"Well, certainly from her perspective. Miss Levy, I do not believe it is a secret that I choose to keep my personal thoughts, feelings, opinions, and practices to myself. I neither volunteer that information nor allow it to be weaseled out of me."

At the moment, Bex suspected that the role of weasel was being played by her.

"However, if a student comes to me with a direct question and asks for advice, not coach to student but simply, in this case, man to man, I feel a moral obligation to do what I can and answer their inquiries honestly."

"Which is what you did with Coop?"

"I simply shared certain experiences that I believed might be helpful to him."

"Which is when Tess blew a fuse?"

"Correct."

"You don't seem upset about it."

"Why should I be?"

"You lost a top pupil."

"It happens."

"And his mother, the way I see it, she pretty much offended you, too."

"That happens as well. Much more frequently than you can imagine."

"Coop and Allie—" Bex began.

But Gary simply shook his head. "I know nothing of that relationship. I believe Cooper and Allison did not begin dating until after he left my tutelage and relocated to California."

"But you know Coop. Do you believe he's the father of Allie's baby?"

Gary hesitated. He chewed his food, swallowed, and dabbed his lips neatly with a napkin before cautiously opining, "Based on some of the issues Cooper and I discussed, as well as the choices he was struggling with . . . no. No, I don't think so, Miss Levy."

So that was four nays (Idan, Sebi, Gary, and Lian) and two yeas (Ralph and Tess) for Coop being the father. Plus Gil's unsubtle edict that he better be—if Bex knew what was good for her.

What she needed was less innuendo and conjecture and more tangible, physical evidence.

Like, say, perhaps returning to the arena, rounding a dark corner leading to the production offices, and coming upon Sebi.

Wrapped in a lip-lock with Coop.

Thirteen

The day of the emergency custody hearing, rather than trying to bully her way into the courtroom and making even more enemies than she already had, Bex simply waited for Gil's reality show crew to return with their footage, then asked the cameraman if she could look.

"Sure." He handed over the Beta tapes. "Just make sure to check them into the library when you're done."

"Anything interesting?" she asked supercasually.

"If you're into breast-beating and soap opera. We did catch a break, though. The judge agreed to do this in chambers and sign a release. Otherwise we'd have been stuck shooting around not just him but also everyone else who happened to wander into the courtroom, which would have been a major pain."

"Everybody signed a release?" Bex had a hard time believing that Idan or Ralph would be thrilled by the notion of having their family calamity televised.

"Everybody. Go figure. Then again, all press is good press, right?"

"I guess . . ."

Bex found a free beta screener, popped in the tape (as well as a pair of earphones so no one would know what she was up to), and pressed play.

Her monitor instantly revealed a wide shot of a wood-paneled judge's office, with the black-robed magistrate seated behind a desk, and everyone else in two rows of chairs directly in front of him. The front row featured Ralph, Idan holding a sleeping Omri in a yellow jumper, Coop, Tess, and two men Bex assumed to be lawyers for various sides. The second row held Pandora, and Sebastian, of all people. Bex wondered if he might be the unimpeachable witness Tess boasted about earlier, and what he could possibly contribute to the conversation.

Idan was the first to speak. He looked directly at the judge to insist, "I do not understand what we are all doing here. I am the legal father of this child. The claims of everyone else, what meaning do they have?"

"Allie was my daughter," Ralph snapped. "I got rights."

"Stepdaughter," Tess reminded from the back.

Lawyer number one indicated a file the judge already held in his hand and reminded, "We have presented the court with a legitimate birth certificate. If Mr. Adler wishes to sue for custody, this is not the correct venue for his petition."

"Guy's a pervert," Ralph leaned across the desk, trying to swipe the file away as inconsequential, but only managing to lose his balance in the attempt. He braced himself with one palm and went on, "Grown man sleeping with a little girl, it's disgusting."

"As you can see by the birth certificate, Your Honor, Ms. Adler was of legal age."

"He should be strung up by the fucking balls for what

he did. Idan's the one that should have been hanging, not my Allie. You can't reward him for being a pervert. My grandson shouldn't be brought up by a criminal. Not to mention that wife of his. What kind of a home is it where the boy's going to know every day his stepmother hates him because he reminds her of his dad's catting around?"

"Mr. Adler." Due to the camera's angle, Bex was only privy to the back of Pandora's head—complete with what Bex presumed was an authentic, diamond hair clip to keep her heavily hair-sprayed ponytail in place. So Bex did not, for a fact, know that actual honey was dripping from between Pandora's lips. She could only deduce it from her dulcet, soothing, patronizing tones. "I can assure you that would most certainly never be the case. Omri is my husband's child. As such, I welcome him into my family with open arms and promise to love him as my own."

"Bullshit," Ralph said. Which, quite frankly, was more or less what Bex was thinking. This certainly wasn't the Pandora she'd encountered the other night. Bex wondered what had changed her mind. Was the woman really so terrified of losing her young—albeit unfaithful—stud, that she was willing to play Mother Bountiful to ensure his not losing custody? Or was something more sinister going on here?

"I'm not certain what I can say to convince you, Mr. Adler. I'm afraid you're just going to have to take my word that Idan and I will provide Omri with a wonderful home—"

"This whole point is moot," Tess interrupted. Her lawyer attempted to rest a restraining hand on her shoulder, but she brushed it off like a stray bang strand across her forehead. "The quality of Idan and Pandora Ben-Golan's home is irrelevant, as the child in question isn't theirs. Allan is my grandson."

"Who the hell is Allan?" Idan snapped.

"Your Honor, this is Sebastian Vama. He was Allison's Dance partner for many years. I'm sure even Mr. Ben-Golan will agree that the intimacy level necessary for partners to succeed on the ice carries over into their off-ice relationship as well."

"So what, now he's claiming to be the dad, too?" Ralph huffed.

"Hardly," Sebi drawled. "What Ms. Devaney is alluding to, is the fact that even more than the other candidates in this room, I was required to be closely attuned to the subtle fluctuations of Allie's body. I skated side by side with her. We had to make hairpin turns where so much as a fraction of an inch leaned in the wrong direction meant the difference between a Gold-medal-winning edge and a complete wipeout. I had to lift her. Her center of gravity was of vital importance to me. I could tell she'd gained or lost an ounce without need of a scale. I realized she was pregnant even before she did."

"What?" Coop woke up. He had to swivel around to confront Sebi. Bex noted the utter shock on his face. "You *knew*?"

"I was sworn to secrecy."

"You knew Allie was pregnant? And you never said anything?"

"Partner's oath. A promise is a promise, on both sides of the skate edge."

"How could you not tell me?"

Sebi made a noncommittal gesture with his hand, bending the wrist this way and that to indicate . . . something obscure.

Maybe it was a quote.

"The point is, Your Honor." Tess tapped her son on the knee, directing him to turn back around and face the judge. Coop did so grudgingly, anger and betrayal fighting for dominance across his features. "The point is, not only did

Allison confide in Mr. Vama that she was pregnant, she also told him that my son was the father."

"Is this true, Mr. Vama?"

"Absolutely, Your Honor."

"How could you do this to me?" Coop demanded. "You saw what a basket case I was after Allie took off. How could you just let me wonder and worry? I thought we were friends."

"Allison and I were friends, too. I gave her my word."

"But I could have helped her. I could have prevented all . . . this. I would have. Think of how much she must have been suffering. You could have helped me to save her."

"I promised Allie—"

"It wasn't your promise to make! Allie was my girlfriend! This is my baby! They were my responsibility. Mine, and mine alone." He crumbled then. The bravado dissipated, leaving Coop as seemingly lost as when he initially heard about Allie and her surprise child. He slunk down in his chair and covered his face with his hands. His back shook, vertebrae bobbing like a one-lane stone road in an earthquake.

"I'm being punished," he said with a moan. "Because I couldn't go through with it. Gary tried to tell me how hard it would be, but I didn't believe him. I thought I was strong enough, but I wasn't. That's why all this happened. It's divine retribution, that's what it is. Because I failed. Because I'm a hypocrite."

Just when things were getting interesting, Idan pulled the plug.

"Oh, enough!" he thundered. "This is getting ridiculous. It is obvious that a legal document issued by the State of California is not going to be enough to satisfy all of your hysterics. Obviously there is only one way to settle this."

Idan reached into his inside jacket pocket and, for a

moment, Bex found herself wondering if Uzis came in size small. But then she figured if a shoot-out had occurred during the proceedings, even the jaded 24/7 cameraman would have mentioned it.

Instead of a weapon, Idan pulled out, rather anticlimactically, a palm-size box of Q-tips and a pair of clear, sandwich-size, plastic Baggies.

He ripped the plastic covering around the Q-tips box off with his teeth, pried open the perforated, cardboard lid, and pulled out a swab. In a single, fluid motion, Idan stuck the cotton into Omri's mouth, rubbed it against the protesting baby's cheek, and dropped the results into one of the plastic bags. He then repeated the process with his own cheek and angrily tossed both across the judge's desk.

"Here," Idan hissed, rocking Omri to soothe him after the incursion. "Let us just end this and move on."

While Idan's lawyer launched into legalese about DNA and such, Bex focused her attention on Tess, who looked utterly bushwhacked by the development.

"This is highly irregular." Her attorney attempted damage control on Tess's behalf, since Coop was certainly in no position to speak or defend himself. He was still sitting glassy-eyed, pondering, Bex could only suppose, the wrath of God against his—what had Coop called himself? A hypocrite?—children. "Surely, a paternity test with such contested results should be conducted within the controlled environment of an accredited laboratory."

"Oh, please," Pandora spoke up. "There are advertisements for such things in the back of tabloid magazines. Send a few dollars and a cheek swab for your verdict. And those tests results are regularly accepted in court. This is practically the Mayo Clinic in comparison."

"Mrs. Ben-Golan has a point," the judge agreed. "I will postpone making my final ruling pending the paternity test results. My bailiff will see to it that the samples are delivered to the proper lab for testing. Until then, court is adjourned."

The tape ended with a shot of every litigant leaving the judge's chamber. The 24/7 cameraman obviously had hustled to scramble out before they did so he could get everyone's head-on reaction, live and in color. Bex made a mental note to compliment him on his fancy footwork.

If it hadn't been for such quick thinking, she'd never have been privy to the shot of Ralph exiting, scowling, mumbling something about the law being a tool of rich, good-looking people. Or Idan and Pandora smiling, both making goo-goo faces at Omri as they strolled down the hall, looking every inch the picture-perfect family.

Or Tess, arm around Coop's waist, head down, hissing under her breath to her son as they headed in the opposite direction, seemingly unaware of just how long of a reach a good, camera-mounted, boom microphone had, "What the hell was that all about in there, Cooper? I thought we talked about this. I thought we understood each other. What you do on your own time and away from the public eye is your own business. But for God's sake, keep your mouth shut about it. We're selling an image here, not a flesh-and-blood person. Believe me, those teenage girls Gil Cahill is planning to attract with our series have no interest in seeing you like that."

They turned the corner at that point, disappearing out of both view and boom-mike reach. But just in case Bex felt she hadn't gotten her daily fill of parent-child conflict, the moment she turned around from checking the tape back into 24/7's makeshift video library, Bex stumbled upon Craig and Jeremy.

They were at the far end of the arena, arguing yet again. Craig had his arm on Jeremy's elbow, but the boy yanked it away, turning to kick the wall in frustration. Craig said something that Jeremy clearly didn't care to hear, because his response was an upturned middle finger and then a sprint toward the stairway.

"Hey, Coop!" Jeremy yelled. "Wait up!" and scurried out of sight.

Bex, who only a few seconds ago had been looking at Coop at the courthouse, had to remind herself that the proceedings had, in fact, taken place a few hours earlier. And if the camera crew had time to return to the arena, so obviously had Coop.

Bex had a few questions she was dying to ask him, but with Craig heading in her direction, Bex's curiosity got the best of her, and she had to ask, "What was that about?"

"Beats me." He threw his arms in the air. "I left home with a polite, mild-mannered eighth-grader, and I arrived with a surly adolescent."

"Interesting time to mature."

Craig took a deep breath. "You could say that, yeah."

"Any idea what set him off?"

"I don't know. All I can think of is maybe instead of distracting him from everything that's happened, like I hoped, Nationals just put him under way too much pressure and the poor kid cracked."

"But he looked like he was having so much fun out there!"

"Don't they all?" Craig challenged. "It's part of the artistic score. These kids practice looking happy and divinely inspired the same way they practice triple-triple combinations. You can't take anyone's expressions on the ice at—excuse the horrible pun—face value."

"Well what does Toni think?"

"She doesn't know what to make of it, either. It's like, after years of begging me to allow him to compete, now that he's here, Jeremy is itching to get the hell out of

Dodge. The rotten way he's acting, I'm this far from saying forget this whole thing and let's go home."

"It doesn't make any sense."

"Yeah," Craig agreed. "What else is new in Skate-Land?"

"You know . . ." she began.

"What?"

"It's only . . . I was thinking . . ."

"Come on. Out with it. At this point in time, I'm taking parenting input from anyone and everyone. A few more of these blowouts with Jeremy and I'll be going to Lucian Pryce for advice."

Bex tried to be as tactful as possible, asking instead of coming right out and voicing her suspicions. "Has Jeremy been spending a lot of time with Coop Devaney at this competition?"

Craig shrugged. "A bit. They hit it off the first day. I think they've hung out once or twice. Guy's been Jeremy's hero for years. He's thrilled someone he admires so much took an interest in him."

Bex said, "Coop is gay, Craig."

"Wow. A gay skater. That *is* a shock. Besides, what about all this commotion over Allie Adler's baby?"

"I'm not sure how that works, exactly," Bex admitted. "But I am sure that I saw Coop making out with Sebi Vama a few nights ago."

"Fascinating. Not sure how that pertains to Jeremy and me, but I'm sure this arena is packed with people who would find such a sighting utterly fascinating."

"What I'm trying to say is, what if Jeremy's recent mood swings are coming from Coop trying something . . . inappropriate . . . with him. I mean, Jeremy's only thirteen. He probably has no idea how to handle something like this. Especially not from someone who, like you said, he admires so much."

Craig appeared to be considering her words. Then he said, "I never pegged you for a homophobe, Bex."

"Excuse me? What? No! I—that's ridiculous. This is TV—skating TV—I work with lots of people who—"

"Some of your best friends are homosexuals? Is that what you're trying to say?"

"You know, Craig . . ." Strange, but now that he was attacking her, Bex actually felt more comfortable talking to the man than the other night, when he was being so friendly. This probably said something about her and the whole male/female dynamics issue. Probably something not particularly good. But Bex had no time to dissect the implications at the moment. "There are a lot of dads out there who wouldn't let their sons figure-skate specifically because they're concerned about the kind of . . . influences . . . those boys might fall under. I'm hardly voicing something unique."

"Unique, no. Unsubstantiated, yes."

"So you're not worried."

"Look, Bex—am I aware that figure skating may attract a higher number of gay men than, say, welding? Yes, I am. Am I aware that the odds of Jeremy turning out to be gay are probably higher than average? Yes, I am. Am I worried about it? No, Bex. Not particularly. Would you like to know why?"

"Okay. Why?"

"Because to date, the straight men of figure skating have beaten a good friend of mine into a coma, driven her practically insane, and murdered my wife. The gay men of figure skating haven't done any damn thing to me."

He had a point. And though she was not a gay man, Bex knew she could freely add herself to the list of skating-related hangers-on who had done serious damage to his family, life, and sanity.

"So you don't think Coop—"

"I don't know. That's the problem, Bex. I don't know a damn thing anymore. It's like there's this viral psychosis running through all of Nationals. And we're it."

Family Court was reconvened the next day. This time Bex didn't wait for an invitation. She simply showed up along with the camera crew and figured no one would question her presence. Only one person did: Ralph Adler. Fortunately, no one paid him any mind. If this were a competition on the ice, Ralph would be the one undeserving of prime-time coverage. He probably would barely warrant a mention during the afternoon roundup. This battle was down to two top contenders. With Omri as the grand prize.

The baby of the hour was, once again, in attendance. This time he wore a white, one-piece jumper with red stripes, making him look like a wriggly candy cane. Pandora was holding him—the better to prove what a loving stepmother she'd be, my dear . . .

No one said a word as they filed inside. Coop accidentally brushed against Idan. Then, when the accident didn't trigger any reaction, brushed against him again. Harder, this time. Without even the pretense of not meaning to.

Idan simply smirked and pulled out a chair for his wife, helping Pandora get settled, baby in tow.

With all of Ralph's talk about his grandson being raised by a harridan from a fairy tale, Bex noted that the one person in the room who had yet to express even token interest in the child was his self-proclaimed paternal grandmother, Tess. She'd come in, one arm linked through Coop's, and taken a seat at the farthest end of the room—even her lawyer was physically closer to Omri than she was—without so much as a glance in his candy cane direction.

Coop, on the other hand, could not take his eyes off the

boy. He reached over and, without asking Pandora's permission, tentatively stoked the back of the baby's palm.

"He's so small . . ." Coop noted.

"He's healthy," Pandora reassured.

Idan cleared his throat. Pan moved Omri to her other arm. Out of Coop's reach. He didn't try to touch him again.

The judge swept in, noted the cameras, and, for a moment, looked as if he'd forgotten agreeing to let them in. However, once Tess's lawyer laid a manila folder with copies of the assembled group's signed releases on his desk, he shrugged, mumbled something under his breath that may have been "publicity whores, the whole lot of them"—or maybe that was just Bex's projection of her own thoughts—and squeezed into the chair behind his desk, calling the hearing to order.

He spewed forth a few legal terms, chastising everyone for taking this case to court when family disputes were always best settled without lawyers getting involved. When no one looked even a little bit chastised, he gave up that ghost and got to the meat of the matter.

Reading from yet another manila folder, this one handed to him by the bailiff, the judge pronounced, "I have the paternity test results. The lab informs me that within 99.9 percent accuracy, the biological father of the child known as Omri is Idan Ben-Golan."

Idan and Pandora exchanged smiles.

Bex wondered why Mrs. Ben-Golan was so thrilled to have proof that her husband had cheated on her with a teenage student. But, as established earlier, Bex wasn't so good at the whole female/male relationship dynamic.

Tess flushed crimson, glaring first at the judge, then her lawyer, then finally at Coop, accusingly. Visibly thwarted, and even more visibly unhappy about it.

Coop, for his part, was the only one merely stunned by

the verdict. The only one whose expression wasn't one of smugness or anger, just confusion.

"How . . ." he began.

"Jesus, you idiot, do I have to draw you a picture?" Ralph all but smacked Coop on the back of the head to knock some sense into him. "You still don't get it. This guy raped our Allie."

"Now, just wait one minute . . ." Idan half rose from his chair, his body language clearly radiating the Incredible Hulk's familiar refrain: *Don't make me angry. You won't like me when I'm angry.*

Ralph, however, was not a Lou Ferrigno fan. He went on, either beyond fear or not fully cognizant of the sort of threat a truly enraged former soldier could pose if properly motivated. "That's right. You heard me, you son of a bitch. I don't give a damn if she was eighteen. I don't give a damn if she even thought it was her idea. Fact is, you're the coach. You're the adult. She listened to every word you said. She did whatever you told her to do. Point your toes, spread your legs—makes no difference in the end, does it?"

"Ralph, please . . ." At first, Bex thought Tess was simply trying to calm the irate man down. But then, when she indicated the camera and whispered to Bex, "Please tell Gil to cut that part out. We don't need Coop associated with this kind of vulgarity," Bex understood her true motivation.

"Please, what? Please don't tell the truth? I'm gonna tell the truth until this bastard is drummed out of the USFSA and banned from ever coaching again."

Ah, Bex thought. Yes, that truly would be a worse fate than, say, oh, jail time?

"Mr. Adler." Idan turned to face the older man, his tone so steely it effectively silenced every other voice in the room. Ralph stopped screaming. Tess stopped fuming.

DEATH DROP

Even the baby took a break from gurgling. The only sound still audible above the tension was the faint bzzz of the video camera. Which, of course, was capturing every word. "Mr. Adler," Idan repeated, "I am genuinely sorry for your loss. Perhaps, after you have calmed down, the three of us might sit down and work out an equitable visitation agreement for you and your grandson. His Honor is right. These sorts of things are best settled outside of court. In spite of your and Allie's problems in the latter years, I know she cared for you, and would have wanted for you to be involved in Omri's life."

"Involved in Omri's life?" Ralph repeated.

"Yes, sir." Now that paternity had been settled, Idan sounded almost penitent. Or, at the very least, respectful, as one must be to a . . . father-in-law?

"Omri's life? *Omri's* life? What about Allie? What about her life? My daughter is dead! Does any one of you give a damn about that? Allie is dead. And you killed her, Ben-Golan. I've got the proof right here."

Fourteen

Ralph jabbed his finger in Omri's direction. "That boy, there. He's the proof. Allie killed herself over what you did to her. If it wasn't for this boy—"

"Oh, enough, already," Tess snapped. It hadn't been her day so far. What better way to salvage the dregs of it than to ruin it for someone else? "Could we drop this pretense of Allie committing suicide, already? It's giving her this aura of a poor, put-upon martyr, which, to be honest, is making me a little queasy. Allie wasn't some starry-eyed innocent seduced and abandoned by her big, bad coach, then driven to suicide over losing her baby. The girl was a slut who hoodwinked my son, got knocked up by the guy she was cheating with, then sold her bastard by threatening to get an abortion. Isn't that right, Pandora?"

Idan's wife blanched. Apparently it was fine to spill this fact in private—she certainly had also told Bex as much; but a quick peek at the video camera still recording the proceedings suggested that Pandora didn't really want to go on the record with calling her new stepson's mother a blackmailing whore.

A qualm Omri's almost-grandmother clearly didn't share. Realizing she wouldn't be getting backup from Pandora, Tess continued with her tirade, this time addressing the camera almost exclusively, and, by extension, the viewers at home. "Allie didn't kill herself, for Christ sake."

"Mom!" Coop tried to stop the torrent, but it was obviously too late for calmer heads to prevail. Or even make a guest appearance.

"Allie was murdered. I would bet because of her, shall we say . . . social habits? I mean, she was sleeping with my son, she was sleeping with Idan. Who knows what else she was up to in her spare time? I will not have her painted as a saint. She was a liar and a cheat. She lied to my son. She made a fool out of him. She—"

"Got killed for it?" Bex interjected innocently, just to see what the reaction would be.

Tess's lips were pursed, tongue touching her top teeth to spit out a triumphant, "Yes!" And then she realized what Bex was really asking.

"How dare you suggest—"

Bex stood her ground. "I'm just following up the obvious. You're the one who wanted the world to know that Allie was murdered. And then you laid out some very convincing reasons for why your son should be a prime suspect."

Somewhere in the ether that was time and space, Gil Cahill was already ripping out his hair over Bex having even brought up such a possibility—despite the fact that Gil had yet to see the tape. Physics and advanced math nevertheless made it possible.

"No, you idiot," Tess raged. "That's not what I meant. What I meant was I will not have the media making Allie out to be some saint. Because, as we all know, where there's a saint, there has to be a bad guy. And that will not be my son. I won't allow you to do this to him. Coop has a golden future ahead of him."

"He also had the best motive for killing Allie. You said it yourself: She cheated on him."

"But I didn't know that," Coop insisted. "Until the paternity test . . . I thought—"

"We only have your word for it," Bex pointed out. "Even if we believe that you didn't know what happened to Allie when she first disappeared, how do we know that you didn't see her at the rink the morning she died? You saw Allie, you saw the baby, you thought it was yours, Allie told you otherwise, and you went nuts."

"I would—I could never do that. Kill someone? You think I could kill somebody with my bare hands?"

If she had to go with the Coop Bex had watched for the past several years—the virile, hot-blooded Coop who could whip off incredible physical feats without breaking a sweat or upsetting his flirtatious grin, Bex would have to lean toward "Yes." However, if she thought about the sniveling, I-want-my-mommy, impotent boy who'd leaked out of the Super Cooper shell over the past few days, well . . .

"It doesn't matter what Bex thinks," Tess reminded. "She's a flunky. A peon. Gil Cahill understands what we're trying to do here. Gil won't let a second of this trumped-up travesty leak out. Everything is under control, Coop. It's okay. We'll put out a statement expressing our deep, deep disappointment with the results of the paternity test, as well as our discovery that Allison didn't turn out to be the young lady we all so foolishly assumed her to be. Liars like her always take advantage of decent people like us. The audience will understand that we're the victims here. They'll understand it all, once we explain it to them."

Idan smirked. "I'm sure you'll do an excellent job. But

unless anyone else wishes to perform a monologue for the camera, Pan and I are taking our son and going home."

"I seem to have misplaced my son. Have you seen him?" Craig popped his head through the open door of the video library, where Bex was most certainly not trying to stick the tape of that morning's proceedings in the back so that while it wasn't exactly lost it also wouldn't be easily accessible if Gil spontaneously decided he was bored and needed something to screen.

"What happened?" she asked.

"Well . . . I grounded Jeremy. I've never had to do it before, so I admit I was a bit fuzzy on the overall concept. What I didn't realize, apparently, is that it's very difficult to ground somebody when your current home away from home is a single hotel room. The close quarters . . . they got a little too close after a while. So I stepped outside to get some air and, honestly, to keep from strangling the kid next time he mouthed off. Guess what happened when I came back?"

"Jeremy was gone?"

"You've heard this one before!"

"Sorry. But yeah, you're right. You were pretty fuzzy on the concept, there."

"I need to speak to him sternly. But first I need to find him."

"Did you try the main rink?"

"Yup."

"Did you try asking Coop Devaney?"

"Can't find him either."

"Oh . . ." Bex said.

"Feel like a little road trip around the perimeter?"

"Sure."

They started by checking out the obvious places, such

as the competitors' lounge. There they encountered only a handful of adolescents sitting on half a dozen couches, playing with their Game Boys; a steely-eyed mother wearing a chaperone badge picking through the buffet of stale pitas, sliced Swiss cheese, and pool-ball-shaped clumps of tuna salad; and a bored volunteer leafing through the official program for what was clearly the umpteenth time that day. Their question as to whether anyone had seen Jeremy Hunt—or Coop Devaney, for that matter—was greeted by a listless assortment of shrugs and mumbled "uh-uhs."

"I actually saw Coop this morning." Bex filled Craig in on the hearing and subsequent round of murderous accusations.

"Sounds like a good time was had by all."

"Oh, yeah. Never a dull minute. Especially once Tess got going. She was so adamant about making sure no one thought Coop did it."

"That it made you pretty certain he did?"

"I don't know. I certainly don't have any proof."

"If she thought he killed Allie, it would definitely explain why she didn't want him giving any DNA samples for a paternity test—too easy to have the sample become evidence in a murder trial. Of course, it turned out unnecessary in the end, but—"

"Oh. You're right. I just assumed she didn't want Coop giving a DNA sample because she knew he couldn't be the father."

"Oh. Right. Your Coop-is-gay theory."

"It's not a theory. I saw . . ." Craig raised an eyebrow, and Bex instantly blushed. "I mean, it's not like I went looking . . . and it wasn't totally . . . I don't usually . . ." I told you before, "I saw Coop kissing Sebi Vama, okay? That's how I know."

"It's okay with me if it's okay with you." Bex wasn't

sure if Craig's amusement was stemming from the story, or just her fumbled telling of it.

"Of course it's okay with me. I mean, it's none of my business what Coop—I told you, I don't care what people do in their private—this isn't about Coop being gay, it's about who killed Allie and—"

"Bex?"

"What?"

"Chill. I'm pulling your leg."

"Oh."

Their next stop was the boys' locker room, where Bex waited outside and Craig went in and returned to report that Jeremy wasn't in there, either. That sealed it, then. They would have to leave the cocoon of the arena and step—gulp—into the outside world. Or at least into the arena parking lot.

Bex asked, "Does Jeremy have access to a car?"

"Not that I know of."

"So we're assuming he's still within walking distance."

"I'm assuming. But that doesn't mean he hasn't gone off with someone else."

"Being a parent is really fun, isn't it, Craig?"

"Oh, yeah. It's a barrel and a half of monkeys. Pays well, too."

"Makes you wonder why Coop wanted to be named Omri's father so badly."

"From what you told me, sounds more like that was his mother's dream, not his."

"Well, he seemed pretty into the idea—in front of the judge, at least. But you're right: Tess thought it would be great PR. Not to mention, I'm guessing, an awesome beard. Nobody's going to accuse a teen dad of being gay, too. And that's what Tess is most afraid of. The public finding out."

"But if she knew he couldn't be the dad—"

"The way I figure it, Tess had Coop date Allie for a cover. Clearly, he wasn't everything Allie was dreaming of—she's no Lian. Maybe Coop couldn't buy her off with some purity ring, so Allie cheated on him with Idan. Tess must have gambled that Idan wouldn't risk his marriage to Miss Cash of the Pan by stepping forward to claim Omri. It must have looked like a slam dunk to Tess, especially since everyone 'knew' Allie and Coop were an item."

"So Tess killed Allie? To protect her son's reputation?"

"I don't know," Bex admitted. "It does make sense, though, doesn't it? Tess would do anything for Coop and his 'golden' future."

Craig's eyes twinkled. "So how are you going to break this case, Ms. Holmes?"

"God knows."

He took one look at her despondent face and burst out laughing. "Oh, cheer up, Bex. No one's really expecting you to do the police's job for them, are they?"

"Only Gil. And, you know, the police." Bex filled him in on Officer Ho and his request of a few days earlier.

"Wow. Your reputation really preceded you."

"Yeah. Lucky me."

"Okay," Craig said. "We can't deny the obvious any longer: Jeremy's not in the arena, and he's not immediately outside of the arena."

"What do you want to do next?"

"Outside of throttle the boy?"

"We have to find him first."

"You're the detective." Craig took a stab, "You want to drive around with me for a few blocks? See if maybe he, I don't know, took a walk to ponder all my failings as a parent?"

"Sure."

Inside Craig's rental car, Bex pointed out the desolate stretch of highway in either direction, with a red and yellow McDonald's sign to mark one exit and a large billboard boasting "Outlet Shopping" along the other. "There really isn't much to do around here."

"Nope."

"Nope," Bex agreed.

And now they'd officially run out of things to say. How could that be possible? Bex never ran out of things to say. Even when to do so would be most prudent.

She looked out one window while Craig started the engine, pulled out of the lot, and silently did the same through the other. Neither saw anything. But for some reason, even that no longer seemed worth noting. He tapped his thumbs on the wheel. She shifted awkwardly in her seat. Something weird was happening. Somehow, without either of them budging an inch, Craig suddenly was sitting much closer to her. Or, at least, it seemed that way. In the silence, she could hear every breath he took. She could hear the slight scrape of his back along the vinyl seat. It should have been uncomfortable, but it wasn't. It was merely ... unusual. She wondered if something similar was happening to him. And then she wondered why she was wondering. And finally she wondered what she wanted the answer to be. She didn't have to wonder long.

After a fruitless fifteen minutes spent cruising by both the McDonald's and the outlet mall on the off chance that Jeremy had gotten hungry and/or desperate for a new yet slightly irregular sweater, they returned to the arena. In the parking lot Craig cut the engine, turned to face Bex, and said, "This is ridiculous."

"What is?"

"How old are you?"

She knew exactly what he was asking, and why. She swallowed hard. She said, "Twenty-four."

"Damn."

"I know."

"You don't act twenty-four."

"My mother says I was born going on forty."

"Yeah, well, that doesn't really count, does it?"

"Sorry."

"Oh, the hell with it," Craig said. And then, in a move that would have been utterly unexpected, except for the fact that Bex had been expecting it for several days already, he kissed her.

She kissed him back because she knew that she would, all along.

And she would have kept on kissing him—the experience was a rather pleasant one—if Craig hadn't pulled away, looked at her sadly, and sighed.

Bex could only guess that he hadn't found their experience equally pleasant. She wondered if she should apologize. What was the protocol for situations like this?

But as it turned out, Craig was worried about a protocol of a different sort. He said, "My wife's been dead for only a few months."

Oh. Now Bex understood. And she instantly felt guilty for her instinctive thrill at the realization that his reluctance was due to that guilt, and not any unpleasant sensations she may have engendered.

"I loved Rachel," Craig said.

"I know. She was lovely. I met her."

"And then—"

"What?"

"You're twenty-four."

"That'll change," Bex pointed out. "Before you know it, I'll be twenty-five. Then thirty. Then forty. I'm looking forward to catching up with myself."

Craig smiled. "Do you realize that there are almost the same number of years between you and me, as there are between you and my kid? And, you know, I wouldn't want you dating Jeremy."

DEATH DROP

"No offense, Craig, but I wouldn't want to be dating Jeremy, either."

The fun-and-games portion of their afternoon was now over. Bex was deadly serious, and she needed Craig to understand that.

"I like you," she said simply. "I like you a lot."

"Yeah . . ." Craig mused. "Now what the heck are we going to do about that?"

"There he is!" Bex sprang up in her seat and pointed.

Dating dilemmas aside, she knew what her priorities were.

At the other end of the lot, Jeremy was climbing out of a stranger's silver Lexus. Stepping out from the driver's side was Sebi Vama.

Craig was out of his own car and blocking his son's path before the boy even knew what hit him. Bex naturally followed.

"Where the hell have you been?" Craig demanded.

"None of your business," Jeremy shot back.

"We went for a drive." Sebi indicated the direction they'd come from. "A young man can get stir-crazy cooped up inside his hotel room all day."

"Who are you?" Craig wanted to know.

"Sebastian Vama. If you please."

"I would please," Craig seethed, "if you refrained from taking my thirteen-year-old son on any more spontaneous drives without my expressed permission."

"I'm not some dumb kid," Jeremy said. "I can do what I want."

"That's true," Sebi said. "You can't keep them pinned to your skirts forever, Mr. Hunt. What are you going to do when Jeremy's Olympic champion? Climb onto the podium with him?"

"At the rate you're going," Craig ignored Sebi to focus on Jeremy, "your getting to skate here at Nationals is a big question mark. I wouldn't be counting my Olympic Golds quite yet."

"Oh, screw you," Jeremy said.

Which was when Bex decided to exit. This seemed like the sort of conversation a father and son would want to have in private. Though, as Bex headed back toward the arena, neither one appeared to notice that she was gone.

Senior competition finally started that night, opening with the Dance event. Bex was glad for the distraction. After all the father/son battles she'd been privy to over the past few days, the thought of just Francis and Diana to berate her, and then on subjects not concerning paternity, rebellion, romance, or murder, were actually things Bex was looking forward to.

She climbed into the booth with them, ready to call the two compulsory dances, despite knowing that the odds of their commentary ever making air for more than just the first-place finisher was slim. Francis and Diana took advantage of this fact by drifting off on an assortment of tangents, confident that since this was just Ice Dance, after all, Gil wouldn't even bother to reprimand them.

By random draw, the first compulsory of the night was the Killian. Bex actually liked that particular dance, since it was at a march tempo, usually skated to peppy, nonsleep-inducing music and in military—thus not too outlandish—costumes. Plus, at 116 beats per minute, 6 patterns took only 50 seconds to complete. It may have driven the skaters to exhaustion-induced asthma attacks and possible backstage vomiting, but Bex found it one of the least offensive options.

As Francis and Diana argued over which couple was conveying the proper march attitude—"How can she be smiling like that? They're supposed to be marching off to war!" "Maybe they're coming home from the war, you silly, old goat!"—Bex allowed herself to just be lulled by the pretty music and shiny lights. She felt no need to say anything or do anything.

Pretty, pretty music . . .

"I don't think anyone smiled like that after storming the beach at Normandy!"

"Maybe they're support staff who never left Fort Dix."

"Damn National Guardsmen," Francis huffed.

Pretty, pretty music . . .

By the time the seventh couple took the ice, both Howarths had run out of wars to deconstruct, Ice Dance style, and had moved on to such nitpicking minutiae that even Gil felt moved to offer, "I think you two are overdoing it just a tad, guys."

Francis said, "The rule book clearly states: 'Start and succeeding steps may be located anywhere around the circle, but once established, no shift of pattern is acceptable on subsequent sequences.' I saw a shift, I know I did. First they went right, then they went left."

"That's because the couple going left was before the couple going right," Diana purred. "You really must stop nodding off between teams, Franny."

"Rule book says: 'The man's left hand should clasp the lady's left hand so that her left arm is firmly extended across his body.' I see no firm extensions. I see spaghetti arms. No, wait: It's more of a fettuccine!"

"Maybe you should eat before you come to the announcer's booth, too."

"And what is with the distance between them? You could drive the entire Pony Express between those hips! Whatever happened to: 'The man's right hand should clasp the lady's right hand and keep it firmly pressed on her right hip to avoid separation'?"

Bex was about to say, "All right, Francis, we get it. You

have the rule book open in front of you, and you possess the ability to read from it. Congratulations. Now give it a rest."

But instead, what Bex realized was that thanks to Francis and his rule book, she now thought she knew who'd killed Allison Adler.

Fifteen

"You killed Allie," Bex accused.

"What makes you say that?" Following the conclusion of the Senior Compulsory Dance event, Sebi Vama was standing by his car—the same one he'd earlier been driving with Jeremy, which is how Bex had been able to stake it out. He held a key ring in his hand, sharp points out, right arm already stretched to slip the key in the lock. The sole light came from a lamppost half a lot away. Sebi's was the only vehicle left in the area. Bex and Sebi were the only two people still there. Which, in retrospect, might not be the best circumstances under which to accuse a man twice her size of murder.

Sebi gazed down at Bex, his expression unreadable, his tone suggesting genuine curiosity. "What makes you say that, Bex?"

"The position of the handprints on her body. Under her left armpit and her right hip. The police found traces of the same red fluff that was embedded in her neck in those two places. They assumed the fluff came from the killer wearing the official, Team USA gloves. That the killer lifted Allie up to hang her in the noose and make it look like she killed herself. But under the left armpit and on the right hip . . . that's a pretty unusual way to lift somebody. Unless you've spent years skating with her in that position, and it just came naturally."

Sebi didn't say anything. He merely finished the act of sticking his key in the lock, and whistled what Bex could only guess was a happy tune.

"The Killian position," Bex pressed. "You use it for a bunch of Ice Dances, don't you? You use it for footwork. You use it for lifts."

Sebi opened the door. He said, "If that's the only evidence you've got, Bex, I don't believe I shall start picking out my black-and-white-striped wardrobe quite yet."

"But it's true, isn't it?" Bex couldn't believe what a rational conversation they were having about this most irrational of subjects.

"What is laid down, ordered, factual is never enough to embrace the whole truth: Life always spills over the rim of every cup. Boris Pasternak—the Russian novelist."

"What the hell does that mean?"

"You're the researcher," he said. "Do some research."

"Why?" Bex demanded. "Why would you kill her?"

"Because," Sebi said, "even the best of spread eagles eventually come home to roost."

"Pasternak, again?"

Sebi smirked. "Pandora Westby Ben-Golan."

"What does she . . ." Bex began. But the truth was obvious.

"Perhaps Mrs. Ben-Golan was not quite as sanguine about her man's affair with a little trollop as her performance in court suggested?"

"Pandora hired you to—"

"Mrs. Ben-Golan sponsored me for a great many years. I owe her a debt."

"And Allie was your friend. She was more than your friend, she was your partner. Didn't you owe her anything? How could you cold-bloodedly—"

"Don't believe me, Bex?"

Well, to be honest, he hadn't exactly confessed to anything for her to believe or disbelieve. Their entire conversation had been built on assumptions, conclusions, and literary allusions.

Sebi shrugged. "Ask your pint-sized pal Jeremy Hunt. The little brat saw Miss Cash in the Pan giving me the money."

"I talked to Sebi!" Bex had to yell the words over Craig's shoulder and toward Jeremy at the far side of the hotel room. When she'd first knocked on the door, Craig had been loath to let her in, and when she asked to *please, it was really important,* speak to Jeremy, the boy had hollered back, "Well, I don't want to speak to you!"

But at her charge about Sebi, Jeremy's head practically did a 180. At the same time, he took a step back, visibly scared. Craig noticed it, too, and dropped the arm that was keeping Bex from stepping inside.

"Jer? What is it?" Craig sounded almost as terrified as his son looked. "What's going on? What happened?"

He allowed Bex to approach Jeremy. The boy sat down on the edge of the bed, looking out the window like he wished he could leap out of it and just fly away. He tapped his lips together in a futile, manic popping, and hugged himself with both arms, shivering. Bex crouched on the floor so that she could look up at him. She dropped her binder and rested one hand, very tentatively, on Jeremy's knee.

She said, "I talked to Sebi. He said you saw Pandora Westby giving him some money. Is that true?"

Jeremy swung his legs. The toe of his right foot connected with Bex's knee, but hardly hard enough to hurt. Bex didn't react. Instead, she merely followed up, "Is it?"

The slightest of a nod. But he did definitely nod.

"What's this all about, Jer?" Craig sat down next to his son.

Jeremy looked at Bex as he answered, "I was looking for Coop. After the Men's Short practice. Coop said we could hang out, you know, talk skating. I went looking for him at the arena, but I got lost. So many hallways and elevators, and the levels all have letters instead of numbers, it's confusing."

"Yes, it is," Bex agreed. Anything to keep him talking.

"So I got lost and I ended up totally the opposite of where I should have been. And I saw Sebi. I thought maybe he could help me get back. But when I got closer, I saw that he was with Mrs. Ben-Golan. She was giving him a bunch of money, just tied up with a rubber band. It was flapping like some stupid fan or something. I didn't think it was a big deal. I didn't know what was going on. But Sebi got real, real mad."

"What did he do?" Craig demanded.

"He told Mrs. Ben-Golan that he would take care of it. After she went away, he told me if I kept my mouth shut, there could be a lot of money in this for me. He said Mrs. Ben-Golan was rich. Filthy rich. And that she sponsored promising young skaters who didn't have a lot of money, all the time. He said it wouldn't look weird at all if she all of a sudden said she wanted to sponsor me. Nobody would get suspicious, and I'd make out like a bandit."

"So that's why she called us," Craig said in understanding.

"Yeah. And then Sebi, earlier today, in the car, he said

we had to go for a little drive so he could remind me of the terms. I keep quiet and Mrs. Ben-Golan pays all my skating expenses from now until forever. Everything's cool. But . . . but . . . if I don't . . ."

"What?" Craig and Bex asked in unison.

"If I don't—he said—Sebi said—he said that he would kill my dad."

Neither Bex nor Craig responded, both too shocked to speak. At the unexpected silence, Jeremy raised his head and looked from one to the other. He stammered, "I—I wanted to go home right away then, I wanted to just get out of here. But I thought if I told you and Toni I was quitting, you'd want to know why, and since I couldn't tell you why, I thought maybe, if I acted like a real brat . . ."

"Oh, Jeremy, oh, God, Jer . . ."

"I did a good job of that, didn't I, Dad? Being a brat?" he asked with the hint of a smile. And then promptly burst into tears.

Bex felt as if she might cry, too, and Craig wasn't looking so dry himself. He said, "Jeremy, dude, guy, come on, some bastard makes an empty threat and . . . what made you think something like that could actually happen?"

"It happened to Mom," Jeremy said.

And now Bex really did think Craig was going to cry. But he pulled himself together and instead grabbed his son into a bear hug, rocking him back and forth and swearing, "It's not your job to protect me, Jer, you got that? It's not the child's job to protect the parent. It's the parent's job to protect the child. I am so sorry, man. So, so sorry. I should have tried harder to figure out what was going on. I should have known you'd never—I should have known there was a reason. Never, ever do that again, you hear me? Always come to me. Always, always. I'm your dad. I'll take care of you."

They separated and looked at each other for a long

moment. Trying to quench the tears, Craig offered Jeremy a smile. The boy smiled back, wiped his eyes, then smiled again, this time more convincingly. Only then did he turn around to Bex and ask, "So why was Sebi so mad? What was that money for, anyway? Sebi didn't tell me."

"Well"—she straightened up from her crouch and sat down on the bed, next to Jeremy—"he told me it was Pandora paying him off for having killed Allison Adler."

"He just told you that?" Craig was having a hard time believing it. "Just out of the blue, for no reason, he came up and told you he was now a hired contract killer. What, was he passing out business cards?"

"Not exactly. I figured out he was the one who killed Allie, confronted him, and while he didn't exactly confess, he did point out that even if I was right, I had no hard evidence, just conjecture."

"How did you figure it out?"

She told him about the incriminating glove fluff.

"Wow," Craig said.

"Yeah. Not exactly something you'd see on *CSI*."

"So that's all you've got?"

"Well, that and him saying Jeremy saw Pandora paying him off."

"I wonder why he did that."

"I assumed it was so I'd know he wasn't the mastermind. He was just paying off a debt. Pandora's the one with the motive."

"What I mean is, telling you about Jeremy just adds one more person who can testify against him. Sounds like a pretty foolish thing to do."

"Not necessarily. All Jeremy knows for a fact is that Pandora gave Sebi money. No big deal—she's been his sponsor for years, everyone knows that. It wouldn't prove anything. I think Sebi told me just so I'd focus the rest of my investigation on Pandora."

"You do that," Craig said, standing up. "You do that. And in the meantime, I am going to track down Sebastian Vama and rip his intestines out through his nostrils for terrorizing my child."

"Actually, Craig—"

"What?"

"I have a better idea. How'd you like to help me nail him for murder?"

Sixteen

The next morning, Bex blew off Senior Men's Long Program practice (Gil would just have to deal) in favor of a return visit to the home of Pandora Westby and Idan Ben-Golan. At first Craig insisted on coming along, too.

The previous night, they'd conferred outside the door of his hotel room, speaking in whispers in case the walls had ears—or Jeremy wasn't quite as sound asleep as he seemed.

"I'm going with you tomorrow," Craig said. "They are not getting away with this. I may have seemed calm in there a minute ago, but believe me, the thought of my kid riding around in a car with a killer—I thought I was going to throw up."

"I know. Poor Jeremy. But it's okay, now, Craig. It's over."

"How do you figure? Sebastian Vama is still out there, walking around, free as a bird, not to mention Pandora Westby and God knows who else was in on this."

"I'll confront her. I'll see if I can get her to confess and then—"

"What? Then what? She can tell you whatever she wants, you've still got no evidence. It's Sebi all over again."

"Give me a chance to play one against the other."

"I'd rather just bang their skulls one against the other. Might yield better results."

"And when you're sent to prison, Jeremy will have no parents left."

"I see your point." He sighed, then smiled ruefully. "Promise you'll keep me posted?"

"I promise. This isn't over, Craig. I meant what I said in there. I'm going to get these guys. And I'm expecting you to help."

"Any time."

"Thanks."

"You're welcome."

"No problem."

"So . . ."

Their conversation was officially over again. To anyone with ears, or even an average ability to read lips, the conversation had clearly been over for about five clichés now. And yet, neither Bex nor Craig had budged an inch.

"So," he repeated.

"Yes."

"You still twenty-four?"

"About six hours more than the last time we discussed it, though."

"Oh, well, sure, I can see the difference."

"You're saying I'm looking older?"

"More mature, is what I meant."

"Well, fine then."

"Good."

She turned around to leave. She turned very slowly.

Which is why she was barely down the hall, not even halfway to the elevator, when she heard Craig call, "Bex?"

"Yeah?"

"This conversation, you know, it's not really over. More like a commercial break."

"I know," she said.

Of course, the entire time that she was being (hopefully) adorable and flirtatious, Bex actually had no idea what she knew, or even what the few things that she did know, actually meant. Something had happened between her and Craig that afternoon, that part was obvious (the kiss kind of gave it away). But what it was exactly, she had no clue. So Bex just stuck with the adorable and flirtatious. Until something better came along.

For her confrontation with Pandora Westby, though, Bex swallowed the adorable and went with stern. Stern was always a good one.

It lasted from the time Bex rang the doorbell, encountered Pandora, and talked her way into being invited inside. It screeched to a halt as soon as Bex stepped into the living room and came face to face with the vision of Pandora sitting on a blue blanket spread out on the floor, Omri on his back, kicking his arms and legs and chortling at the various colorful objects Pandora was goo-goo-ga-gaaing in his face.

Bex's first thought was . . . *Aw, cute baby.*

Her next one was . . . *Aw, cute Pandora playing with cute baby.*

Her third was . . . *This doesn't seem right.*

At that point, Bex decided to speak. She said, "I had a very interesting chat with Sebi Vama yesterday."

That name definitely got her attention. Pandora looked up with a start; the cute bunny on a string (in light of what had happened to Omri's mother, it seemed a bit in bad taste to Bex) went slack.

"Sebi," she repeated.

"And then I followed up with Jeremy Hunt. You know, his dad, Craig, was very surprised when you just called out of the blue offering sponsorship."

Pandora's voice shook as she insisted, "That was sincere. Jeremy is a wonderful skater."

"He is. Probably why you and Sebi shouldn't have scared the hell out of him right before his first National competition. You know, being afraid for your dad's life can make anyone a little unsteady on the ice."

"What are you talking—"

"You mean Sebi didn't tell you? Yeah, he threatened a thirteen-year-old boy with killing his father if Jeremy didn't keep his mouth shut about witnessing your little financial exchange the other day."

"He didn't—"

"Feel free to call up Jeremy Hunt and ask. His father has a few words he'd like to share with you as well."

"Sebi . . ." Pandora stood up, stepping over Omri and lowering her voice, as if the baby could understand a word she said. "Sebi told me he just promised Jeremy money for his skating. He didn't say anything about a threat."

"Yeah, who would have guessed a hired killer could be a liar, too?"

"A what? Who? What are you talking about?"

"Sebi Vama."

"Yes, I understand, but what about him? Why did you call him a hired—"

"Sebi told me you hired him to kill Allison and make it look like a suicide."

At that, Pandora actually stumbled. She didn't move, her legs simply gave out, and she needed to grab a couch's armrest with one hand and the glass coffee table with the other to steady herself. While down there, she looked guiltily at Omri, then quickly away again. She opened her mouth as if to speak, but no sound came out.

Bex decided to help. She said, "I know Sebi killed Allie. The handprints on her body were in Killian position. Who else would automatically lift Allie in that position, except for Sebi?"

"Sebi killed Allie?" Pandora asked, gasping.

Her genuine confusion inspired uneasy stirrings of the same in Bex. "If you didn't believe he went through with it, why did you give him the money?"

"Went through with what?"

"Killing Allison."

"I had no idea Sebi killed her!"

"What, did you think you got lucky? That she beat him to the punch and hung herself before he could go through with it?"

"Why would I want Allie dead?"

"Because she had an affair with your husband!" Bex wondered why she was the one left to point out the obvious. "I mean, I know what you said and how you acted in court. But I also remember what you said here the night before that. You acted all Stepmother of the Year for the judge so Idan wouldn't lose custody of Omri. But you were furious; you told me so yourself."

"That was just so you'd believe us."

"Believe you about what?"

Pandora straightened up and swept Omri into her arms. With great effort, the baby lifted his wobbly head to check who it was, caught sight of Pandora, and, with a contented sigh, nestled against her neck. She covered him with the blanket they'd just been playing on and told Bex, "You don't understand."

"Explain it to me."

"We didn't think Ralph Adler would take this to court. Quite frankly, we never factored him into the equation. It was wrong of us, we should have known, considering how obsessed he was with Allison, that he'd be obsessed with Omri, too. But we naively believed he'd washed his hands of her completely. Idan and I thought the only challenge would come from Coop. Well, Tess using Coop, anyway. And we needed people to believe that Idan was the father. We thought, what better way to drive our point home than to have me be up in arms about their affair."

"You mean you weren't?"

"I mean"—Pandora sighed, kissing the top of Omri's head—"there was no affair."

Bex said, "Okay. You're right. I don't understand at all."

"That's enough!" The male voice booming down a flight of stairs, complete with accompanying footsteps, was unmistakable.

Idan told Bex, "That is enough browbeating of my wife. Sebastian Vama is a liar and an opportunist. You cannot believe a word he says. Certainly not about Pandora."

"Sounds like you guys have done a share of lying yourselves recently."

"We had reasons."

"Idan . . ." Pandora began.

"No. She will listen, and she will understand. Miss Levy, my wife is a wonderful person. She is the most loving, generous, caring woman I have ever known. Think of all of those skaters whom she supports, and asks for nothing in return."

"Well . . . Sebi said—"

"And asks for *nothing* in return," Idan thundered. "Not a penny, not a favor, not even a thank-you note. She does it because she loves skating and because she wants to help talented young people reach their potential."

Bex thought of Allie swinging dead from a belt, and said nothing.

"For a woman like this, I would do anything. Anything, do you hear me?"

And suddenly, Allie swinging from that belt took on a whole new meaning.

"Idan, are you saying that you're the one who actually—"

"I am saying that Pandora Westby Ben-Golan deserves anything her heart desires. Unfortunately, the one thing she has been wanting this last year that she has not been able to have, is a baby."

Bex looked at Omri. And very disparate puzzle pieces slowly began to drift toward each other through the swampland of her brain.

"So you and Allie . . . for Pandora?"

"No! Will you please remain quiet until I finish speaking. Your wild guesses are not only intrusive, they are also inaccurate."

"Okay," Bex agreed. No way was she missing the conclusion to this tale.

"Pandora very much wanted a child. She has for many years now. We were on the waiting list of several private adoption attorneys, but the wait, it was getting very difficult. And then Allison came to us, already pregnant—"

"So the baby isn't yours?"

"*Already pregnant*, Miss Levy. She didn't know what to do. She was terrified of telling Ralph. She knew how invested he was in her career, he would be furious. And she did not want to tell Coop."

"Why not?"

"Because he would insist on their getting married. And if he didn't, well, then, she knew that Tess would. And it's not what Allison wanted. The marriage would have been a complete charade. Not to mention the fact that she was nineteen, she truly had no interest in raising a child at all."

"So you and Pandora decided to adopt Allie's baby?"

"She lived with us. We paid all of her expenses. She

helped Pandora design the nursery, and she signed all the papers in advance, giving us custody."

"Did she change her mind at the last minute? Is that it? Is that why you killed her? Because she decided not to let you have the baby?"

"I did not kill Allison. She gave birth to Omri six weeks ago. She recovered from the birth in our home, and once she was back on her feet, we gave her money to leave Los Angeles and start a new life. It was all worked out. Allie would leave town, and Pandora and I would introduce the world to the baby we'd recently adopted. There should have been no reason to connect the two."

"But then Allie was murdered."

"Yes. She was at the arena to say good-bye. It was her idea; she wanted to see everyone for the last time. Even if they did not see her. She was saying good-bye to her old life before starting a new one. She had Omri with her for the last time. She was not conflicted over giving him up. She knew she had done the right thing."

"Except that then somebody killed her. And suddenly everybody knew that your new baby was Allison's."

"Yes. This is correct. Once that information was out, Coop became a problem. Even with Allie's signature on the adoption papers, he could still challenge us. That is why we decided it would be easier simply to claim that the child was my own. Allie had even planned for this possibility by listing me as Omri's father on the birth certificate. There, you see, even more proof that she wanted us to have him. She would have never named me as the legal father if she was reconsidering giving Omri to us. We thought that would be enough."

"I don't understand," Bex said. "The paternity test, it showed you were the—"

Idan shrugged.

Pandora said, "That's where Sebi comes in."

"What?" Bex shrieked. "Sebi is the father?"

At that, both Idan and Pandora couldn't help laughing.

"No," they said nearly in unison, then quickly quieted.

Pandora said, "He helped us. That's what I was paying him for. That's what Jeremy Hunt saw. We asked Sebi to help us fake the paternity test."

"I don't understand. I saw you swipe your own cheek."

"I was very careful. The Q-tip was prepared in advance. It never touched my mouth."

"But . . . the box was sealed. I saw you open it."

"Yes, Bex, glue is a very difficult task to master. There is no way that anyone could open a box, put in a pre-prepared swab, with the appropriate DNA, and reseal it."

Okay, so she was an idiot, that part was crystal clear. But she still wanted to know, "How did Sebi—"

"We needed Coop's DNA. We needed, preferably, some saliva and cheek cells from him. So Sebi—"

"Kissed him!" Bex exclaimed. She may have been an idiot, but she also knew what she saw. "Sebi kissed Coop and got you the DNA sample you needed."

"My understanding is that he also bit him," Idan confessed distastefully. "To ensure a sufficient amount."

"That's gross."

"He was adequately compensated," Idan snapped.

"But if he was working for you, why, at the hearing, did he make such a big deal of Coop being Omri's father?"

"Mr. Sebastian Vama works for the highest bidder. I can only assume Tess also offered him adequate compensation."

Pandora said, "If you believe Sebastian killed Allison, I really can offer you no evidence to the contrary. All I can tell you is, it was not at my behest."

"Sebi says—"

"Fuck Sebi," Idan offered, this time without raising his voice. "Sebi claims that my wife hired him to kill Allison because she was jealous over our affair? Fine; I shall take a second paternity test to prove that I am not Omri's father. That should blow his ridiculous accusation out of the water."

"You could lose Omri," Bex pointed out.

"Yes." His face was grim. "I know."

"You weren't there the first day," Bex told Craig later that morning as they waited for Jeremy to finish getting changed in the locker room after practice. "When Idan came busting in on us and the police, looking for Omri, he was crazed. I really believed he was Omri's father. I really believed he loved him. But if he's not the biological—"

Craig asked, "Does Idan love his wife?"

"Sure sounded like he did."

"Does this child make his wife happy?"

"Sure looked like he did."

"Then he loves the kid. It's real simple."

Bex said sheepishly, "I guess you'd know."

"Yup."

"No one would ever guess you weren't Jeremy's real father."

"Yeah, yeah, yeah, I'm a prince, that's neither here nor there," he said. "How are we going to nail Vama? Because, whether Pandora paid him off or someone else did—"

"Someone like Tess maybe? Idan said Allie didn't want to marry Coop, that she didn't want to live a lie. Maybe Tess saw his coming off like a deadbeat dad to the public as a problem for her press kit. A problem she could only think of one way to fix."

"Doesn't matter. Sebi's the one I want. He's the menace here. He's the killer. I want him off the street, by any means necessary."

"Well, maybe I can get him to confess to me again. He

was pretty forthcoming the first time I asked. I know he was just messing with me, he knew there was nothing I could do about it, he even said as much. But maybe now that I've got his guard down, if I could get his confession on tape and—"

"Still inadmissible," Craig said. "A person has to give you permission to be recorded for it to count."

"You know a lot about the law."

"It's screwed me over enough times."

"You mean Rachel?"

"Yes. I mean Rachel." From the look on Bex's face at the mention of his wife's name, Craig added, "We can talk about my late wife at length some other time. We can rehash all of my feelings for her and about her death. But not now. Now we are going to nail Sebastian Vama's sick, twisted, bastard hide to the wall. You with me?"

"I'm with you," Bex said. "And actually, I think I have an idea about how we can do that."

Seventeen

"What are we doing?" Craig asked.

"Breaking and entering."

"The door was unlocked."

"Okay, then," Bex conceded. "Just entering. But quietly."

Two hours before the Men's Short Program was about to start meant one hour before the 24/7 crew started assembling in the production truck to get ready for the broadcast. It also meant that the entire staff, both above and below the line, were currently on break, trying to eat, drink, be merry, and live their entire nonskating-related day in the space of these precious sixty minutes. It also meant that the truck was deserted. The better to rifle through Gil's files.

"It's got to be here somewhere," Bex said, sifting through the manila-covered mound. "If it's not back at the production office, it's got to be here."

"What? You still haven't told me what we're looking for."

"Gil's paperwork for Coop's reality show."

"Coop has a reality show?"

"He will shortly. It was Tess's idea."

"What does it have to do with—"

"Here." Bex located the file and let her fingers do the walking through the multitude of pages before finding what she was looking for. "Here they are, just like I thought. Look, everybody who was in court yesterday, Sebi Vama included, signed a release giving permission to have his voice and image recorded in conjunction with Coop Devaney's reality show. It doesn't have an expiration date."

"Which means—"

"Which means that if Sebi Vama confesses to murdering Allie as a part of Coop's reality show, the recording is not illegal."

"So we're what, going to ambush him Jerry Springer–style?"

"No, no. Nothing like that. Sebi signed this waiver in perpetuity. There is nothing here that says he has to be reminded of it every time he opens his mouth."

Craig got with the program real quick-like. "Or even that he needs to be made aware that he's being videotaped."

"Exactly! I knew I liked you for a reason."

"However, to be legally binding, doesn't this mean that Coop Devaney needs to be somewhere in the vicinity while you are filming Sebi's confession?"

"I think so, yeah."

"Which means Coop Devaney needs to be in on this."

"Yeah." Bex sighed. "I think so."

"You said they were romantically involved."

"I saw them kissing."

"So what makes you think he'll turn on Sebi like this?"

"Well, Sebi had no problem selling out Coop's son and DNA."

"Doesn't mean Coop is equally easy."

"We'll never know until we ask, I guess. But maybe we'd better wait till Coop's in a receptive mood. After the Men's Short this afternoon. If he skates well, he might be feeling magnanimous. And if he skates badly, maybe he'll be out for blood."

For the actual competition, Bex was back in the broadcast booth with Francis and Diana. The arena, about half filled to capacity, nevertheless looked practically covered in "Super Cooper" posters and prepubescent girls wearing new sweatshirts with "Flying the Coop" silk-screened across the front over a picture of him midtrick. Bex could just imagine Gil and Tess counting up their potential audience and wondering how much advertisers would be willing to pony up for such a coveted demographic. According to the pages she'd skimmed while looking for the legal releases, Gil was thinking of calling the show "Cooperstown." Because it had a very manly ring to it.

They had two different monitors at the announcer's table. One to watch a live feed of the skaters on the ice, and another so they could see the actual broadcast, complete with commercials and rolled-in personality features. Which was how, while Jeremy stroked around with his group of four other Senior men in the warm-up prior to their skate, Bex was able to watch the up-close-and-personal piece Mollie put together on him, using footage Bex had shot both earlier in the week, and a few months before, in Pennsylvania and Connecticut.

The four-minute overview wasn't all about Jeremy and his precocious quadruple jumps, however. It also was about his mother, Rachel Rose, a onetime champion Pairs skater who was abused, raped, and eventually murdered by her partner, Jeremy's father, Robby Sharpton. Bex had interviewed Rachel before her death, and Robby, too. Seeing them both onscreen now, before the tragedy, reminded Bex how careful she should really be when digging around in people's personal histories and secrets. This wasn't just a game—prove that Sebi killed Allison and get a pat on the head from Gil. This also could get very dangerous, very unexpectedly.

Warm-up over, Jeremy got ready to take the ice for his very first Nationals.

"Your boy better not screw up, Bex," Gil warned over the headset. "Or else that piece was a major waste of time. And money."

The audience, who had yet to see the potentially wasted piece, clapped politely when Jeremy's name was announced. For the hard-core fans, he was the ultimate enigma. A boy who not only hadn't competed on the international circuit to date, he also hadn't so much as made a National appearance at even the Junior or Novice level. (Plus, Jeremy's behavior at practice over the past few days was hardly the kind that marked him as an up-and-comer.) The assumption was that he'd qualified due to some sort of fluke, like maybe the defending champion from his section was injured, and that Jeremy Hunt should enjoy his time at center ice; it probably would be his only opportunity.

Jeremy's music began and, after a lightning-fast combination spin that prompted a few fans to applaud in surprise, he set up for his first jump. Based on the way he turned and dug in his toe pick, the crowd was expecting a triple Toe Loop, probably in required combination with a double. Instead, what they got was a quad, followed by a triple Loop. For a moment the audience didn't realize what they'd just seen. And then they exploded in a roar of surprise that only got louder as, twenty seconds later, Jeremy followed that trick up with a quadruple Salchow.

For the rest of the program you could barely hear Jeremy's music as the spectators clapped, hollered, and stomped their feet. Even Diana and Francis seemed unable to find something to argue about.

Francis feebly offered, "Well, the young fellow is awfully young. His presentation isn't as mature as some in this—"

"Oh, shut up and enjoy it," Diana said.

Francis happily did.

Jeremy skated off to a standing ovation—"Not bad, Bex," Gil grudgingly admitted—and, ignoring the kiss-and-cry area where a 24/7 cameraman was frantically gesturing for him to sit, instead slid over to the barrier where his coach, Toni Wright, was still standing, seemingly frozen with shock at what they'd just done, and threw both his arms around her.

"How wonderful," Francis said. "How wonderful for Toni."

Antonia Wright, who, for years, had been dismissed as an also-ran, as the coach who could get skaters to a certain point, then needed to hand them over because she, it was widely understood, didn't have what it took to train a champion, had finally shown them all.

"Astounding," Diana said.

"Remarkable," Francis agreed.

And it was clear the praise was meant for both coach and student.

Jeremy finally sat down and waited for his marks. Which put him firmly in first place among those who'd already skated.

But no matter how phenomenal he'd just been, nobody seriously expected Jeremy Hunt to remain at the top of the standings for long.

Because Coop Devaney was the next skater.

He came out of the tunnel with Sebi by his side. Coop was wearing the same Short Program outfit he'd been competing in all year, the skin-tight red T-shirt and equally snug black pants. His hair was perfectly moussed to fall rakishly above his eyes, his makeup expertly applied to look like no makeup at all. And yet something was off. Bex couldn't put her finger on it, but the sense of imbalance was definitely there.

Coop rested one hand on Sebi's shoulder while he removed first his right, then his left skateguard. Coop linked his fingers behind his back and raised both arms to shoulder level, stretching. He took a swig of water from a bottle Sebi was carrying, then set it on the barrier. He stepped out on the ice, head down, bending first one leg, then the other, as if testing whether his knees were working.

"Representing the Figure Skating Club of Southern California . . ."

At the announcer's voice, Coop's head jerked up, Pavlovian-style.

"Please welcome . . ."

Arms out to the sides.

"Cooooooper Devaneyyyyy!"

Big smile, and five smooth glides to take him to center ice.

Everything was exactly as it should be. And yet . . .

"He's not focused," Francis said, with, Bex noted, his mike firmly in the off position. The truly insightful comments he liked to keep to himself.

Diana agreed. In response to Bex's query as to how she knew that, Diana pointed at the monitor, which currently held a tight close-up of Coop's face. "Look at his eyes— they're darting all over the place. You can always tell, from the first minute, if it's going to be a good performance or not. A focused skater's eyes never budge. If the eyes are all over the place, the body will be, too."

Coop's first jump in the Short Program was scheduled to be a quadruple Toe Loop/triple Toe Loop combination. As he prepared to enter the jump, his left, vaulting leg bent just a bit at the knee, prompting Diana to gasp and Francis to shake his head in anticipation of a wipeout. For her part, Bex couldn't imagine how he would ever get the necessary height to attempt four revolutions in the air.

He didn't. But Coop, despite having less spring to work with than usual, did manage to whip around three times, rotating faster than Bex had ever seen him, through seemingly sheer force of will. He ended up completing an adequate—if not spectacular—triple Toe Loop. Which would hardly cost him any points, but also wouldn't earn him nearly the score that a quad in combination would have. Especially since, due to the weakness of the first jump, Coop didn't have enough oomph left for a second. Meaning that now he would still have to find another place in the routine to do the required combination jump.

"That," Francis intoned, "will not hold him in very good stead."

The rest of his routine, Bex had to admit, was letter-perfect. The screwup with the combo seemed to have lit a fire under Coop, making him realize that he was fighting for his life now, and this couldn't be just another phone-it-in performance.

His spins were tight, quick, and perfectly centered. His footwork hit every bit of the music. When he whipped by the camera position and it caught another close-up, his eyes weren't wavering an inch.

Which was good, because coming up was what, in the original scheme of things, should have been Coop's required triple jump, a triple Axel. But if he was going to turn anything into the combination he'd missed earlier, this would be the place to do it.

Coop took off forward, pulling his arms into his chest and spinning around three and a half times before landing cleanly on his right foot, instantly digging in his left toe to squeeze out a triple Toe Loop for the combination. It was a gutsy, unrehearsed move, and the knowledgeable audience rewarded him with a round of applause.

However, as Coop took his bows and headed toward the kiss-and-cry area, the ovation noticeably diminished. There weren't the usual cheers of "Super Cooper" and cries for a perfect score. The audience knew this hadn't been his best effort. Judging by the tight grimace on Tess's face as she sat up in the parents' section, clapping fiercely as the applause died down in order to get a second round going, she knew it, too.

His marks reflected the unevenness of the program. But he was still ahead of Jeremy Hunt in the standings.

"Francis, Diana," Gil ordered over the headset, "tell the audience how outrageous it is that the Hunt kid, with his two quads, is behind Devaney and his pitiful triples."

Francis turned off his mike to speak to Gil in private. He said, "Now hold on there. Coop Devaney's other elements were clearly superior to Jeremy's. His spins, his stroking, his presentation—the Hunt boy still skates like a child. Coop is—"

"Just say it," Gil huffed. "Or else we've got the same boring show we've always got, with everybody knowing who the winner is in advance. This way, we can hype up the Long Program. Can the little brat from nowhere topple the defending champion, yadda, yadda, yadda. Come on, folks, we all know the drill."

Francis sighed, exchanged a shrug with Diana, and did as he was told.

Afterward, Bex sat through the interminable press conference where Coop did the usual, smile and *aw, shucks, don't know what happened out there, I guess I just lost focus* rope-a-dope, complete with the promise to do much better in the Long Program and *show the judges just what I'm capable of*. Jeremy, meanwhile, looked somewhat lost in the glare of the media lights. He referred most questions to Toni and, when asked the secret to landing the quad, guilelessly said, "I just jump as high as I can, turn around really fast, and land on one foot." If he'd been even a year older or an inch taller, it would have come off as obnoxious. But for now, it was still charming.

As the press dispersed, Craig sent Jeremy and Toni off to celebrate, promising he'd be there as soon as he could, and turned to Bex.

"Now?" he asked.

"Now."

They shanghaied Coop as he was exiting the dressing room. Bex said that Gil needed him to shoot some exclusive footage for the reality show.

"Well, actually, my mom is waiting for me—"

"We'll be quick."

She led him into a side office far removed from the main action. And had Craig block the door. Coop, they'd decided earlier, wasn't getting out until they were through with him.

"What's going on?" Coop didn't know whether to go for bravado or confusion, so he settled for a mélange of the two.

Bex cut right to the chase. "Your friend Sebi killed Allison."

Confusion knocked out bravado. "What did you say?"

"Sebi strangled Allie, then hung her up to make it look like a suicide."

"Why—why would he do that?"

"That's what we'd like to know."

"And you think I know?"

"We think you can help us find out."

In as few words as possible, Bex laid out the scenario, including evidence, Sebi's inadmissible confession, and their belief that if Coop could get him to repeat it on tape, the law would be on their side. At the very least, they'd have every right to broadcast it on air, which would certainly put pressure on the police to investigate.

"Think about it, Coop," Bex urged. "You'd be a hero. The guy who solved his girlfriend's murder—even after she cheated on him. Think of how great that will be for your image. Your mom will be thrilled."

"You're sure that Sebi—"

"There's only one way to find out. Maybe he didn't do it. Maybe he was just messing with me. If that's the case, then, well, he'll probably tell you, and you guys can have a good laugh about stupid, gullible Bex, and that will be the end of it. But if he did—"

"Sebi is not a bad person."

"Look, Coop. I know—I know that you care about Sebi." Bex realized she was treading on very thin ice here. She couldn't give away what she knew about Coop and Sebi's real relationship—he'd probably freak and run straight back to Mommy with the news that 24/7 was on to them, and what should they do now? On the other hand, she had to make him understand that if Sebi was a killer, he probably wasn't someone Coop should be locking lips—or any other body parts—with anyway. "But you cared about Allison, too, didn't you?"

"I loved Allie." It was Coop's story, and he was sticking to it.

"So don't you want to get to the bottom of who killed her? Don't you owe her that much?"

Craig spoke up for the first time. "Listen, man, she's never going to rest in peace until this thing is settled. You can help her."

"For Allie," Bex urged.

Coop made up his mind. "For Allie."

Afterward, Bex asked Craig, "How did you know what to say to him, to make him throw in with us? How did you know that thing about Allie resting in peace—"

"After Rachel was killed, all I could think about was ripping out the eye sockets of the guy who did it to her. I just felt like Rachel was still there, waiting for me to do something. I'd let her down when I didn't protect her. I couldn't let her down by not seeing her killer go to trial, testifying against him. I figured it would be the same with Coop. Only he's not the ripped-out-eye-socket type. That's why I went with the kinder, gentler, rest-in-peace rap. I figured he'd feel like he let her down, too."

"So you really believe that he loved her?"

"Sure. Why not? Especially if your theory about him using her as a beard is accurate. He probably wanted to love her really, really badly; it sure would make his life a lot easier if he could. And the fact is, Idan Ben-Golan said the baby was Coop's, right? So it wasn't all a lie."

"You seem very at ease with all the twists and turns this story is taking."

"You've poked around my family tree enough. Anything here that a guy like me would find out of the ordinary?"

"I see your point."

"And speaking of which—considering that you've been around for practically every dark moment of my life for the past few months—"

"Yeah. About that, Craig, I am sorry—"

"How would you like to participate in a lighter one for a change?" Craig offered her his elbow. "How about joining Jeremy, Toni, and me for our celebration?"

"Oh—I—thank you, but—isn't that a private family thing?"

"Jer wouldn't be at Nationals if it weren't for you. I think you've earned a seat at the table. Besides, I owe you a rain check for that drink."

"Well . . ."

"There's nothing else for you to do tonight. Coop and Sebi aren't talking until morning. Loosen up, Bex. Have some fun."

She took Craig's arm and let him lead the way.

Eighteen

Waiver or no waiver, Bex figured Sebi Vama wasn't just going to spill his guts if there was a camera around. They needed to hide it. The question was: How?

She could hardly drill a hole through the wall, Norman Bates/Porky's style, nor could she drape it with a festive cloth and hope Sebi would think it was the latest in lamp couture. In the end, it was Craig who came up with the idea of hiding it in plain sight.

"The room where 24/7 keeps their cameras."

"We store them in the tape library. What about it?"

"In a room full of cameras, who's going to expect one of them to be on?"

"You are very devious man."

"Just trying to help."

"Of course, this begs the question of how we get Coop and Sebi inside that room."

"I have faith in you, Bex. You'll think of something."

With a vote of confidence like that, she thought extra,

extra hard. And what Bex came up with was that Sebi should believe he was breaking into the 24/7 tape library.

After Bex had all but written out his lines for him, then had Coop repeat them back several times until they sounded, if not natural, then at least feasible, she listened, hidden around a corner, as he told Sebi, "We've got a problem, man."

Bex hoped the high pitch of Coop's voice would be attributed to nervousness about "the problem" rather than to his overall terror. "Someone must have seen us."

"Seen us?" Sebi was sitting on a bench in the arena, poring over the scores Coop received in the Short Program, analyzing each judge's marks.

"The other night . . ." Coop jiggled up and down nervously.

"Impossible." Sebi waved his concerns away. "You're just being paranoid."

"It's that researcher. She keeps giving me all these cryptic hints."

"She's fishing."

"No. I think she knows."

"How could she?"

"It's the reality show my mom's got me in. They have cameras following me 24/7. What if one of them caught you and me—"

"Impossible."

"Then how does Bex know?"

"I'm telling you she doesn't."

"And I'm telling you she does. And I bet you they have video of it."

"Video . . ." The faintest hint of discomfort crept into Sebi's placid features.

"We can't let anybody see it. My mom will kill me!"

"Forget about your mom." Sebi closed the protocol booklet. "You're certain she has video?"

"I don't know. But how else would she—she saw you kissing me. She knows. What are we going to do?"

"Just let me think for a minute."

"This'll ruin me, you know it will. I can't let anything go wrong, especially not after the way I skated yesterday. I almost got beaten by the Hunt kid."

"I know. I saw the numbers. Way, way too close for comfort."

"The Federation is just looking for an excuse to dump me so he can be their new Golden Boy. You heard his story, right? I mean, his mom got murdered. How lucky can you get? That's the kind of stuff that puts you on the front of Wheaties boxes. Not to mention TV specials, endorsements. We've all worked too hard for this, you and me and my mom, to just let some stupid bitch researcher take it away from us."

All right. Bex hadn't written the stupid or the bitch part. But she told herself it was all for a good cause. If her hunch was right, Sebi would be chomping at the bit to be named Coop's official coach, and ride him all the way to Olympic fame and fortune. By now he had as much invested in Coop's image as Coop and Tess did.

"Video?" he repeated. "Actual footage?"

"She sure sounded that way. Kept asking me if there was anything I wanted to talk about, anything I wanted to get off my chest, if I wanted to, you know, tell my side of the story before she let viewers make up their own minds."

"Crap," Sebi said.

"What are we going to do? We can't let her get away with it."

"There's only one thing to do." Sebi stood up. "We've got to steal that tape before they decide to put it on the air."

Coop appeared to be mulling over the proposal. Then, hesitantly, he offered, "I think I know where they keep them."

* * *

As a rule, the tape and camera library was manned at all times by an intern. The contents were too valuable to leave unattended.

But Sebastian Vama didn't know that.

When he encountered the barred door, he thought it was his fine lock-picking skills that got them in, lickety-split, rather than Craig's jiggering the apparatus to unhinge at the slightest touch, then lock securely behind them. And when he found the place deserted, except for five file cabinets full of tapes and half a dozen cameras lying on their sides, Sebi thought that's how it always was, rather than that Bex had specifically told the intern to scram. All six of the cameras looked equally harmless. Except that one of them happened to be on, with a cable running under the rug, out the door, and into an adjoining room, where Craig and Bex could watch the entire proceeding on a monitor.

"So where do you think it could be?" Coop asked.

Sebi said, "They probably file stuff by date. You start with that cabinet, I'll look through this one."

They worked silently for a few minutes. Then Coop surfaced, holding a gray Beta tape in his hand. He said, "Look. It's Allie."

Sebi didn't bother turning around. "Old news."

"I still can't get over—"

"That she cheated on you? Well, get over it. DNA don't lie."

"That she's dead," Coop said softly. And, in the pure horror of his voice, Bex recognized that he wasn't acting. "Who could have done something so horrible?"

"You want my best guess?" Sebi turned around, resting an elbow casually on the filing cabinet, as if discussing the most offhand thing in the world. "Ol' Cash in the Pan. When a crone like that buys herself a sexy stud muffin, she's hardly going to get all Jesus Saves and turn the proverbial other cheek when he goes out and knocks up another bimbo."

"Don't be blasphemous."

"I'm just saying, Pandora's got the motive, and she's got the money to make it happen."

"What would she need money for?"

"What? You think Pan would string Allie up herself? Hardly. Rich people don't mow their own lawns or pump their own gas or change their own sheets. Why would they commit their own murders?"

So softly that Bex had to strain to hear, even with the volume up at maximum, Coop asked, "Did you do it, Sebi? Did you kill Allie because Pan paid you to?"

The camera Bex planted in the library was equipped with the most sensitive microphone money could buy, plus a lens big enough to encompass the whole room. What it was not equipped with was a temperature gauge. But Bex guessed that if it had been, she would have seen it drop to zero in a second.

Sebi clearly did not appreciate Coop's query.

But then again, maybe he did. Because in response, rather than getting angry, or denying, or even pleading ignorance, Sebi decided to laugh.

He chortled as he asked, "Is that it? Is that what all this was about?"

Now officially off-script, Coop didn't know what to say.

"You weren't scared about some videotape of us Frenching that doesn't even exist. You've been listening to that fucking researcher, and you thought you'd get me in a quiet spot and ask me if I knocked off your precious Allie-poo."

Coop merely nodded.

"Well, what do you think, Super Cooper? Do you think I killed Allison Adler, Her Royal Highness, Princess of the Ice?"

"I don't—I don't know why you would. Was it because of Pandora?"

"Oh, fuck, Pandora." Sebastian elaborated, "Which I'm sure she would have loved for you to do before she found out about your . . . issues."

"So it's true?" Coop started trembling as if the temperature really had dipped to unbearable levels.

"Oh, grow up. You can be so gullible, Coop. Really it's not at all attractive."

"Tell me," Coop demanded. And, to his credit, it wasn't a whine but a command. Skating's Closeted Stud was growing a backbone as they spoke. Quite an impressive sight to see, really.

"Figure it our for yourself. Or let Tex-Mex-Bex draw you a picture."

"Tell me!" Coop howled and, without warning, lunged at Sebi, knocking him to the ground, tapes scattering every which way.

Stunned, Sebi didn't have time to react or defend himself. Coop had him pinned flat on the ground, Coop's knees smashing Sebi's arms, his hands around Sebi's neck within seconds.

Sebi smiled lazily. "Admit it: You always knew we would end up this way."

Coop smacked Sebi across the face with an open palm. That sure wiped the smirk off.

For the first time, Sebi looked genuinely scared rather than amused.

"Tsk, tsk." The scolding prompted a trickle of blood to drip out his quickly swelling mouth. "Now *what would Jesus do?*"

"Leave Jesus out of this," Coop warned.

"But how can I do that, Super Cooper, when He's the one who got us into this mess in the first place?"

Bex and Craig exchanged looks. Neither one had the slightest idea what Sebi was talking about.

But Coop obviously did. "Shut up."

"Oh, do make up your mind, sweetie. Is it *shut up* or *tell me*? Rather tricky to do both, especially with your crotch in my face. Not that I'm not enjoying the view."

"Tell me what you know about Allie's death."

"Only that you and your Jesus freakiness set it in motion. You thought your mom was the only one who blew a gasket when you went all holy on us and found religion? She thought getting you away from Gary and his own craziness—"

"There is nothing crazy about being a religious Jew."

"There is when your lifestyle contains a certain sexual preference that both the Old and New Testament frown upon."

"Gary has made his peace with that. That's why I went to him for advice on how to—"

"Reconcile your new Born Again passion with your Old Again desire to screw Allie every chance you got? Oh, yes, she told me. We were partners. We shared every little thing. She told me how Tess thought that getting you away from Gary and his corruptive, religious influence would nip your little 'problem' in the bud. When that didn't work, she encouraged Allie to keep throwing herself at you as a reminder that the pleasures of the flesh outweigh any prayer breakfast, any day."

Charming, Bex thought. Coop's mother pimped out Allie. No wonder the poor girl didn't want anything to do with that family.

"Ironic, no?" Sebi mused. A tough act to pull off lying prostrate on the ground, but, to his credit, he did manage to do it with a modicum of panache. "Tess sics Allie on you, and I'm the one who suffers."

"You what?"

"Her pregnancy, you idiot. Apparently, while you still managed to screw her—"

"It was so hard. I loved her so much, and to just stop . . . I was weak, I know that now. I should have been stronger."

"Yeah, well, you should have used a condom, too. But hey, I hear you guys are against birth control, right? Sex for procreation only. Well, congrats, Jesus Junkie, you were a good little be-fruitful-and-multiply drone."

"What are you talking about? Allie's baby was Idan's."

"Oh, God, you are dense, aren't you? The other night, when I kissed you out of the blue. What, do you think I was suddenly overwhelmed by lust, unable to stay away from your hot little body a moment longer? Wise up. I was getting a spit sample Idan could use to match to the kid's DNA."

"So Omri is—"

"Yours. Of course he's yours. I didn't lie in court. Allie was head over heels, heels over head, crazy about you. That's why she let Tess push her around. She wanted to be with you—so not a hell of a lot of pushing required. Allie also thought you'd get over this Deity doldrum. Until she got pregnant, that is. Then she changed her tune real fast. Suddenly, instead of just fun and games, she was looking at a lifetime as Mrs. Jesus Freak, tied down to Baby Jesus, and she didn't want any of it. That's why she ran off, that's why she didn't tell you she was pregnant, and that's why she went to Pandora and Idan to adopt your baby."

"My baby," Coop repeated. Bex couldn't tell if he was pleased or horrified.

"Yeah, your precious baby. So now Tess has proof for the media that you're a red-blooded American boy who only lives to screw—in a wholesome, All-American boy way, of course. Pan and Idan have their brat to coochie-coo over, and you're on your way to the World Championship unencumbered by diaper duty. Everyone gets their happy ending. Except for me. This was supposed to be *my* Worlds. *My* turn to be champion. I worked my entire, fucking life for it. Only to have Allie and her female troubles snatch it all away."

Coop said, "You killed her, didn't you?"

"Damn Skippy. Bitch deserved it. Wasn't anything I planned ahead for, mind you. At first I was as in the dark as anyone. Had no idea where she was or what she was up to. But then she called me. Said she was coming to the rink that morning and wanted to say good-bye. She said she owed me an explanation. You bet she did. She owed me that and a hell of a lot more. She owed me my life back. The life I lost because of her. I figured it was only poetic justice that Allie should perish at my hand in return."

For a moment, Coop didn't do anything. He didn't even appear to be breathing. And then he raised his right arm, bringing it down to smash Sebi across the face again, this time with his clenched fist.

Sebi howled, and Bex, realizing that enough was enough, sprang from her seat, heading for the tape library, Craig hot on her heels.

She flung open the door, allowing Craig to dart past and grab Coop's arm before he completely obliterated Sebi's nose.

Allie's killer looked dazed, blood no longer trickling but gushing from his mouth, one eye already starting to swell shut.

But not so dazed that he didn't understand exactly what it meant when Bex smiled down at him and politely informed, "Surprise! Sebastian Vama, you're on *Candid Camera.*"

Epilogue

After Sebastian Vama's media-saturated arrest, the Men's Long Program proved to be somewhat of an anticlimax, made notable only by Coop Devaney's flawless performance, complete with three, clean quads (one in combination), and Jeremy Hunt's surprising podium finish—third place, behind Coop and Lucian Pryce's well-spun student.

At the press conference afterward, of course, the reporters wanted to talk about only one thing. The tape of Sebi's confession—and Coop's less-than-subtle method for extracting it—had been dominating the airways, well, 24/7, since Bex had breathlessly delivered it to Gil and received as a reward after screening, that rarest of the rare, highest of the high, compliments from her executive producer.

"Air it as is. Break into regular programming."

Now, in theory, Bex was a liberal arts major, well versed

in the well-documented oppressiveness of the patriarchy that glorified violence as a means to any end.

In practice, she had to admit that her tape made damn exciting TV. And Coop look like an action hero.

Tess, naturally, was ambivalent. She'd flown into Gil's office after the initial airing, huffing that they'd made her sweet boy look like a Neanderthal. How were they supposed to sell him to the preteen audience, not to mention their cautious parents, if his image was now of some hot-tempered, fist-flying bully? Gil simply let Tess go on and on until she ran out of steam and demanded to know what 24/7 was going to do about this travesty. He then handed her a sheet of paper listing all the major corporations who had called, inquiring about sponsorship opportunities for Coop's upcoming reality show.

After that, Tess not only shut up, she might have even smiled at Bex on her way out of Gil's office.

"That," Gil told Bex, "is how it's done, kid."

It was the first piece of Cahill advice Bex actually expected to use someday.

The evening of the press conference, she stood in the back, Craig on one side, Tess on the other, as they all watched Coop and Idan, Lucian and his student, and Jeremy and Toni up on the platform, wincing slightly from the television lights pointed right in their faces while the assembled reporters all but shouted over each other in their quest for the whole story.

"What are your feelings toward Sebi Vama, Cooper?"

"I'm angry, I'm devastated, that goes without saying. But I also feel sorry for him. A human life in exchange for a ruined skating career is an obscene justification, and anybody who believes it's warranted is clearly a person in need of serious, professional help. I hope that Sebi's arrest helps facilitate that."

"So what happens now?"

"Now?" Coop smiled. "Now we're all off to Worlds."

"About the baby. What happens now with the baby?"

Coop looked at Idan. "After a great deal of thought, and consultation with both my mother and Mr. Ralph Adler, we've all decided that the best place from my son to be is with the parents Allie chose for him. Mr. and Mrs. Ben-Golan. Omri deserves the best and, at this point in my life—and my skating career—I am just not capable of taking care of him as well as Pandora and Idan can. While it's very difficult for me to give up my child, I have to do what is best for him. I owe Allie as much."

It was a moving speech—as the one about Sebi had been. Though Bex might have been a bit more impressed if she hadn't already read both in the notecards Tess prepared before the conference and run by Gil, to see how he thought they would play.

However, Coop obviously decided to improvise, as he added, "One of the new friends I've made at this competition, and now, one of my new World teammates, Jeremy Hunt, told me how great it is to have parents who you know wanted you so much that they were willing to go through hell to protect you. Jeremy's the one who convinced me that, in the end, the best thing you can do for a kid you really love but can't take care of is to let them be adopted by somebody who can."

Next to her, Craig was squirming with embarrassment. And also beaming with pride at the same time.

On Bex's other side, Tess was musing, "Okay. Okay, that's not bad. Shows that Coop's been mentoring an up-and-coming skater. That's good. We can work with that."

At the conclusion of the conference, as Coop and Jeremy posed for pictures, Bex and Craig remained at the back of the room, completely ignored by all the other agendas swirling about.

"So," Bex said.

"So," Craig agreed.

"Same time next year?"

"Oh, no." His eyes danced. "You're not getting away from me that easily."

Bex smiled in return. She told him, "Good answer."

Penguin Group (USA) Online

What will you be reading tomorrow?

Tom Clancy, Patricia Cornwell, W.E.B. Griffin,
Nora Roberts, William Gibson, Robin Cook,
Brian Jacques, Catherine Coulter, Stephen King,
Dean Koontz, Ken Follett, Clive Cussler,
Eric Jerome Dickey, John Sandford,
Terry McMillan, Sue Monk Kidd, Amy Tan,
John Berendt…

You'll find them all at
penguin.com

*Read excerpts and newsletters,
find tour schedules and reading group guides,
and enter contests.*

Subscribe to Penguin Group (USA) newsletters
and get an exclusive inside look
at exciting new titles and the authors you love
long before everyone else does.

PENGUIN GROUP (USA)
us.penguingroup.com